S<small>IR</small> H<small>ERBERT</small> R<small>EAD</small>: "Alive with passion and beauty; it has a poetic quality that reminds me of Emily Dickinson, so precisely does it register a special kind of experience."

K<small>ATHRYN</small> H<small>ULME</small>: "A rare book, so infinitely tender, with its wild little warrior children, so deeply revealing of the creative spinster soul who wins their hearts. A whole new world opens up in these pages. A thousand thanks for sending me this beautiful and original story."

L<small>EWIS</small> G<small>ANNETT</small>: "It creates a world of its own, dewy-fresh, with an accent of its own, and a passionate and unforgettable character who is at once all woman and inspired teacher. *Spinster* both delighted and disturbed me."

A<small>NGUS</small> W<small>ILSON</small>: "Excellent. . . . Mrs. Ashton-Warner, with fine creative imagination, speaks from inside the character and gives us in result an exhilarating and enthralling account."

By Sylvia Ashton-Warner

Spinster
Incense to Idols
Teacher
Bell Call
Greenstone
Myself
Three

Spinster

A NOVEL BY

Sylvia Ashton-Warner

A TOUCHSTONE BOOK
PUBLISHED BY SIMON AND SCHUSTER

A TOUCHSTONE BOOK
PUBLISHED BY SIMON AND SCHUSTER
ROCKEFELLER CENTER, 630 FIFTH AVENUE
NEW YORK, NEW YORK 10020

SECOND TOUCHSTONE PRINTING

SBN 671-20916-7 TOUCHSTONE PAPERBACK EDITION
LIBRARY OF CONGRESS CATALOG CARD NUMBER: 59-5492
MANUFACTURED IN THE UNITED STATES OF AMERICA

To K

Spring

"*I want the one rapture of an inspiration.*"

*W*HAT is it, what is it, Little One?"

I kneel to his level and tip his chin. Tears break from the large brown eyes and set off down his face.

"That's why somebodies they tread my sore leg for notheen. Somebodies."

I sit on my low chair and take him on my knee and tuck his black head beneath my chin.

"There . . . there . . . look at my pretty boy."

But at night when I am in my slim bed, away from the chaos and hilarity of my infant-room, it is I who am the Little One. Before I turn out the light above me and open the window behind I take out my photo. It is pillow-worn, finger-worn and tear-worn, yet the face of the man is alive. I read into it all the expressions I have known; and the attention my spinster heart craves. But memory only loosens the tears. No longer does Eugene take me on his knee, tuck my black head beneath his chin and say, "There . . . there . . . look at my pretty girl."

Not for many long virgin years.

But here is the spring again with its new life, and as I walk down my back steps ready for school in the morning I notice the delphiniums. They make me think of men. The way they bloom so hotly in the summer, then die right out of sight in the winter, only to push up mercilessly again when the growth starts, is like my memory of love. They're only shoots so far but I can't help recalling how like the intense blue of the flowers is distilled passion. Living the frugal life that I do I am shocked at the glamour they bring to my wild garden and at the promise of blue to come. With no trouble at all I break apart into sobbing. What luxury is self-pity! How blessed to weep in the spring!

But you can't get this sort of thing to last and soon there is only sniffing left. And confound it, here's my face to wash and powder again. Also I'd better take some brandy to make my legs go. Yet as I come down the back steps for the second time these tender shoots are still hard to pass. They've got so much to say. There's something so mature about them, as if there was little they didn't know.

However, you don't drink half a tumbler of brandy for nothing and soon I'm severely immune. I walk out and away from the garden, singing an orderly tune.

Yet, when I have crossed the paddock between the rambling old house and the school and reach the cabbage trees that divide them, and when the pre-fab where I teach comes into view, I run into something that does more than renew life in a garden. It is something you find on your shoulders with tight legs clasping your neck. I thought I had forgotten Guilt. I thought he was gone for good, and not merely into hiding for the winter. But oh, these precarious springs! Is there nothing that does not resume life?

My song stops. So does my step. I lurk among the trunks like one of my five-year-old newcomers. If only I had done all that inspectors had told me in the past—whenever they wanted me to, in the way they wanted me to and for the reason! If only I had been a good teacher, an obedient teacher and submissive! If only I could have remained in the safety of numbers that I knew when I was young! But no, I've always been wrong.

4

Yet it can't be too late. True, the mistakes have all been mine, but this is the ground I'll build on. Plainly the inspectors are all good men and all I need to do is to co-operate. What could be easier or more profitable? Slowly I will recover my lagging professional status and prove myself a thoroughly useful force in the service. Then maybe this Old Man Guilt will release my throat and I'll be one with others at last. How fortunate to have these chances! After all everything else comes up new in the spring: flowers and guilt and love. Why not my teaching? With a new courage, not wholly originating in my plans, I walk forward again.

. . . or try to, through the clusterings and questionings and greetings of my Little Ones.

"Miss Vorontosov," inquires Mohi, "how old do you weigh?"

I can see that I'm not going to like this young Vercoe who has been appointed temporarily to the school: a teacher-in-training fresh from the Emergency Course in which teachers are trained in half the time to meet twice the difficulties of the staff shortages since the war. How he comes to be selected at all can only be put down to the desperate shortage of teachers. Where has he come from, anyway? From what strange soil of life has evolved that mixture of culture and gutter in his voice? Why has he chosen children? Why isn't he married, with a surplus of women after the war? Why hasn't that face taken him to the front line of a chorus on a New York stage? He's young but he's still had time to try and fail in other things. Yet, as I emerge from the trees between my house and the school and see him standing uncertainly there by the Big School steps, the sun touching his hair and outlining his story-book features, my general dislike for bachelors does not wholly take over. I can't help feeling touched at his youth, and his strangeness to the world about him.

So that as I make my way across the frost to the pre-fab where I teach, through the greeting hands of my Little Ones, and their dark upturning eyes, I still see him in mind. And although it is far from comfortable for me to think of men, I cannot escape the interest they bring. The faultless blue of his eyes reminds me of the delphiniums and the glamour of my garden in spring.

"Miss Vorontosov," cries Whareparita from the Big School, running gaily up to me as I mount the dingy steps of the pre-fab, "how old are you?"

"Good God!"

"It's my turn to take the quizz session in class this morning and it would do for one of my questions."

I plough through all my talking, laughing, pulling Little Ones . . . the brown, the few white and the brown-white of the New Race . . . across the spare pre-fab to the piano the Head has bought with his last Show-Day funds and unlock it for the day. If you don't lock it you'll find apple-juice on the precious keys and crumbs of biscuit and lolly papers. Next I put my pen-box on the table. Then I unlock the storeroom where I keep the guitar, away from boys who can't play it, and reach down my box of pre-war chalk from behind some books where I hide it. I stoke the fire which has been lit previously by a boy. Then I tuck up my sleeves, damp the sand in the container, send Blossom and Bleeding Heart out for a bucket of water for the trough, tie the flared fullness of my short red smock behind me in a business-like knot, pull on a sack apron and get to work on preparing the clay. No. I'll mix the paints first before I wet my hands.

"Matawhero, get out the pencils. Waiwini, put out the books. Little Brother, use your handkerchief. Reremoana, go and tell Mr Reardon the wood boy has not brought the wood. One-Pint, get out of the sand. Hine, put the papers on the easel. Who's got my . . . where's my . . . who is this dear wee boy? Did you come to see Miss Vorontosov? Here. Patchy, show this wee new boy a picture book. Sit him by the fire. Where's my . . .? What are you laughing at, Bleeding Heart? You mustn't laugh at my little New One. Who's got my . . .? Are you big enough to open the windows, little Dennis? Look at the big long legs and arms Dennis has got! Ani, tidy my . . . I mean dust my table. Who's got my . . .? Tuck in your shirt, Matawhero. . . . Seven! Don't you frighten that little boy! Look, who's got my . . .?"

6

"Miss Vorontosov," inquires Bleeding Heart, "what for those smell by your breff?"

"Aa . . . hair-oil."

I suppose, I reflect, picking up a bundle of tears and toes and fingers from the mat, that my mate God will see fit to excuse this brandy in the morning; He'll arrange for some measure of forgiveness in His extravagant way. I stroke the fat brown finger with the mark of a high heel upon it.

"You tread my sore han for nutteen."

"There . . . there . . . look at my pretty boy . . ."

He may pardon me for drinking myself to school. I demand it, expect it, and will even accept it. But for blundering in my art I don't. My bastard art. For lack of precision I want no pardon. Don't ever forgive me for that, God. Save it up for the age of oldness and haunt me with a shoe. Save up a finger, a child and a scream, and for punishment that will do.

In my unsteadiness I place one foot carefully before the other, balancing my way to the new piano, through the others, watching for more little pieces of trusting humanity on the floor. Although my comforting hasn't worked, Schubert's will. Sitting Little Brother across my knees I grope round him to the keys.

Together we take an Impromptu, to get over the fashionable shoe, and by the time the tears on his face have dried, the tears on my heart have too.

"Miss Vorontofof," says Mohi, "you got ugly hands."

"That's because I'm old."

"You shoulden be old!"

"Why not? I can be old if I like."

"Nanny's old, but she's not ugly."

"Well I am, and I like it."

"You should be new."

"Why?"

"Because you're lovely."

The thing about teaching is that while you are doing it no yesterday has a chance. If only I could get here! Why waste a half-tumbler of brandy in the morning in order to lose the past when you lose it among the Little Ones anyway? Is this drinking necessary? After all I have only to cross the paddock through the trees and here I am saved. Why is the setting out so hard? Do I actually want memory, as much as it wants me? Are Eugene and I still so engrossed that even time and oceans fail? Ah, these intricacies! They're too confused for a drunk teacher to solve. I only know that the call of the bell each morning means a dangerous crystal tumbler.

Yet I teach well enough on brandy. Once it has fired my stomach and arteries I don't feel Guilt. It supplies me with a top layer to my mind so that I meet my fifty Maori infants as people rather than as the origin of the Inspectors' displeasure; and whereas I am so often concerned on this account with the worst in children, I now see only the best. Never do I understand them more, and never is better creative work done. As the legs release my throat some magnificent freedom comes to us all and the day leads off like a party. More and more I learn to see what a top layer can be. You can bear more. The encloistered soul may sally without risk. It is sheltered: it is buffered. It can endure more of the feeling in this exhausting art. Indeed, the only thing that seriously upsets me is this unpardonable loss of precision in my bastard art and the damage to my nylons when I walk too inaccurately between the stove and the easel. Which means another fifteen-and-six, which has a relation to my freedom when I come to think about it. Fifteen-and-six less for my ticket. Fifteen-and-six further away from that boat steaming out through the Wellington Heads. Fifteen-and-six more of this bell . . . hell or whatever I mean. . . . Intoxicating . . .

"Can I sit with Patchy again?" asks Matawhero.

I look at him from my low chair in perplexity. This question has a significance of some kind if only I could put my finger on it. But although we have all been in school for about half an hour this Monday morning I have not yet wholly made the change from the world of the week-end to this one. I draw my hand across my eyes, trying to brush away the mornings of intense work in Selah and the evenings of music and church.

"Can I?"

"Can you what?"

Really, it's confusing, this overlapping of two worlds. Does it amount to a fall or a rise, this crossing through the trees?

"Can I?"

"I beg your pardon?" I brush my face again more severely as though there were cobwebs collected upon it, obscuring my view. And to an extent it works because whereas before I felt there was some significance in this thought of Matawhero's, now I realize there is even more to it. If only I could see what's under my nose. I take a deep breath and concentrate. "What did you say, Matawhero?"

"Aw, hell, I said it a hundred times. Can I sit with Patchy again?"

Ah, I see it! Why doesn't he just get up and go and sit with Patchy under his own power?

The children have broken away from the morning gathering on the mat and are finding their favourite things to do. Voices are rising and the noise of feet. There are shirts that should be tucked in and noses that should be attended to. Matawhero grasps both my knees and trains the full force of his brown eyes upon me. "Can I can I?"

So much asking! Who am I, the law or God?

"Why not, Little One?"

Patchy is pleased. His fair face lights up and every freckle sparkles. "You always want to tit wit me," he says.

Ah, I see something else! The brown and the white meet. Even though they can't mix. I brush my face again more effectively. Steadily those evenings of reading, Beethoven, Schubert, thinking, working and remembering, move inland. Only in blood and by blood, claims my mind, can the races mix. Yet communication of any kind must be a step towards understanding of some kind, which is the only path I know towards toleration.

But I'm still not wholly myself. Not only the echoes of the music come back to me: the lethargy following the long and hard hours of work in Selah this morning follows me. Plainly there are two worlds, and in which do I truly belong? Must I really drink myself through the trees over into this room of raw reality five times a week? No other job in the world could possibly dispossess one so completely as this job of teaching. You could stand all day in a laundry, for instance, still in possession of your mind. But this teaching utterly obliterates you. It cuts right into your being: essentially, it takes over your spirit. It drags it out from where it would hide.

Unerringly the inner restlessness provokes a bodily one. The sense

9

of conflict brings me to my feet and drives me stepping carefully among the fingers and toes on the floor. What exactly am I? To what world do I really belong? The intoxicating one of paint and music, memory and wine, or to this jagged-edged one of rough reality? To phantasy or to . . . Small hands find mine or pull at my smock for everlasting attention. "Miss Poppoff, Twinnie's she's draween on my side!" cries Twinnie.

"Miss Vontopop," shouts Tame, "Bleedeen Heart he won't learn!"

"Make him then," I answer from one half of me, while the other half, from its unease, sees a picture of a big boat steaming serenely out of the harbour of this country out into the open sea.

"He won't listen."

"Make him listen."

"I teached him and he won't listen."

With a sense of saving myself I cling to these accusations of Tame's. Diligently I apply myself. Something tells me that this stormy pre-fab is the real and the right and the safe half of my world. "What did you say, Tame?" I ask anxiously.

"Bleedeen Heart he won't learn! Bleedeen Heart!"

"You'll have to make him." These children will have to just teach each other for the time being. I'm busy.

"Shall I biff him, or just teach?"

I haven't got an answer for the moment and I look up across the sun-streaked pre-fab-full of vivid, black-haired life, to Bleeding Heart's face smiling at us with that grand and enviable toleration of a situation, so wonderful in a Maori. I manœuvre myself through the desks and blocks and bodies to where he holds his indulgent court. His mouth is the biggest thing in or out of this school and therefore his smile is too. Honestly it would be a shame to biff him.

"Why don't you learn, Bleeding Heart?" I ask reasonably.

He leans back in mature relaxation, crossing his legs, and smiles back at me with far more wisdom than I'll ever know.

"Me, I'm dumb."

Crash comes my laughter and in no time all the Little Ones have joined in. Gone is the picture of the pleasant laundry with my hands among the soap-suds and my mind to myself. Gone too is this regularly recurring picture of a big boat. I forget about the conflict within me and about how many worlds there are. I'm utterly lost in the present, and the time comes during the ensuing hour when I am back into my teaching on the surface level as usual, and working out on a lower level this interesting question of communication leading to understanding, and understanding to some degree of toleration, so that when silence falls, and loud yells bring me from my reading and writing groups, out into the spring frost, to find that dirty white Boy has gone home after a thrashing from brown Seven, I think, taking yellow Lotus up in my arms, that even this thrashing is communication of a kind and could lead to understanding of a kind and thence to a measure of toleration. After all, Boy did apparently feel Seven's hand, under whatever circumstances. Indeed I see not inconsiderable evidence that I should have allowed Tame's biff.

Not that I believe the hiding sent him home; not the hiding alone. It may be just a rhythmic reaction to the passions of school. There may well be, in these first few months, a swing back sometime. But I could have tempered the retreat had I not been in this no-man's-land between the week-end and school. I could have done the necessary comforting. But Boy is gone, and as an Infant Mistress I fail.

If there's anything new in that. Fail seems to be my nom de plume: Miss Anna Fail. Pretty. I should use it when signing my cheques. I'll put it on my Maori Books: "by Anna Fail." Standing among the Little Ones outside in the trodden frost, and with infinitesimal Lotus in my arms I look back into those years of Inspectors . . . yes, as an Infant Mistress, I fail all right.

Although, as a person, I consider, I don't. Fumbling back from another world, making the journey from phantasy to reality, is never an easy thing, and there is a . . . an allowable blindness. Still, brown sent home white and I have a ghost to lay.

I look across the frosty enclosure to the walnut tree beyond the pre-fab for Seven. He is a slight child with an uncommonly long face and big eyes like the children draw. He looks far more like a sad neurotic than the aggressor he is. His clothes, though expensive, are put on all ways; he has the same trouble as all the other little Maori boys of keeping his trousers up which hang half way to his feet, and his boots plain frighten you. But he comes when I call him, which means a lot to me, and in no time, as I kneel to his level holding Lotus on one knee, we are surrounded.

"Was it you, little Seven, who thrashed Boy?"

"No."

"Course!" supplies the chorus. "Course" is their abbreviation of "Of course."

"He was cheeky for me," defends Seven.

"He dong him," supplies Tame. "He dong him and dong him and dong him."

"You liar!"

"Not!"

"Course!"

"Not!"

"Course!"

I straighten and take Seven by the hand. "Come in, Little One," I say, leading him into school. "Tame, you come in too for a mate for him."

You don't want to let them brood in loneliness. In fact you mustn't let them brood at all. They'll get enough of that anyway, later on. We don't want more sad Annas than we can avoid. There's only one thing to be done about Seven at this malleable age and I do it. I've got to start on this boy sometime, and force and punishment is not the answer. In the world behind my eyes I see a hazy picture of a volcano with two vents: one is creativeness and one is destructiveness. I sit the little chap gently down in his small desk with Tame beside him and give them each a board and clay.

Then I pick up my yellow spot of a Lotus and return to the crater of the infant room.

What was I thinking about . . . what was it that I was upset about now, when I first came over? I've no idea. . . .

Intoxicating . . .

Just as intoxicating are these infants themselves. Silently the inebriation of ferment has glided into that of teaching; of the vitality about me, at my feet, in my arms, behind me and before. As the hour pulses on I lose myself in others, deeply in the personalities of others; more utterly than ever I do in the personality of brandy.

As for my breath, only Bleeding Heart smells that and he compliments me on my hair-oil.

Not everyone understands my artist's smock, flared and short to the knees, with a tube skirt below, and Riti, who is new and only half-past four and God knows shouldn't be here in the first place what with the rising numbers, takes most of the morning to work it out. However after hours of staring and following me about she at last sums it up.

"Miss Vontopopp, your petticoat it's showing."

"My apron's pinched."

Mark tugs at my red smock. He's a little white boy who likes the right things in the right place at the right time.

"Good."

He stares up at me perplexed and I kneel to his level.

"It's not in my desk," he declares, "but I put it there."

It is brown Matawhero who answers. He is fine-boned Maori and fine-minded, just like his grandfather, the Chairman, and, like him, feels racial frictions. "You said, you said," he accuses Mark above the noise, "you said you were taking it home on Friday to get it washed." He misses nothing, just like his grandfather. "It's at your place. It's at his place, Miss Vorontosov!" Ah! He can say my name . . .

"It's not!"

Ah, Maori versus Pakeha.* Which side am I on?

Matawhero slams down his book and stamps his way through the children to the porch and sure enough returns with the apron. "He didn't even look for it," he splutters. "It was in his bag!"

All Maoris are thieves, I quote myself, to the Pakeha.

"Miss Vorontosov," says white, nervous Dennis, with the classic whine of the incorrectly disciplined, catching me kneeling, "someone's pinched my duster." How well his little tongue gets round my name!

"I—I know where it is!" sings out Matawhero. "It's by the dead rat!" He has big beautiful eyes in a big beautiful head, set on a small body, set on smaller legs, just like the Chairman. He slams down his book again with the resignation of an old man.

I look from one to the other. Dennis has the shifty eyes of the child thrashed too early by his mother, and the disgusting cleanliness of the respectable. He can't dance like my filthy disobedient Tamatis. "Why," I say, "where is this dead rat?"

"By the hole," answers Matawhero.

"Where's this hole?"

His voice rises in his Nanny's exasperation with the Education Board

* *Pakeha:* Maori for "white one."

when they stall over the improvement of the school buildings. "By the lavatory door, of course!"

I look from brown to white; whose side am I on?

"He left it there!" storms the Maori. "He didn't look for it either!" His English is considerably better than that of the Pakehas, and he fights with all the gusto of the Maori warrior. This is the way to stand up for the rights of the brown race. This is the way to wring buildings from the white Board. ,

"I didn't leave it there," lies Dennis conscientiously.

All Maoris are thieves and all thieves Maoris. Is that how the Board feels about our Maori school? Anyway whose side am I on in these racial interchanges? What colour am I?

What colour am I? . . .

I edge my way to the window and lean over the piano and look out over the long plains to the hills in the distance. I'm like those hills. They're blue some days, and grey other days, and white in the early spring. It all depends on the weather. . . .

But they can both say my name!

"What is it, what is it, Little One?" I kneel to his level and tip his chin.

"Thas why Seven he pinchded me. Seven."

"But he's out in the shed. I sent him out there for kicking Hine-waka's foot."

"He camed inside and pinchded me."

"Where is he now?"

"In those shed. He camed inside and pinchded me."

"You don't mean to say he came inside and pinched you, then put himself back in the shed!"

"Yeah. He camed inside and pinchded me."

When the bell has called all my Little Ones out I go to the mirror in the storeroom to repair my face before I meet the men at morning tea. There's a good bit of work to be done on it. There's wear and tear on a face in an infant room, what with chalk and dust and feeling. Especially your hair. My hair, being black, picks up anything in the air. I comb it proudly; it's like my mother's. It masses in curls on top, as my father says hers did. Then I help my mouth along with a bit of lipstick and brush the powder from my eyebrows. God knows why, I'm sure. Men mean nothing to me. Just personal pride. Besides, a senior woman teacher should give a lead in dress to the big girls. There's all sorts of reasons really. The spring, for instance. It's impossible not to be in keeping.

But I can't do anything about painting on cheerfulness. The brandy has worn off, the children are outside and there's only the depression left. By the time I go over to the corridor in the Big School I'm no more than my sad self again. Sitting in the chair the Head has brought me from his own room, among the coats and basins and lost shoes, I seek refuge in the elm tree outside the window. I apply my eyes and my mind to its unclothed branches, realizing the wealth of new green life tucked away in its buds, and trying not to hear the conversation of the men.

The Head is here and Paul Vercoe pours the tea. Although he is fabulous to look at his nearness irritates me; I feel the conflict of generation. Yet, as he passes me my cup I can't help seeing him. He is tall and young and apparently perfect. His dark hair is brushed back from a wide forehead; his broad deep eyes, like framed delphinium petals, are darkly lashed and browed, the lids flickering eloquently while his mouth says everything in immobility. As for his nose and the wonderful lower jaw, they are straight off a magazine cover. Now what chance has a spinster against this? Yet, to me, features of the body run nowhere in the race with features of the mind. Having learnt at least a few lessons in my life, so that I see no more than just another of these sissy bachelors who giggle among themselves about frustrated spinsters, I return to my elm tree in bud.

But the hope in them causes me to recross my legs unhappily. Don't they know that winter follows? You see it in the flowers the Head plants for me too, this hope; in the way they flaunt themselves. All colour and tossing of heads! You would think they could bloom for ever. Yet what can they do about the autumn? It's as much as I can do to walk in my garden in the evenings, knowing what I do and they don't. . . .

". . . and so I think, Paul," the Head is addressing the younger man, sitting on the low form opposite looking up at him, "that you and I can manage all the playground duty on our own. Between us we should

15

be able to relieve Miss Vorontosov of any obligation there." He lays his legs gently together and takes out his tobacco and papers as though life were the most uncomplicated of issues.

Paul Vercoe's face lowers contemplatively upon me, and my cup halts on its way.

"Will that suit you, Paul?" asks the Head.

But he is still looking down upon me. "Blessed are they," he observes in an unnecessarily loud voice, "who have their battles fought for them. I—I mean, Miss V'ront'sov," he says, missing no less than two syllables of my name, "that the wind blows you good luck."

He has mutilated my father's name! "It's not good luck!" I flash back, spilling my tea. "It's good management. I always pick a head-master who is married! Always a man who is married!"

Surprisingly he smiles, in a way that is old for a young face. He should have flared up with wounded pride, so developed in New Zealand men. Plainly he is not one of them. But it saddens me: such detachment belongs to the old.

The Head lights his cigarette. He is a man of medium height, well and quietly dressed, somewhere beyond the forties, and his head is permanently inclined in attentiveness. "Well, shall we settle that, Paul? I'll take before and after school, and you take morning interval and lunch? It's better that way with my home just up the road."

"I'll give the orders," he says, the trace of gutter accent at variance with his choice of word, "if they, if they . . . shall we say . . . give ear to them."

"They do, don't they?"

"I can't remember when anyone last gave ear to me." He turns to me once more, a clinically detached smile on his face. "I was obliged to chastise the baby of your irresponsible Tamati crew yesterday. I told him to pick up the cabbage-tree leaves and he thumbed his nose at me. In short he failed to . . . to . . . shall we say . . . give ear to me."

"The Tamatis are not built to obey God or Man," I reply with my usual unnecessary feeling. "What makes you think they can obey you? What makes you think they can obey you?"

His smile expands delightedly. "I love that mood of yours!" he exclaims.

The Head rises. "Now, that's another thing," he mentions mildly,

"I mean to get my Committee on to. The removal of those cabbage trees. Really, as they are, a tidy playground is impossible."

"Only over my dead body will those trees go, Mr Reardon!" I cry. "Only over my very dead body! I haven't been here long but I claim all the trees!" But the outright laughter of young Vercoe is too much. I have no idea of what I am saying until I hear it. "You've got no occasion to strike a small child!"

"These grounds," goes on the Head in a soothing tone, "would be an easier job to keep tidy without the constant dropping of the leaf-blades. If only they would stick to one season for it like other trees. But they do it all the time." The Head is new here too.

"I'm only just beginning to bring that Tamati baby round to understand what obedience is. To thrash him undoes my work!"

Suddenly the young man standing here, plainly enjoying the moment, wheels and disappears through the door of his classroom and immediately I see what I have said. Am I still so blind that I can hurt the young?

"It wouldn't be so bad," ploughs on the Head, "if, as trees, they still looked nice; but they appear so pathetic and underfed."

"He's wrecked all my work on that child!"

"No one can say they add beauty and dignity to the place."

"You mean the Tamatis?"

"I mean the trees."

"The trees . . ."

Tears promise in my throat. They come easily with Mr Reardon about. Married men are so pleasant to weep to. But my cosmetic wouldn't take it. My age would show up. I look up at him where he stands, glancing through the glass top of the door of the assistant's classroom and my eyes follow his. Mr Vercoe is poised there, a glamorous irresolute thing. I have let too much of myself go; I have shown too much. "It's just that he's got to be gentle with my Little Ones," I justify myself softly.

Mr Reardon's eyes are still thoughtfully on Paul. "Yes," he says, as though not meaning particularly my young ones but his own new young one on the staff, "we've all got to be gentle with the young."

"I'll organize my big girls on those leaves," I say. "I'll see that you are not worried by the appearance of the place."

"I have every confidence, Miss Vorontosov," he replies, taking up the used cups himself, "that you will help me all you can. But I can't have you doing too much."

"I'll see to those cups, Mr Reardon." I turn to a big girl, a very beautiful Maori girl, peeping through the top of the door at the young white man in there. "Whareparita, be so kind as to take these cups from Mr Reardon."

I pick up my pen-box before the bell and set off down the corridor in my high important heels, thoroughly at variance with myself. As I make my way through the laughing assembling children across the grass to the pre-fab my neck is red with shame. I have hurt a young man who, even by his annoying presence alone has afforded me the one blessing I desire: an obliteration of memory. Poor young chap standing there alone in his room: a "stranger within the gate." There . . . there . . . look at my pretty boy. . . .

"My mother," says white Mark, "said I'm not allowed to take off my shoes in school."

Down we come to earth with a crash. Down from the elm buds, the hope and offended young men. It really is curative if you can take it.
"Why?"

"Because yesterday I came home with my laces undone."

Certainly there's no power like the present. There might have been some acute past before school, and a touch of it at interval, but here beneath the rafters with snails hanging in them and frost melting from them, it's all urgent *Now*. "Why didn't you do them up? Tuck in your shirt, Matawhero."

"I can't do them up."

"I beg your pardon?" It's hard to hear against the reading.

"I can't."

"Everyone else here can do up their laces. . . . Use your handkerchief, Blossom. . . . Bring your slippers then, Mark."

"I'm not allowed."

Now I'm peculiarly and particularly susceptible, if not even allergic, to this phrase "not allowed," and the very last echoes of the encounter at morning tea, the too close range with the self of another, together with the last shred of regret connected with it, quite vanish. A rage moves into its place, and it's for this white mother who has a little boy who has shoes he can't do up and who is not allowed to bring his slippers. Like the old war horse lifting its nose, I warm up. I kneel to his level. "So you're not allowed, Little Mark."

"I'm really not allowed. She said that, and I know when she means it too."

But I don't want Mark to feel the division between his teacher and his mother. It's not fair to a little boy. But at my age there is a limit to fifty or sixty—or forty if I must be accurate—pairs of shod feet crashing round the pre-fab. It's all too much of the present. Yet the feeling I have about this mother must not be let go on Mark. Reluctantly I separate my rage for her from my tenderness for him. "Well," I say, taking his little pink hands and dragging my voice down to a low level of patience, "I can't teach with all these noisy feet, you know. You still have to take your shoes off in here, Little Mark. You still take your shoes off in here."

He nods, poor little chap, but I know he has seen, and also felt, the conflict.

"Dennis," I continue gently, "used to bring his slippers each day. And now his mother has bought him a pair of crêpe-soled sandals he can leave on." What a rest that was to see a parent trying to understand a school situation, even if not the child himself. At least I prefer to see it as an effort at understanding rather than just routine respectability. Now what was I thinking of again? What was I red in the neck about when I came back? I've no idea.

"What school did you come from, Little One?"
"Whakamaharatanga."
"And what was your teacher like? Old or young?"
" 'ung."

If there's anything I can't stand it's stopping work in the middle of the day. All this great big hour for unnecessary eating. Playground duty would be better after all. It breaks the mood coming over here for lunch. Lunch! I'd far rather walk round with a cup of tea in my hand at school. When I start work I mean it and keep full out until I have done. It's a wrench coming back here; a wrench in the climate of the mind. However, I put the jug on for tea, reach for my cigarettes and poetry, lift my legs to the table and have a look at how other people handle their memories . . .

Strange Power, I know not what thou art,
Murderer or mistress of my heart,
I know I'd rather meet the blow
Of my most unrelenting foe
Than live—as I now live—to be
Slain twenty times a day by thee . . .

Oh . . .! The bell! Really these lunch hours are too short. . . .

"Hark, hark, the lark!" I teach earnestly, beginning on my lark theme for the spring. "Say, 'Hark, hark, the lark!' "
"Cluck, cluck, the lark!"
"Hark, hark, the clerk!"

"I was talking to the new Senior Inspector last night at the Headmaster's meeting," the Head tells me as he steps his way zigzaggedly through the maze of my Little Ones. He has come, I guess in advance, to collect my Roll, which is not up to date. The names of the new entrants are not in, the attendance for the week not marked and the classifications forgotten. I lift my hands from the keyboard observing his gentleness; the gentleness of a man with a woman to care for and small children of his own, of a man who finds time to plant flowers. Waiwini's little brother is bawling his brains out on my knee and dropping his tears on the notes. "I don't want to hear about Inspectors," I say.
"I asked him," he goes on, his head inclined attentively, "for a junior teacher to help in this room. Regulations or no regulations."
I can't help laughing. I look round the crowded pre-fab, at big Hori copying out music on the blackboard, at Waaka practising on the sewing-machine without cotton, at Wero and Tai working out the D Major chord on the guitar and at the dozens and dozens of infant Maoris toiling and playing from one corner of the room to the other beneath the rafters, and laugh again. As if I were still within the range of help! Even if I wanted it.
"But, Mr Reardon, there's plainly no room for a Junior in here."

20

I struggle tardily to my feet. After all, nice teachers do stand when the Head comes in; they train their children to do so also. Nice teachers keep their records and rolls up to date too. Where are those resolutions about co-operating with the inspectors I made this morning? Ah, these tight legs of Guilt on my shoulders!

The Head looks round too, guardedly. "There's far too much work in this room for one woman."

"But I like it. I've got to be doing ten things at once or I start thinking. I like it. I like all this."

"I'd never expect it, or allow it, for my wife."

I look round the child in my arms. "But Juniors get like landladies. They check on everything you do."

He laughs like anything. It's lovely to see all the care vanish from his face; the care for others. "Anyway," he says at length, "what's the matter with this little chap?"

"He's just having his daily bawl."

"He's taking a big interest in it."

"Hey! What are you crying for, Little Brother?" I have forgotten to ask him. I had just picked up this mass of tears to help with my afternoon Schubert.

"Thas why Seven he punch my stomat for notheen. Seven."

"There . . . there . . . look at my pretty boy . . ."

"He's far too heavy for you."

"I like things too heavy for me. I like things too heavy for me."

He strokes his chin. Of course we would never be able to understand each other. "Well I'll just take this roll of yours along with me. Don't worry about it not being done. I'll do it myself." He looks round the pre-fab again, the several layers of children, the water trough and the sand-place blocking the door from nowhere else to put them. "But I'm jolly sure I'm going to get something better than this for you out of the Board."

My Headmaster. He is susceptible to "poor dears." And there's no "poorer dear" than me at times.

"But I like rafters in pre-fabs!" I wish that he could see it the way I do.

"I'm going to stand my Infant Mistress up in a first-rate modern infant room before a year is out."

The Head does like "poor dears." I wish that I could really wish for a new classroom if for no other reason than that he could extend himself. But how could he know why I like rafters; the earliest memory of my mother. I look down at the child in my arms. "There . . . there . . . look at my sweet boy . . ."

"I had a good day last night," writes Mohi.

It is the last hour in the afternoon and the flowers and tears and brandy of the morning are long since left behind. I've completely forgotten all that. I've mislaid who I am. Sensuously and accurately I vibrate and respond to the multifold touch of my Little Ones, and to the Big Ones who invade at this hour. I am made of their thoughts and their feelings. I am composed of sixty-odd different pieces of personality. I don't know what I have been saying or what I will say next, and little of what I am saying at the time. It is a potent drunkenness, an exhilaration, and it is one that does not leave depression in its wake. Indeed it is not unlike, in its effect, the intoxication of Beethoven for three hours the night before.

"Miss Vorontosov," says Whareparita, a senior from the upper school, a calm, brown and beautiful girl, "Mr Reardon he sent me over to help you."

That's what I like about Whareparita: she can say the name my father left me. And that's what I like about the Head: he sends someone to help me and he chooses someone who can say this name.

"Miss Vottot!" cries little brown Ara, "Seven he's got a knife! He's cutteen my stomat!"

"Whareparita, disarm Seven."

That's another thing I like about a big girl to help me. They can take orders and smart ones.

"Miss Vontofoff," claims Waiwini, six and brown and girl, "I'm going to write a letter to Mr Reardon when I go to Health Camp."

I kneel to her level; it's the least of the courtesies. "I thought you would write to me, Waiwini."

"Your name's too long."

"Miss Voffa," inquires Twinnie, "how do you spell 'boko'?"

"What are you writing?"

" 'My twin she dong me on the boko.' "

"What is a 'boko,' Whareparita? Tame, use your handkerchief. Irini, have you brought your fourpence for your pencil?"

Irini is half Chinese and very five. "My muvver she haven got fourpen."

And this is the home where eighty-four pounds went down in drink one night last week; the child allowance for a family of ten and all the wool bonus for mothers.

"Miss Vorontosov," complains brown Matawhero, "I'm sicka writing." A little Maori boy of six can say my name. I kneel to his level. "Well, write, 'I'm sick of writing.'"

"Miss Foffof," points out brown Wiki, all eyes and smiles and curls, "you sayed I could play the piano when I camed in."

"That's right. Tuck in your shirt, Matawhero. Handkerchief, Blossom."

"Can I play it now?"

"Have you finished your reading, little Wiki?" I kneel again.

"No, that's why I hates readeen."

"Well, finish it, then you can play the piano. Really, Whareparita," I say, standing again, "the things these children say I have said! The things they say I have said!"

"You do say a lot of them, Miss Vorontosov."

"Not all?"

"No, not all."

"You've heard me say things that I have denied after?"

"Oh. Yes!"

"It's time for my practice, Miss Vronsof," says Hori, coming barefoot and brown from the big school. A big gentle Maori boy.

"Carry on then. Scales and arpeggios first."

"Miss Foffof," insists Wiki, "you sayed I could play the piano when I finish my wort."

"That's just it," I reply kneeling. "I didn't."

"Yes, you did, Miss Foffof!" Eyes and teeth and curls all flash.

"Did I, Whareparita? Did I, Whareparita?"

"I heard you say that."

"All you little new ones," I call, straightening again, "come here to me."

"Do you want this Kowhai?" asks Ata, a senior girl who wants the table for her dressmaking, "or shall I put it out?"

"Miss Foffof," calls Wiki, "come an hear me read. Here I am ahind the piano!"

"Play those scales with both hands, Hori. Handkerchief, Blossom. Shirt, Mohi. Handkerchief, handkerchief! Shirt, shirt!"

"You said, you said I could paint this afternoon," accuses white Mark. He is ugly and earnest and respectable and distressingly clean and forgets nothing. I kneel. "That's right, little Mark. Get your colours mixed."

"I haven't got any paper."

"I thought I told you to bring some paper."

"Somebody pinched it."

I stand. "Wrong fingering, Hori. One, two, three, thumb."

"Riti is crying!" reports Waiwini's little brother, sensationally. "Riti!"

"What for? Ata, that seam is too close to the edge."

"Seven he put sand in her neck. Seven."

"Whareparita, bring Seven to me. Bring Seven to me."

"What's this word?" asks Hine, who stinks.

"Between."

"Atween?"

"Between. I told all of you little ones to come here. Wiki, Mark, Tame, bring those new ones to me."

"My pencil's pinched," charges white Dennis.

"Whareparita, have you ever heard them make up anything I didn't say?"

"Yes, sometimes."

"Somebody's pinched my pencil," repeats Dennis, a threatening note lowering his voice.

"Don't say, 'Somebody has pinched my pencil.' Say 'I have lost my pencil.'"

Two more big Maori girls come in from the big school, silent in their bare feet. "Who is the captain of the B Team for the competitions, Miss Vorontosov?"

"I have lost my pencil," says Dennis, his hands still in mine.

"But I sold you one this morning, little Dennis."

"Who is the captain of the B Team, Miss Vorontosov?"

"I haven't picked one yet. I haven't picked one yet."

"You picked Hirani."

"I most certainly did not. I certainly did not."

"Well, who is?"

"I'll pick one later. Ata, that seam's too near the edge. Take that child out of the water trough."

"I've lost my pencil." I find I am still kneeling with the small pale hands of Dennis in mine. I examine them. How did they get here?

"Miss Vorontosov," he nags. The way these little white tongues can get round my alien name! I smile at him gratefully. He is still nervously ill, Dennis. "I've lost my pencil."

"Good, Hori," I say, standing. "That bass was right. Hang on to the last note. Style, that's what's missing. Style, man, style!"

"Shall we nominate the captain?"

"I beg your pardon?"

"Shall we nominate the captain?"

"I can't hear."

"Shall we nominate the captain?"

"No, I'll do all the picking of the captains. I'll pick someone who has been regularly to practices and who doesn't sulk."

"You picked Hirani."

"Why have you brought Seven to me?"

"I've lost my pencil," cries Dennis, pulling at my smock.

"Seven he put sand in Riti's neck. Seven," reports Matawhero, who is the keeper of our morals, his grandfather being the keeper of the School Committee.

"Who can lend Dennis a pencil? Lend Dennis a pencil?"

"Here you are, Dennis," says Mark. "But give it back to me, no one else, or it'll get pinched."

"Who is the A captain for the competitions then?"

"Why can't you wait till I pick one?"

"Mr Reardon wants to know now so he can send in the entries."

"I got nutheen pencil," comes in Irini with the chorus, sepulchrally, from the eighty-four-pound-party background.

"Can I play the piano now, Miss Foffof?" asks Wiki confidently, "I've readed my readeen."

"Who is the captain of the A team, Miss Vorontosov?"

"Here's Seven, Miss Vorontosov."

"I wonder if you would mind," says Hori courteously in his deep man's voice, "composing me a little music, Miss Vronsof?" He approaches me respectfully, barefoot.

"Riti she's cryeen, Mitt Vottot. Riti."

"I've got my paints mixed, Miss Vorontosov. But I've got no paper."

"Now all you little new ones get a blackboard and duster and chalk and come and sit by me on the mat. Sit by me on the mat."

"Arn you comeen to hear me read ahind the piano?"

"What shall I do with this Kowhai?"

"Here's Seven."

"I'm sorry to disturb you," goes on Hori gallantly, "but you promised to write me some new music." He puts pencil and paper in my hands. . . .

"Please tune this guitar, Miss Vrontossup."

"I'll shoot that ghost," Matawhero assures us. "It jumps on my back."

By three o'clock in the afternoon the intoxication of the infant room wears off suddenly, especially when the big girls come in with their brooms and loud voices, and the past threatens me again. There was a time when I could postpone this a little longer by a quiet cup of tea with the Head in the corridor among the coats and basins and lost shoes; gently summing up the day over a biscuit. But now there is a stranger with us. And here he is, when I come over, standing indeterminately about, hitching on to whatever we have to say and telling us both what to think. There's only one thing to do and that's skip the tea and get on with my basketball practice. I wheel on my high heels and stalk off down the steps and whisk out my whistle and off we all go, those who are not sulking about something, out on to the rough plain. I don't know anything about basketball but I do know the shortest distance between two points; two goal-posts: a straight line. Moreover the competitions are not so far off and the Vorontosov does not like defeat.

Now what we want is smart clothes. Short brown rompers to show off these incomparable legs, and brilliant yellow pullovers. Not only because yellow suits their eyes but also it may hasten play. The yellow I see in mind could be caught out of the corner of the eye. Moreover when I take my girls out among the august infant mistresses in town who always do the right thing, stand up for the Head, complete their

Rolls, and prepare meticulous work-books, I don't want them to know what I really am. I might be able to fool them with a successful basketball team. I sigh heavily between whistles. . . .

"It's time you were gone, Whareparita." Now what's this girl still dawdling about the top of the corridor for? I hear Mr Vercoe's steps moving away into his room.

"I'm—I'm just doing the cups, Miss Vorontosov."

"Thank you so very much. That's very nice of you." We'll have to work out a rota among the girls for tea-duty. My job really. If only I had time to think of it. I pick up my pen-box and set off through the disputed cabbage trees, homeward. I'm still thinking of the two men at school when I come within sight of the bulk of the house where I live. Full to the top with emptiness it is; full of a waiting past. And in no time I have taken up the tears again where I left them off during the morning interval; not so much because of memory lying in wait as because of this very present. I hurt that young lad this morning, and again after school in the corridor; a lonely being who dispenses to me freely the greatest blessing; a relief from this memory . . . and because you can't leave good weeping unfinished anyway; especially in the spring.

But my weepings, luxurious though they are, can never manage to last long: I enjoy them too much. When I arrive in my own ground and see the garden beneath Selah window that the Head, for some reason, some secret untold reason, keeps yellow for me through three seasons the whole thing falls through. And here I am drinking flagons of colour from the delicate freesia, the higher daffodils and jonquils and the taller hollyhocks against the wall that he has told me will be a pale lemon. Tears easily dry up before it. True, the weeds are doing well too, but so do my weeds in the infant room. Indeed, far from carrying my collapse to a proud conclusion I take a walk through the long grasses to greet the blue garden at the garden wall near the back door, the red one along the length of the house and the orange one near the gate. Everywhere, I note, the grass and weeds are doing equally as well. And so they can, as far as I am concerned, except the thistles. They'll get the carving knife. As I return through the trees to make the holy coming-home cup of tea, the hydrangea buds and the geranium beneath the hedge have a word to say, and the nasturtium beneath the tank, so that, as I lift one foot after the weary other up the back steps I have forgotten what the recent drama was about and am reflecting on the ways of a married man and a headmaster, marvelling that he should find the mind-space, apart from the time-space, to succour me with flowers; that this should come my way at all; this garden full of flowers.

"I frighteen of those ghostes," says my spot Riti. "They's eat all us up."

The days happen along in their inadvertent way . . .

I plan, but this is the surest way not to do a thing. Some other deeper mysterious plan takes over. I look for it sometimes, thinking I might submit my own will to it; thinking it would prove easier, if only I could put my finger on it beforehand. But I never can. I only recognize it when my intentions break astray, when something unexpected yet fundamentally gratifying takes their place. Then I hear myself saying, "But of course! Of course!" And I find myself wishing that I was more accessible to this thing so that it could substitute for the brain I haven't got. The brain I haven't got.

Yet I still plan in my wan way. I find some element of security in seeing ahead of me a definite arrangement. It's a framework that amounts to a spacious shelter, and even though little eventuates that I have thought out first, I still do it. And as fast as my deliberations come to no fruition I make them again, while, to the extent that they fail, I sense this other inexorable direction in my life; so that although I am chained to a memory I am sometimes struck with the triviality of it, and feel that any affair of the heart has nothing to do with the ultimate destination. And that I am as clay in the hands of this force, this something that told my delphiniums when to bud; this will that is frighteningly present in my infant room, deeply at large beneath the lid of orthodoxy and discipline, that breathes up through the cracks in moments of outburst. I sense this other intention and am afraid to touch it.

Yes, the days and nights happen along, happen along; "neutral-tinted haps and hazards." But I must not touch this thing. I must go no nearer to it than to think about it. The next time I go to church I'll think it all out during the sermon . . . think it all out during the sermon. Yes I'll think it all out during the . . . but I must not touch this thing.

"What's this word?" asks Waiwini.
"Brother."
"Brother?"
"Yes. Like your little brother over there."
"But he wasn't always my brother."
"What!"
"See, he used to be my cousin."
"How does he come to be your brother if he was once your cousin?"
"Mummie knows."

A picture persists in my mind as I lie on the rug in the drawing-room firelight, holding up the transition from the school life to my own. I can see Whareparita standing on the basketball field after school, poised with the ball. She is my strongest and quickest player and I have placed her centre centre. She stands, finger-tipping the ball, waiting for the whistle. What a beautiful sight! What perfection of form, feature and physical strength! She could win a match on her own.

Something strange comes over her and the ball lowers. I delay the whistle. The ball lowers still further then drops to the ground. Then before all our eyes Whareparita crumples and falls to the ground too.

I open my eyes and look at the flames. Yet she got up and walked home afterwards. I've been playing her too hard. I play them all too hard. As indeed I play myself. I must remember that other people don't necessarily need to live as I do. Oh! Shut your eyes and forget school and get on with your rest!

It wasn't playing her too hard. There was something else the matter with her. What was it? Oh, something right under my nose, I suppose. Something right under my nose.

"Mitt Wottot."
"What is it, Little One?" I am preparing the clay in the storeroom for the day and am covered in it up to my elbows.
"Look what he gived me." Patchy shows me a florin; no, a foreign coin of some kind, and his freckled face is a glow of pride.

"Who?" I kneel and take a hand.

"Mitter Wertoe."

"Does he still live with you, Patchy?" His parents are the Head's Number One helpers.

"In the back woom."

So he can be kind to children.

"He roided me on his boike to 'chool." Look at that now! What about that hiding he gave my Tamati baby? Just nervousness, I suppose. It must have been something like that. Young people just out of College are usually, yes, usually, so gentle. How slow I am to understand him! There must be a lot of good in him since he was accepted in the first place. And I know that the Head sees possibilities in him. In fact there is an improvement in his work already, so he says. I sigh. Will I never learn not to assess a person on first sight? Anyway I do see this small thing now; even though under my nose; or big thing. Kindness to a little very ugly boy.

"You put clay on me han'!"

"Good gracious, so I have. Well, look, you help me now."

Then I forget all about it, all through the full chaotic day until I rise in the evening from my table in my little room that I call "Selah," detached from the house at the back, where I really work. Then, as I fill my colour pots with water so that they will not dry out the next day when I am away at school, I find myself wondering why. For working with paint never fails to stir the different assortments of urgent curiosities I go in for and lead me to calm enquiry.

I throw the faded cover over my paper and pages and brushes to protect them from the dust of this unlined shed until I come this way again. The "why" has multiplied itself. Why has he come to New Zealand in the first place? Why has he plunged into teaching so late? Why does he board at Parent Number One's rather than at the pub across the road from them? Why does he drink anyway? And, above all, why does he smile when I am angry and why does he not defend himself when I attack him?

The way I attack him! Can't I see he is young? The desire of a woman in the forties is to protect and nurture the young.

I close my window and draw the curtain so that the morning sun when I am not here cannot dry up my work on the table, and as I set the small fire for the morning, soiling my red gown as I kneel, my thinking follows the route I don't want it to; so that by the time I step out into the night, unreal with scent and loud with the talk of flowers, the biggest why of all confronts me like a man: why am I cruel to him? I, a normal woman of hardly over thirty?

But some flowers are cheekier than others; they're not all well-behaved like the rose. Because he can't say your name! calls out one of them. That chatterbox, the phlox, I suppose.

"I was obliged to chastise the descendant of our redoubtable Chairman this morning," says Mr Vercoe when I meet him inadvertently in the playground.

"Have you struck a child again?"

"He failed to, to . . . shall we say . . . give ear to me."

"Maybe with good reason!"

His mouth, and his eyelids also, twitch in that both nervous and fascinating way and he doesn't reply.

"Didn't you have time in Training College to discover other ways of disciplining children?"

He smiles appreciatively.

"D. H. Lawrence advised the smacking of a child if it annoyed you. He was on the reading list. Besides," he expands a little, "these five-year-olds coming into the world throwing their weight about, have, have . . . shall we say . . . to learn the winds."

I hurry on. I'll tell the Head on this monster. I catch him at the bottom of the steps just as our hundred and a quarter children are bursting out of doors for Friday afternoon sport. He inclines his head attentively and thinks actively of something else. "Pepi," he says, "round up a gang of boys and pick up those cabbage-tree leaves. By God I'll rid myself of those trees yet!"

"Don't you touch those trees while I'm here! I use those trees. I use those trees!"

"But they've lost their beauty, Miss Vorontosov."

"That's why I like them! That's what I like!"

But he never knows what I really mean and continues in all innocence. "They're no longer worth the ground they take up."

I try four tears, but give another reason. "That Shall-we-say of yours gave Matawhero a thrashing. He's been far too good since. Concentrating and so on. I can't stand it. I honestly can't stand it."

"What did he do?"

"I didn't ask."

"Very well, we'll leave the trees for the time being. It is not the child he is striking: it's the situation. He'll get over it."

But this evening when I am shopping in town, being Friday, and as I am resting a moment in my car at the kerb, a strange figure takes my attention. It is a tall man in a long dark tailored coat, the kind you see in the navy. Both hands are deep in the pockets and, quite oblivious to the parade of people about him, he is striding along the pavements close to the shops, his head set to the windows. A solitary desperate figure, pacing with speed, his face to the passing windows; like a big black moth obsessed with the light. What particular classification of derelict is this? I wonder as he approaches. Then I see it is Mr Vercoe.

Impulsively my hand reaches to the door, but by the time the searching eyes are close enough to see I have withdrawn it. I press back in the shadow as he passes and until he is lost again. Only just in time have I recognized the "Thee and Me" between us.

"Miss Pop-off, Seven he's trying to kill us all with the axe for nutteen. Seven. Seven!"

"Hori. Seven . . . axe . . . please."

"I wonder," I mention to the Head, "if the axe could be put away."

"The axe?"

"Either the axe or Seven. One of them needs putting away."

"Rauhuia is at the door!" report the Little Ones.

"Tell him to come in then. Tell him to come right in." Why doesn't he walk in as usual?

"That's why he said he want to see you."

I step over high and low and finally reach the door, and look over the heads clustered about me. The Head's Chairman of the School

32

Committee is profoundly and seriously fat, and unwieldy upon the short legs. The fattest man I have seen, whereas his grandson is the smallest. But they meet on one thing: Thee and Me.

"I just wanted to see Matawhero," he says gruffly. Well, why call me?

"He's here." He must be upset about the hiding his grandson got from Mr Vercoe.

"I just wanted to give him his lunch." The fat hands jerk about uncontrollably, and he looks at me so sadly.

"I've got to cut that boy's lunch," he says. Now what is he trying to tell me in his subtle Maori way?

"Why doesn't his mother cut it? Or his father?"

His voice drops even another octave. "I've got to cut my grandson's lunch."

"Oh? Oh?"

"Oh? Oh?" echo the Little Ones. I blush.

"And it's I who have to get his breakfast."

"You do? You do?"

"You do? You do?" comes the chorus.

"It's my toast he likes, Miss Vorontosov. He says I get it just how he likes it. The toast his mother makes is not quite right."

He is asking me to protect Matawhero. "I see. I see."

"I see. I see," comes the chorus. I blush again.

He passes Matawhero his lunch, turns, and shuffles off slowly down the steps and across the frost. He is overweight and has a "heart." For all his visits to the Board and his wrangling over buildings he is a delicate man. And for all his bluster in the corridor he can become a lamb over his grandson. Also, I reflect, as he takes his lonely sick bike from the elm, for all his expensive clothes he still does not, like Matawhero, wear his trousers high enough. I sigh as I stand and watch him, and within me I think, I see.

"I stayed outside," writes Matawhero who can't stand the bell and who keeps emotional time more accurately than he can keep chronological times,

"because I don't
like school. I don't
like blocks but I

like clay. I don't
want to read
I don't like
Miss Vorontosov."

But Rauhuia can be a lion too, as well as a lamb, over a precious
grandson, and he shuffles his rage along to the Head one morning
when Matawhero turns back from school to go home again and runs
into his Nanny at the corner, taking the bus to town. Rauhuia doesn't
go to town after all but brings his bald head, his bulk, his big, trembling mouth, his smart clothes and his grandson back here. So that
when the Head has a discreet talk to young Vercoe about the national
and racial implications of a white hand raised to a brown child, the
assistant follows me as far as the trees after school, and, for some reason, there is no longer any hectoring in his voice. If anything, it is
wistful.

"I cannot overlook," he says, looking down upon me, "the consistency
with which the Head fights your, fights your . . . shall we say . . .
battles for you."

I look up at him, a risky thing to do. But I can hardly look down at
him as with my Little Ones, even though my feeling is much the
same. Somehow I must find time to help this young teacher with his
classroom. The Head does. Also, although I am tired of this recurring
remark, I am tardily beginning to read some reason for it; some history
of irremedial neglect, some inflammation back in his life that has not
wholly cooled. My habitual irritation in his presence gives way, momentarily, to a wary softening. But from my intense experience with
men in the past, knowing how unprofitable it is to let them know you
are softening, I conceal it and say something else. "I haven't always
had my battles fought for me."

Away flies the disarming wistfulness and he lights up again. "That's
the very first time," he exclaims with excitement, "that you have ever,
have ever . . . shall we say . . . communicated anything to me!"

Away flies my softness also. I am alarmed. I have allowed an in-
excusable relationship to arise. It can't be true that it is I who have first
spoken the fatal Thee and Me between us. I, who have so viciously
beaten it off. Suddenly he is too close. Absolutely and absolutely is he

34

too close! Violently I jettison my patience with the young. "The first time," I whisper in unnecessary emphasis, "and the last! The last!"

And it is not until afterwards when I have left him and am looking in the mail-box for Eugene's letter that I remember the young man under the trees of an hour ago to be the same desperate derelict pacing the shop windows in town of a week ago; and I am saying within me, unwittingly and unguardedly, "What is it, what is it, Little One?"

"Miss Vorontosov," says Mark definitely, "I can't draw any one of the things in that story. Not one single one." Mark is one of these "can't" children whose mothers taste everything first. But he can say my name.

"You could draw the rope, I suppose. Handkerchief, Blossom."

"Just a straight line?"

"Well, a little wiggle in it, you know. And as for the rat, just a round thing like this and another line for the tail like that. Tuck in your shirt, Matawhero." His Nanny the Chairman could pull his trousers higher too. But within me I watch suddenly. Here I am on the old worn track of telling a child how to do a thing instead of leaving it to his own effort and his own way. I'm tasting things for him first, just like his mother. But tradition dies hard. It involves personal sacrifice and courage and a cause. Mark goes on:

"Just a little round thing for a head and another little round thing for a stomach and a line for a tail?"

"And a few legs," I add, unable to pull up and watching the animal grow that is not his conception but mine. "Get out of the water, One-Pint. Lift that boy out of the water!"

"Miss Vontov," complains Twinnie, "my sister she's cheeky. She's draween on my side."

"And a few legs?" continues Mark.

"And a dot for his eye." Ah, no original thought from Mark. "Who's that crying?"

I can't break the habit at all it seems. I even pin this rat monstrosity, which might have been an engaging sketch from the child himself, on the wall beside me where Bleeding Heart comes to gaze at it raptly. Then I hear that noise which boys make in their throats for gunfire. It cuts through someone's singing and the conversation and laughter and through every nerve I've got concerned with sound. It's this new boy drawing his guns. I plunge over and smack his leg, as hard as I can, forgetting my fingers for Schubert. "Don't make that noise!" I gasp.

As I return to my low chair Mark is making another of my rats. "Give that to Bleeding Heart," I say from the surface of my mind. It might, I justify myself superficially, help to promote a little toleration between the brown and the white. But on the lower levels a deeper pondering is under way. A boy drawing his guns with the appropriate gunfire: what could be truer expression? It is a powerful creativity from the very storeroom of his being. Indeed this is the very issue that has begun to dominate my thinking this spring: the lifting of the lid from the young mind. Heard as an explosion of inner pressures, seen as the flowering of an impulse, the noise, as a sound, becomes endurable. It is no longer an ugly noise that hurts me personally but just the sound of a boy drawing madly at his guns and supplying the spit of the bullets.

Brown Wiki brings up a page of rats. "Oh, so you can draw too, Wiki?" Who is that crying?

"No me mate she done this. Me mate."

"Oh?"

"Can I have a scissor to cut it out?"

"No. You make your own rat then you can cut it out."

"I can't make those rat."

"Mark can. Tame, go and see who is crying."

Matawhero doesn't draw. He is reading "The Blue Jug" to Patchy on the steps. Composing the story from the pictures, Matawhero is too closely concerned with the personal relation to do anything with only himself in it. Always the "Thee and Me" for him, first and last. It slows down the ability of his fine hands. I look back into the dark past of that dark-souled man, his grandfather; reflecting on the passions therein. Now, he has no wife. How does he live? Doesn't live, I suppose . . . like me. However . . . brown reading to white. A little more understanding, a little more racial understanding, maybe.

"I've made me piggie, Miss Vontof." Wiki's brown face has a surplus of smiles.

"Where's its legs? Where's its legs?"

36

She turns it round another way. "Here's some legs. Can I have a scissor? Look, Riti, she's cryeen. Riti."

. . . I sit in my workroom in the evening as the cold turns colder, planning my pictures in my third try at these Maori infant reading books. The thing is to draw freely, letting out these images that have intense meaning for me. Just like the new boy spitting over his guns. I put down my pencil and look at the hand that has smacked a child for illustrating in sound something of intense meaning to him also. This, moreover, is the hand that strikes in word at that poor young chap Vercoe on the staff. Ah, mistake, mistake! All my hundreds and thousands of mistakes . . .

How in heaven can I free myself from the tyranny of traditional thinking? Plainly, I see, as I pick up my pencil again, it means effort. But effort involves sacrifice and I'm too old. Besides I have no cause, and no courage to support a cause if I did have one, and how can you rise to sacrifice without a cause?

Fancy a hand that has struck a child presuming to pick up a brush and paint with it! I'm no artist if I strike a child. Even less a woman. How do these things happen? I didn't plan them. Ah, next time I go to church, I decide wearily, I'll think it all out during the sermon . . . work it all out in the sermon.

"Miss Foffof," squeaks Ani.

"What is it, Little One?"

"When I comes to this word 'basket' in my book I never says 'basket.'"

"Oh?"

"I allays says 'kit.'"

"Why?"

" 'Cause 'basket' it's too much like swearing so I says 'kit.'"

"Oh? Read to me then."

" 'So the three likkle kittens all jumped into the ba . . . kit.'"

"Does Riti cry like this at home, Rupeka?" I ask Riti's big sister. Riti is a brown wisp of a four-year-old and her place is at home. Rupeka is at the machine trying to sew herself one of the brown and yellow uniforms that I have designed and insisted on, and arranged with a shop in town to supply the material for, and teach the big girls to use the machine about. She is one of the large poor Tamati family. She is ten, with long curls, and as beautiful as phantasy.

"Yes, Miss Vorontosov, she's always crying. But no one is allowed to give her a hiding. She's Daddy's pet. When he goes away to the Shed and comes back and finds out anyone hit her he growls."

"What are you crying for, Very Little One?" I tip her chin.

"That's why Wiki she's cheeky for me. Wiki."

It's always relationship they cry over. She has a long thin face like a starved rat with little black eyes like peep-holes: straggly black hair all over her face like the rest of the Tamatis, a long dress over her knees and bare feet.

I have been taking a group of sixes and sevens through a page of the Maori book I am trying to make at home, so I sit down again and try to teach over her head and her noise. I am just beginning to see success with the phrasing when there sounds another long high wail. So I put Riti on top of the piano, where she stops immediately for some reason, and track my way through other Little Ones reading on the mat, and between the water and the sand containers, to pick up Hinewaka, who has also broken the five-barrier and who has had treatment and operations on her inturned feet since birth. I pick her up, forgetting altogether that she has not been born of myself, and carry her under my arm back to my chair. She and Riti are so small that how they can meet the requirements of living at all, I just don't know.

But before we have got much further with the testing of the new page I have completed the night before, Riti has been demoted from the piano and back into currency and Hinewaka is there, and between marvellous feats of bawling I am hearing from Waiwini's little brother how Seven has punched him in the stomat for nutteen. He is heavy to lift but I can't resist the physical impact of him on me, on a person that has never been touched by man since I left Eugene. So although his roars are deafening and his tears phenomenal I stagger beneath his weight as best I can, and although I feel his paint brush wet through my smock I also feel that big something, that influences me and frightens me at times when my plans fail, like a great instinct, unidentifiable and uncontrollable, take over. Something that makes me prefer to endure the weight of a heavy child so that holding him becomes the way of least resistance. I can't do anything about the strength of the compulsion any more than Seven can about his violence. I am shocked to have to recognize the volcanic force beneath. We are all caught up in the eruption of energy. Ah, I think, if only all this could be directed creatively!

But soon I am aware of a second weight. It's a moral weight. It's the guilt upon my shoulders like the Old Man of the Sea. His legs round my throat I feel almost physically. What if there were an inspector outside and he heard this din? What if he should come in and see the children in this fluidly moving state, and the teacher acquiescent in the middle of it all? Maybe there is still time to recover orthodoxy again. For there actually will be another inspector . . .

In the evening, however, as I sit in the little back room at the back of my house where I really work, I do no more about it all than pick up my 6B pencil with the softest black lead and draw a small girl crying. True, there are no such things in the new Imported Books, with which the Maori infant rooms have been supplied, no such things as tears, and nothing so unrespectable as emotion. Neither is there dancing nor punches in the stomat, nor screams of laughter and embraces. But there are these things in my books. I make this little girl. I draw her in pencil first, a few lines-worth of long dress, bare feet, straggly hair and tears. I choose the finest of my pre-war brushes to turn the paint the colour I mean and, by the time the rain has settled down heavily on the low roof, here is this little girl wailing from the page.

I'm portraying child drama in these early books. Open-eyed I'm going into another sure mistake. Another avoidable mistake.

DAY by day as the spring days beat by, this one in sun and frost and this one in wet, I sink deeper and deeper into my infant room. No provocation from men may follow me here. I forget all about the young teacher fighting away with his children over there in the big school, and my unexplainable feelings about him, when I am teaching. Never do I hear again or feel again, in here among the children, the voice and the hand of the Reverend as I do over a meal in my house. I don't even recall Eugene. Indeed the only male presence in the pre-fab with any power to disturb me is the shadow of an inspector. But is there anything new in that? Anything new in that?

I pick up a child and sit on my low chair. A heavy lesson has just staggered to its close on the imported reading books. What a dangerous activity reading is; teaching is. All this plastering on of foreign stuff. Why plaster on at all when there's so much inside already? So much locked in? If only I could get it out and use it as working material. And not draw it out either. If I had a light enough touch it would just come out under its own volcanic power. And psychic power, I read in bed this morning, is greater than any other power in the world. What an exciting and frightening business it would be: even that which squeezes through now is amazing enough. In the safety of the world behind my eyes, where the inspector shade cannot see, I picture the infant room as one widening crater, loud with the sound of erupting creativity. Every subject somehow in the creative vent. What wonderful design of movement and mood! "What lovely behaviour of silk-sack clouds!"

An organic design. A growing living changing design. The normal and healthful design. Unsentimental and merciless and shockingly beautiful. But this, I look nervously about the room, is not inspector fare. It is not even my own fare. Indeed, I still have a token of professional status to me, still a few grading marks to hang on to; I've still got something to lose, without the courage to lose it.

What a lot I see, both behind my eyes and before, as I sit on this chair! What a lot of time I spend on this chair.

"Everyone go to sleep."

"Aren't you goin' to wead the B'ue Jug, Mitt Wottot?"

"Do we got to go for a sleep?"

"Matawhero, you go for a sleep. Miss Foffof sayed we got to go for a sleep."

"Wead the B'ue Jug, Mitt Wottot."

"Miss Vorontosov, Bleedin' 'eart won't go to sleep. Bleedin' 'eart."

"Do we got to lie down? Twinnie, lie down."

"Aren't you goin' to wead the B'ue Jug?"

"Twinnie's eyes they're open. She's looking through her eyes. Twinnie."

"The other Twinnie's eyes are open."

"Not!"

"Course!"

"Not!"

"Course!"

"What about the B'ue Jug, Mitt Wottot?"

"Go to sleep!"

Silence.

I take to singing to them as they lie with their eyes closed. True, it must be bad teaching to be singing them to sleep in the Board's time, and the Old Man of Guilt on my shoulders all but puts me out of tune. But memory will have her way, so also will the instincts of a woman, and up come all these little English songs of my mother's that my father sang to me when I was little and which I have not had the occasion to use myself. On this spring afternoon in the pre-fab with the fire humming in the little stove and the sun's fingers reaching, I am for a while no longer the imperfect teacher but the perfect mother and all these children, brown, white and yellow, are my own.

"Oh where, Oh where, has my little dog gone," I sing in my silly voice.

"Oh where, Oh where can he be?

With his hair cut short and his tail cut long,

Oh where, Oh where can he be?"

In time, after I have sent Waiwini's brother and Seven outside and later Blossom, the nursery rhymes make their appearance and then the Maori love-songs that are graduating into Maori nursery rhymes. And the poi* tunes and the melodies they use in canoes, and even my own little song about Ihaka (the central character in my Maori reading books) and his dream that I have made myself. But by the time Patchy has risen and sneaked out under his own power, the habit of wanting to get outside overruling any pleasure he may have felt, back come the songs of my childhood again. "Oh, going down the river in the old steam boat . . ."

Pussy uses my singing to get herself off to sleep, which affronts me somewhat, and lulled with the music I droop a little too, and the world of children on the mats before my eyes gives way to the world behind. With a hand over my face I stop singing and watch the pictures within; flashing, sliding and interchanging in their own order; an order where first is first and last is last in proportion to their significance, and where no outer consciousness interferes.

Yet are there among these wilful pictures none of the men I meet. No wonderful blue eyes follow me into the austerity of my thinking in the infant room. No radiant voice from a pulpit penetrates my spirit here. No passionate interchanges with Eugene track me down from the past. As ever, my mind in the pre-fab is sacrosanct, cloistering nothing other than my absorption in my teaching. The image that jostles forward and upward demanding my inner eye is one of an in-

* *Poi:* Maori dance.

fant room that has achieved the organic order; a seed-bed where children grow and expand and bloom, where there is an end to don'ts and bells and where the Old Man of Guilt no longer dominates my being. It's a noisy happy place with much free coming and going through the door. Children dance spontaneously like leaves in the wind and learning is a matter of preference.

But soon the restless ones stir and some sit up and look at me. More wake. Some stand. But all look at me to see if I am going to say no. It makes me ashamed, and I keep my face in my hand and say nothing. I cover my face and say nothing.

In time they take things into their own hands. Two fight, two embrace, some draw, some move to the sand-container and many sneak outside. All this energy, I think! Why can't I use it? Why must I curb it? Ah, if only I had some courage I'd change it all!

Where is the way, anyhow? How do you do it? I get that feeling I have had before on occasion that the answer is close. Just nearby somewhere. All I want is some kind of influence; some touch. "I want the one rapture of an inspiration."

But two have a place in the birth of something new. If only I could relate this academic life of the infant room with the one of sensuousness beyond. Consciously I summon these men that admittedly divert me to my cold presence. Paul Vercoe is one big take, even though there is some quality common to us both. The Head is one big give, but he understands me not in the slightest. The Reverend appears to be madly in love with God. And Eugene . . . what power can a dark-winged memory have from so long and so far ago? Indeed there is only the shade of the inspector left . . .

I sigh and take a child. I need something else like the rain, like the sun: you need two for inspiration but I am only one.

"and not breed one work that wakes."

$\mathcal{J}$T takes me from eight till nine to dress in the morning, I don't
know why. After my eight o'clock cup of tea, summing up a couple
of hours at the piano or at work in Selah I begin on this pantomime
and unnecessary performance. Anyone would think, by the thought
I put into it every morning, that I went in for a lover every night. Why
in heaven do I do all this? Who sees me?

At last I get out the crystal tumbler I keep for before-school duty
and half fill it with brandy. So that the flowers won't upset me as I
pass and Guilt about inspectors won't halt me at the trees.

I sigh deeply. Why do I do all this? I wonder as I drink. Is it just
plain force of habit, a hangover from my youth, that I care how I
look? Is it hope? Is it the spring? Is it that, even after all those years
of unforgettable lessons, I am still actively in love with life? Or is it the
manifestation of that unseen force that makes me do things I don't
understand?

I walk down the back steps with my pen-box into the sunny spring
garden and sure enough, here are these flowers all set to tease me. How
they love to make me cry! Maybe it is because they are so beautiful
when life to me is not. So fulfilled when life is not.

44

The brandy burns intimately. It releases tensions and softens feeling. Because I myself do not happen to have found life lovely, does it necessarily follow that it isn't? Maybe it is happy and I have been too lonely to see it.

The fire within my body takes possession. This is the kind of time when I am likely to step over the frontiers into phantasy, and it is the kind of time when my flowers are just as likely to do the same thing. With no surprise at all I hear these flowers talking. If only I knew what they were talking about! After all, their conversation can't be so unrelated to that unfathomable design that puzzles and frightens and propels me, and that I take to church with me, since they show it so simply themselves. I kneel to the level of a delphinium bud and tip its chin. "Why do I try so hard to look beautiful when my life has been so sad?"

Her voice is confused with the others and I lean a bit nearer to catch it. Life is in bloom, she is saying, and you're only trying to match it.

"What can I do for you, Madame?"

Good God! It's this Vercoe! What's happened? Ah . . . this is the Head's work! He has spent a lot of time with this boy. In his classroom, in the playground, in the porch. Gentleness plus persistence pay apparently. More than my old-maid spitting.

"I beg your pardon?" He has penetrated the holiness of my infant room for the first time, where I am damping the sand for the day with water, having already dampened my brain for the day with brandy.

He doesn't answer. Fancy Paul Vercoe without an answer! If ever a blue-eyed rueful child stood before me, one does now. He's like a new-boy. It's as much as I can do not to tip his chin and say, what is it, what is it, Little One? But, as before, his gaze slides down into the low neckline of my smock as I bend forward, and at once he is a male. Suddenly and furiously I straighten. "You can take my A and B basketball teams for a practice. They're waiting out on the field for me this very minute. There this very minute!"

When he has gone I reach to my blazing neck. What am I? What is he? Is he a child to my teacher, or a man to my woman? How can a nice sober . . . I mean almost sober . . . teacher, a diligent orderly Infant Mistress begin the day with a conflict like this? I must beg the Head to spare me visits from this man!

Yet I have my obligations to help him. I must pull my weight in training a young teacher. The Head said that the Senior Inspector said that we each have definite obligations here. Observation lessons, demonstration lessons and example. Not that the Head or the Senior need to remind any woman of forty-four of the ordinary graces of humanity. But even if I could find the time, the patience or even the resistance to train him, what could I train him in? My ways? Is it fair to drag a young assistant down the drain with me? Into oblivion with me?

What can I do for you, Madame, indeed! You can stop trying to see beyond my neckline. You can stop trying to find my person beneath my smock. God knows it is voluminous enough, isn't it, my smock? What concern is it of yours that the necks are low? They're low because I get hot in here what with the fire and the sun and the children! Besides a woman of thirty-four doesn't have to dress like a nun. What can I do for you, Madame? Paul . . . you can embrace me.

Poetically . . .

"I saw," writes Mohi,
"Miss Vorontosov
and Mr Vercoe. She
was going home
when They got to
the trees they
Stopped and Talked."

I take my Little Ones for a walk this morning down the stopbank along the river through the poplars, and, since Hinewaka is the one above all who must not be left behind on account of her injured feet, I carry her on my back. For some obscure reason I take Seven too, although the Head offered to mind him.

But as we leave the road and get through the fence I am thinking of other things. While the Little Ones break out in loud song as they plough through the lovely grass, dance wildly beneath the poplars, study the calf in the next paddock and slide down the steep bank, I am thinking of that lonely bewildered wanderer back at school.

If only the man and the child were not so confused in Paul Vercoe!

I know how to deal with a child and I have learnt how to manage a man; at least I should have, by now. But, confronted with a child when I am resisting an adult, and alarmed by a man when comforting a child, I wonder if I know anything at all. What I should do, I reflect, my eyes roving over the farthest child, if I really wished to understand him, is allow him nearer me. Then, possibly, his annihilating conversation, seen as the protestations of an injured child rather than as the predatoriness of a male, would cease to offend me.

Amazingly, Seven is walking meekly at my side. Plainly he is timid. Like all bullies; like all loud talkers; like, in fact, Paul Vercoe. Believing at last that he is secure in me, Seven relaxes at my side, no longer knowing the need to attack. For a moment, stumbling along under the weight of Hinewaka, I'm hardly sure who exactly I am thinking of: Seven or Paul.

The child in Paul increasingly engages my attention. I have had time during his anxious and inefficient stay here to find the oldness and sadness behind the petal-blue eyes hanging like water colours in his face, hidden behind the authoritative poses he strikes; from the references in his conversation; from the regular drinking I hear about and from the revelation of that Friday night in town; all so at variance with youth. Indeed, there could well be a third person in the concoction that is Paul: besides the child and the attacking male, plainly there is an old man. If it were not for the way he manages to touch me so accidentally as we wend through the carpenters, walling off the corridor for a staff-room, and the secrecy with which he watches my legs when I am obliged to cross them, I would get to know these three people and maybe ease him.

I settle down in the cushiony grass with Hinewaka and Seven beside me. If only he could learn that, for me anyway, there can be interests other than men; that there can be romance outside desire; that with me, in spite of the reputations of the unmarried, relations with the male come second to my relations with my work; that the need for the physical engagement, the "trivial ritual of love," so featured in the talk of New Zealand men as being the driving factor in the life of a spinster, can at my age, in some women and to a workable extent anyway, lift to the realm of the mind to be partially consummated there; if only, I insist, looking through the rich shade to the blue river beyond, he would get it out of his head that I am necessarily and automatically and always racked with physical tension; that I am, in that stock phrase "starved, hungry and bitter"; that my mind, as the Head and the Reverend apparently see, is able to conceive and bear fruit as cheerfully as any body of a smug married woman and that my heart, in spite of the insubordinate responses of my person, can be ineffably gayer; if only he could approach me with the respect and fellowship of the two older men! Ah! but he is young, he is young. . . .

When we arrive back at school, the Little Ones in time for milk and I in time for morning tea, I avoid the public corridor and return to the cool of the pre-fab with Hinewaka. Here I put her down at the long low wall blackboard with some chalk and I sit down to rest.

I don't expect anything from Hinewaka; she has never put pencil, crayon or chalk to paper or board before, being too wholemindedly so far sounding out, checking and verifying any security to be found in me; but her feet sorrows must come out some time.

Without a moment's hesitation she draws a little girl, in blue, with feet turned in. Then a yellow one beside her with feet turned in. Then a green one in line with the others until from one end of the board to the other is a troupe of small coloured girls with their feet turned in. She works with energy and precision as though she had handled chalk for months, changing the colours in her tiny brown hand with the dispatch of the possessed.

"Who are those?" I ask when the space on the board has finally run out.

She turns to me with a lovely smile. "All them kids on the stopbank."

So of course I cry. I go into the storeroom to do it. I'm not clear who I am crying over: Hinewaka, Seven, Paul or myself. Indeed, considering the volume of my tears, it could be over many others: all the young with grief in their being that I ever knew. I may even be weeping for my own lost youth, for my own lost love. It could even be because of the growing presence of Paul in the world behind my eyes, reminding me of what life with a man might have been. And goodness knows how long I am likely to go on. But it is safe enough to cry in my infant room: we all do.

So that when steps sound in the pre-fab, the shod steps of a man, I don't believe it. But when I hear the lock of the storeroom door and smell the rum on Paul, I have to. I look up at him, forgetting how dangerous it is for a woman to look up.

He is different from his image in the world behind. In the blue paintings of his eyes I see no outline of a child, of a man or of an urgent lover. I see only someone else; someone to share the moment with, and I hear only, "What can I do for you, Madame?"

"You must go over to my house, Paul," I sob, using the "Paul" for the first time and without thinking, "and bring me some brandy. I'll never get through the rest of the morning like this."

"You're tired," he says with unfamiliar softness. "You've been carrying that child for miles."

I get to work with the hem of my smock on my face. He leans an elbow high above on the shelf above me and looks down. Suddenly in his attitude I feel the man. And he is far, far too close. Alarmingly too close. "Go, go, Paul," I say nervously. "Let me get on with my crying. I'm . . . I'm busy."

"What can I do for you, Madame?"

But he has to be saved from me; he's young. Temporarily, the glamorous thirties switch to the vague fifties. I must sacrifice myself for the young or I do not exist at all. I must not allow myself the sweetness of his sympathy; I must not help myself to his youth. I must go without it or . . . perish.

My cosmetic has all washed off and my eyes are the red ones of grief. Grief for myself now rather than for others. I turn this appalling face of mine up once more to the glory of youth above; looking up with this can have no hazards . . . then I turn away. "Go, Paul," I whisper. "There's a good boy. I want to get on with my middle age."

"Me and my sister," struggles Twinnie, trying to write because she saw Tame at it,
     "played
marbles when it was
nearly dark. Then we
went inside and
slipped on my coat."

"Mr W. W. J. Abercrombie, Senior Inspector of Primary Schools," begins the Head portentously at morning tea . . .

"Don't say that terrible word! Don't speak like that in front of a woman!"

"The new Senior Inspector," carries on the Head, beginning to laugh, "is on his rounds. Making the acquaintance of his teachers."

"Oh no no no, don't say that! Oh no no, you mustn't say that!"

Paul Vercoe looks up from his tea at me. "We heard it last night at an Institute Meeting."

"Oh you shouldn't go to those meetings when you hear such things!"

Both the men laugh like anything. The carpenters coming in for their hot water join in. "I heard," goes on the Vercoe, "that they were actually in this district. In fact, in fact," he warms up, "I heard they were looking particularly, particularly for, for . . . shall we say . . . unorthodox Infant Mistresses!"

"Oh, spare me these realities!"

"Actually," tries Mr Reardon, "I am looking forward to seeing him myself. I want to . . ."

"Who-what you want to do," plunges in Vercoe, "what you want to do, Madame, is to scratch a big hole in the playground and you and all your crew, including, not omitting the stock, Pussy, Ginger Rooster and Sammy Snail, bury your heads in it!"

"I suppose," the Head addresses the two carpenters, all agog with the staff talk, "you are ready to put that bench of yours in the shed. I've had the boys clear it." For a moment he converses easily with them, then we are alone again. "As I was saying—" he picks up what he began in the first place—"I want to see him to show him the conditions here. He's sure to . . ."

"We'll give him his tea here in the porch!" crows Vercoe. "Sit him on this form! Let all the kids, let all the kids thunder round! Leave the outside door open for the south wind! Fill the basins with lost shoes and invite him to wash his hands! Pile up all the coats on the . . ." But he collapses with laughter. "Who wants some more tea? Madame? What can I do for you, Madame? Allow me the honour!"

He still does some frightful murdering of thought sequences but the tone on our staff is so much better. So, so much better. No one would offend the Head with bickering. No one wants to now. I give him my cup, his fingers unnecessarily and accidentally touching mine. "Make it strong! Make it strong! Put real tannin in it. Put brandy in it. Put bromide in it! Put anything in it. Shoes, coats, cats, chalk. . . . Must I meet this man, Mr Reardon? Save me from this monster, Mr . . ."

"Madame, Madame V'ront'sov. Drink this and you will be monster-

proof. You will be, will be . . . shall we say . . . obsession-proof. I,"
he claims grandiloquently, "am the Tender of obsessions!"

We all roar with laughter. Paul included.

"I want to let him see," ploughs on the Head from where he left off,
a cup of tea ago, "the conditions under which . . ."

I look up into these eyes above me and stay in them for once. I forget
my appointment with the elm tree and I overlook altogether to cross
my legs. Eyes obliterate trivialities like age.

"Where's your father, Nuku?"
"In gaol. Where's yours?"

The infant room rocks along like a dinghy in a storm. It nearly always has a boy in it practising on the piano, a girl dressmaking, someone looking out the window, someone looking in the window, some
children sitting on the top of their small tables doing their work for
lack of room on the floor, several dancing if I happen to be playing and
dozens of infants talking and working and playing and laughing and
crying and embracing and quarrelling and singing and making.

I like to hear the crying break out but actually I like the singing just
as much. More join in. Sometimes I play an accompaniment to their
crying as well as to their singing. Beethoven fits in. But both crying
and singing have the same essential quality. They draw us together.
First one, then two, then many, with always the natural social outcasts
on the fringe. Sometimes they run up and cluster round the piano to
sing and sometimes they just carry on where they happen to be. But
when I light on a favourite tune they sing themselves inside out. "Big
enough for two, my darling, big enough for two," and "Sleeping, sleeping, Ihaka." Then so strong is the air that I am in the position to play
an alto, and that's about all I ask for a moment of joy. Waiwini
squeezes as closely to the keyboard as a six-year-old humanly can and
tries to follow this part. Then when it is over they flow back to what
they were doing. Lovely movement. Lovely grouping. Talks on the
way; fights on the way. And pushing. And caressing. . . . All sorts of
involved caressing.

But these are not the kinds of things to recover professional favour.
Bad teaching . . . ah, bad teaching. If only I could rid myself of this
dream in my mind; this picture of the real infant room. It reminds me

51

of the wolf in the wood. It might devour me as it might have devoured Little Red Riding Hood.

Ah, yes. Here we are in a dinghy on the high ocean. Where's the port? . . . We all seem to be heading somewhere but what's the name of the port?

"Tell me, Madame," says Paul, as I pick myself up after falling over in the corridor on a pile of lost shoes, "do you live with your eyes open or, or . . . shall we say . . . dream with your eyes shut?"

"I dream, Paul," I answer in a fury of humiliation, "with my eyes open and, and . . . shall we say . . . live with my eyes shut!"

"Can I go outside?" asks Matawhero.

I look down upon him. He is very small and his head is very big but his upward brown eyes are beautiful to a white woman. To a childless woman. I kneel to his level. "The bell," I remind him with the ease of tradition, "hasn't gone yet."

"Can I?" he whines.

I knew what Rauhuia's visit to the pre-fab was the other day. I saw it all in the pleading eyes over his grandson's lunch. I haven't worked among Maori infants for so long without learning to read the unspoken word. He was telling me that he trusted me to care for his *"moko-puna."** If he were here now . . . to see this desperation of his little boy's to get outside. It offends me but I compromise. I fingertip his chin. "Have you done your work?"

He scatters away on his thin bandy legs and brings it: screwed-up-little-writing-all-stuck-together-at-a-rising-angle. "Can I go?"

"Why not?"

At last our lord the bell rings, freeing all the other little prisoners. It rings and rings and rings as though school were over for ever. Patchy runs in eagerly from the step where he has been sitting reading; my spindly-legged, spindly-brained classic of the "poor white trash." "It playtoime, it playtoime?" he cries anxiously.

Matawhero runs in eagerly too. "It was me ringing the bell, Miss Vorontosov! I rang it eight times!"

Yet I had thought that Patchy was happy enough reading on the step.

* *Mokopuna:* grandchild.

Pussy strolls in sinuously. At least she seems to be pleased with school. Is it because she chooses her own time to come and go? Or is it because we don't try to make her learn anything unrelated to her own interests?

Running, running everywhere. This energy in children. Little ones running out and big ones running in. Sounds of feet. Sounds of feet And chattering like the flowers.

"Can I play the piano?"

"Can I stay after and teach the Little Ones?"

"Somebodies they taked my paper for after play."

"Look, here's the Pussy!"

"Mohi he stealed the dice. Mohi."

"Twinnie's cryeen. Who donged you, Twinnie?"

Then Hirani plays *Pokare kare kare ana* and singing coheres it all. . . .

I pick up my little Riti and sit on my low chair pondering. I feel ashamed that my Little Ones are dying to go outside. Why this prepossession to go outside? Why not the prepossession to come inside?

I put down Riti and pick up Pussy and a book and set to work teaching her to read until the screams of laughter unnerve her and she also flees away outside.

"Last night," writes Tame reminiscently,
"I felled out of
bed. So Daddy told
Mummie to
shiff over."

The little dinghy riding the high waves of the ocean runs into some benign weather. The pre-fab is full of sun and a calm, rhythmically beating creativity. There is noise, of course, but these are children. There is conversation and crying, towers rising tall, bombers on the blackboard, flowers on the clay-boards, a graveyard in the sand table, wharves made of blocks in the water trough with precarious ships sailing, and strange shapes in chalk and paint. I am aware of the spring myself and feel like a little Schubert, so I try to run through the crosscurrents to the piano and there I play this favourite "Hark, Hark, the Lark!" tune of theirs, forgetting the world about me, even to the inspector in the rafters, there being no room for him on the floor.

But whether it is the genius of Schubert speaking down the century, whether it is the quickening in the air after the cold winter, or whether the time is ripe anyway, something new comes to us. There is a flash of yellow on my left and I look round. Twinnie is dancing. It is not the usual hula or any native dance. It is some fine expressive movement such as is cultivated on the stage these days as something new, but which belongs before time. Body-talk that is the "true voice of feeling."

Up rises the other Twinnie and their movements merge. They dance to and from each other and in and out of the chairs and tables. Two yellow jerseys like two yellow daffodils. Two brown spirits of the spring.

Tame rises and Matawhero. Then Ani and dirty Hine. Waiwini finds room upon a low table. And here, all at once, we have a rending in the creative vent, widening it. Here we have another escape for the wild spirit within. I am watching an organic movement such as I have not even dreamt of, even over my paints in Selah.

I play it right through to the end and then sit with my hands on my knee. Humble and afraid, I give the flowers to Schubert. I rest with my hands on my knee and leave the flowers for Schubert.

"I frighteen of those p'lice," says brown Rangi. "They take me away in the fire-engine an hang me up and kill me with the butcher knife."

"What can I do for you, Madame?"

Here is Paul's face at the window of my car in town on Friday night as I am resting a moment. He is drunk.

I don't answer, because, sitting here in the mixture of light and shadow, with the beat of humanity about me, I am feeling not a day over my thirty years, not an hour over, and my blood is sparking for absolutely nothing at all. I'm not watching for any face I can bear to see and not listening for any particularly sea-going stride. Neither am I hoping foolishly to hear a raucous voice. At least so I have convinced myself so far. And feeling this way I know all too well what Paul can do for me: what any young man can do for any young woman sitting alone in her car on a Friday night with her blood sparking for nothing. Gone is that moral old spinster and her young.

"I am one of God's lost children," Paul opens cheerfully.

"A handsome lost child," I improve, feeling disappointed. I don't want to be a teacher-saviour at the moment.

"I know."

I laugh; I can't help it. But he goes on, pushing his face right in my window. "No one knows how lonely I am." He breathes beer, or rum, I think, all over me an inch or so off. Six inches off. I must be accurate.

"I've known, Paul, from the first time I saw you."

"If only one person, only one, understood me!"

"I understand you," I reply steadily, feeling momentarily a little older, and rescuing my face from goodness knows what. But he is too well on. "No one understands me," he claims. "I'm one of the lost children of the earth. If there was only one who understood me!"

"There is one. Not more than six inches away." His face approaches. "Five inches," I correct myself. "Four, three . . . two . . . really, Paul, I must draw your attention to my middle age."

"That ravishing perfume you always wear!" Twitching lips.

That's better. But I'm alarmed for all that. He leans rummily and cheerfully closer. "You are," he whispers, as I press back to my limit, "the most fascinating woman I have ever met! If only you were twenty years younger we could, we could . . . shall we say . . ."

"No, we shan't say."

I hold myself back not only because of his breath but because he is a stranger. He doesn't do this at school when he is sober. I've never seen his eyes so close; great blue perfect things with lids like lips. What chance has the unravished, the undespoiled, against this? My sober, frugal person, silent for so many years, begins to say . . . something unpoetic.

"Fascinating . . . intoxicating . . ." says the rum.

I'm relieved to hear this. I have often regretted, since, that I showed my ravaged face in the storeroom that morning. But I don't reply. I can't tell him what I'm thinking.

"You disapprove," he says, "because I am drunk."

"I prefer you drunk."

"Yet your pose does not, does not . . . shall we say . . . confirm that." Flickering eyelids.

"It's only because you are not drunk enough."

"I'm primed to go till four next morning."

"Only four?"

Now he is in my car beside me. And the next thing, here I am driving him home with me to the village. I am flooded with talk, obliterated with philosophical exposition, all the way home to the bridge. But although he is touching me for the very first time, I find my age ascending. Then I find myself feeling the big week at school: the ball preparations, the basketball practices, the orchestra practices, the hard early morning work in Selah, all on top of the infant room. I feel my feet tired from the shopping. So that by the time I pull up at the bridge where the lane leads away to the pub and Parent Number One's place, my silly murmuring person, in spite of his proximity, loses interest. I'm already bored by this lost child of God.

I know he is dreadfully hurt when I stop and let him out, but I'm very tired on Friday nights. After all, is it my fault that God has been mislaying his children? And that they are primed to go till four next morning? Not after nine on Friday night anyway. Besides, now that I come to think of it, I don't know that I quite like this "If you were twenty years younger" part.

"Mr W. W. J. Abercrombie, Senior Inspector of Primary Schools!" booms the Head, looking at me. How he loves to tease me! We are in the porch among the shoes and coats and basins, the gear and odds and ends of the carpenters.

"It leaves me cold. It leaves me absolutely cold."

"Not really," observes Paul.

"Now don't let me down, Madame," reproves the Head. "Aren't I going to raise some response from the mention of the Senior Inspector? Don't disappoint us now. You have brought us up on sparks for morning tea."

I don't blame the Head for taking a rest from the name "Vorontosov." After all he has had a good turn. More than anyone else really. Several times a day actually. Moreover he has proved that he can say it. To be frank, it takes me, myself, all my time to sign my cheques, and to write it at the Booking Office every time I want to run away. Yes, he's qualified for the Madame. Which is more than Shall-we-say has. "It leaves me cold," I repeat. "Freezing. If that will do for a response."

So it does leave me cold. The Senior Inspector, so what! There's a rhythm even in fear. Besides, I feel different . . . temporarily anyway

. . . since church on Sunday night. What power has an inspector against the gift that God has put in my hands . . . teaching?

"I saw," writes Twinnie,
"the fantail in.
The tree It was singing.
Mr Vercoe was telling.
Miss Vorontosov.
About the fantail.
He was looking at.
Miss Vorontosov."

"My word, you are growing a tall girl, Whareparita," I remark as I meet her coming out of Paul's classroom after school, late after school. "How old are you?"

"I'll soon be thirteen, Miss Vorontosov," she replies. There is more than physical beauty in her face. It's blazing from within. Blushing.

"Thirteen? I thought you were nearer fifteen." I should reprove this girl for being on the premises so late. But she is my right-hand man in the infant room and she clears my name like a hurdler.

"You should be home by now," I offer gently.

"I waited to make the tea for the teachers, Miss Vorontosov. And then wash up after."

"That's very kind of you, Whareparita. But you had better hurry home to Nanny. She will be wondering where you are."

Not thirteen yet. These Maori girls are big. "Good afternoon, Whareparita." If you treat these big difficult moody Maori girls with meticulous respect, they treat you with the same. It's my ace card in controlling them, when I'm not in a rage.

"Good afternoon, Miss Vorontosov. I'm always so glad to do anything for you."

See how it works?

It's Thursday and it's raining. I make my way through the cabbage trees very upset. Even the brandy doesn't work. Also I have headache;

not having slept well since Paul was not there last Friday. Somebody younger, I suppose. What is happening to this glamorous present that was pushing back the past? Are spinsters not allowed to enjoy excitement? Fancy me expecting anything from a youth as though I were not a day over twenty! Man-sick misery that I am!

I push furiously up the steps through the porch into the rocky old raftered barn, barely fit for roosters and cats, and get on with all that I am good for: damping the sand, mixing the colours, softening the clay, seeing to the fire and unlocking the piano. *Men!* I actually spit.

Wouldn't you think I had picked up something about men by now? God in Heaven, will hope never stop springing in my human breast! *Men!* What have I ever learnt about *Men!* Get on, get on, you fool, with the only thing you do know about: paints, clay . . . sand! It's Thursday and it's raining and that's all there is for you!

Twenty indeed. . . . You're eighty!

A rainy Thursday . . .

I sit on my low chair with my back to the stove and with tiny Lotus and trashy Patchy in the crook of each of my arms, since they are afraid of the recurring thunder. The rain is heavy on the low roof. I wonder what my flowers are thinking about it. It'll be heavy over there too. Everywhere for that matter. On the high pointed roof of the big school that the Head hates, drowning the singing in Paul's room, on the church in town, on my house where Eugene's photo waits in my secluded room and on the iron of Selah. Everywhere. That is what I like about the rain: it unites all the divisions of my life into one, as nothing else and nobody can.

I look about the crowded room. All these differing personalities and faces and colours make me think that if ever I had borne children I would have wanted it this way: offspring of many sires. Then I would be like the rain, uniting them all in my motherhood. Yet I cannot help but see that for the very reason that I have not borne children I have achieved this state: fifty or sixty souls of varied kinds and sires bundled together in my precarious dinghy on the tumultuous seas, and all encompassed in me.

As the thunder hammers once more and the Little Ones glance up, some wondering, some delighting and some fearing, I marvel at the variation here; at the multitudinous facets of this infant-room soul. It is like the divisions in me. To the Head I show a difficult yet vigorous infant mistress, to Paul an adventurer with possibilities, to Eugene an inaccessible mistress, to the inspectors an inefficient teacher, to the flowers simply a lonely woman, while only to God do I show the passionate toiler in Selah. All the kaleidoscopic personality revolving, flashing irrelevant facets. Ah, if only one love controlled the whole!

True, I consider, twisting a strand of Patchy's fair head, there is a little relating coming. Paul, for instance, from the school presses little by little into my private life; my Maori books find their way over here into my teaching; also the music for the ball and the orchestra I prepare at home in the evening, but can you call this cohesion? I lay my cheek on the black head on my other side. Ah, I'm tired of being a cheap flirt to Paul, an eccentric to the Head, a refusal to Eugene, a failure to the inspector and an artist unto God. I long for one vast rain to encompass my all. To embrace my all. Just as the numberless facets of childhood here are tenderly combined in me. But only the rain does that.

A rainy, rainy Thursday . . .

Seven, my future murderer, if I don't do something effective about it, is shouting in a ring of his enemies. Tame, the brightest all-round brain I have encountered in any of my infant rooms, brown or white, is reading exhaustively to himself. Mark, the disciplined, the righteous, is copying pages and pages. Mohi, my professional lunatic, is dreaming on the mat, and the Twinnies, with a ukulele between them, are singing together. And Waiwini is working out a private dance step upon a table. Whatever, I think selfishly, the life patterns of the future, the Pakeha success or the Maori doorstep-sitting, whatever is coming up through the school, the discovery is first for me. Yes, if there is anything new and of note coming up through the infant room, the discovery is for me.

A rainy, rainy, rainy Thursday and I talk to them all day. They ask ten thousand questions in the morning and eleven thousand in the afternoon. And more and more as I talk with them I sense hidden in this converse some kind of key. A kind of high-above nebulous meaning that I cannot identify. And the more I withdraw as a teacher and sit and talk as a person, the more I join in with the stream of their energy, the direction of their inclinations, the rhythms of their emotions and the forces of their communications, the more I feel my thinking travelling towards this; this something that is the answer to it all; this . . . key.

59

But often I feel the noise is too big a price to pay at my age. Not as noise, I repeat, but as this Guilt that persists on my shoulders; born from What Other People Think. Although I struggle with him I just can't get him off. I wonder if I will ever see the last of him in this short life. It seems to me that getting rid of him is not a matter of courage after all, as I so often think, but that it has something to do with surgery, in the way that one has a life-long growth cut out.

Only a dream can contest his hold; a dream pounding about within like the thunder banging without; a dream of a real infant seed bed where the abstract pattern of growth is allowed all its variation.

A rainy, rainy Thursday . . .

By the afternoon I have seniors in knitting, dressmaking and the orchestra practising, all on top of the infant room. A holocaust of noise. Strange forms of behaviour coming up through the consciousness and tight legs round my throat. And somewhere, not very high above me now, and not too far out of reach . . . a *key*.

The mind flashes, many-faceted. To one circumstance it throws up one mood; to another a second. Turning again it shows another, and again, another. Revolving, revolving, as the hours beat by. This mood, that mood. This thought, that thought. This passion, that passion; this memory, that. How can you keep track of the changes during an entire afternoon? Of the smile, the tear, the tenderness, the rage? Of the thinking, dreaming, hoping and regret? By the time I close the piano and lock it for the day and hide my own coloured chalk high on a shelf in the storeroom where little fingers cannot reach it, and where the big boys preparing the fire for the morning will not notice it, and take one last look across the plains to my favourite hill, blurred with the enclosing rain, only the storm reminds me of something I was thinking on early. Something about the rain . . . or was it about men? I still register a mysterious feeling of a necessity to pack small baby clothes in a trunk to prepare for a birth, like any other mother . . . But what was about to be born? As so often it happens when I come over here into this crater of children, my personal affairs are blasted away. I don't know what I was happy about, or what I was unhappy about either. I've forgotten that earlier mood.

I pick up my pen-box and walk cheerfully out, forgetting the earlier mood; out into the storm-rains homeward, washed, as it were, and renewed.

But the immanence of a key comes back to me.

Sometimes when I am working late at night over my Maori reading books I almost see this key. Sometimes I think it has traffic with violence. The colours make me think that. They make me think of the passions in their homes, in their ways, and tucked in alongside of the gentleness. The way these colours flash and merge and disobey! The way they suggest to me! Their decisions and combinations remind me of the way children go on.

Thoughts come in clear sequence late at night with a moving brush. At the fluidity of the colour on the pages the pictures in my mind tend to run. They slip forward and backward and repeat themselves, and jostle and change places, until one would never know that outside of Selah the world is dark and quiet.

A picture I am seeing increasingly is myself in the age of oldness, shuddering in my wheel-chair, to think that I had done nothing with these five hours a day. Then I see myself being sacked because I do. Then I see the instincts in the raw in my infant room and the beauty of organic growth, and repeatedly I see the agony of minds expanding beneath pressure. And I see the wildness of the *pa* and my bad name in the inspectorate; indeed, possibly, even in the Directorate. They interchange and interweave, the pictures, and I see brown and blue and black eyes peering out from beneath a heavy lid of respectability and tradition like the eyes of prisoners in a dungeon.

I rise and go to the door, but as I feel the cold of the spring night the pictures vanish and I am sprung upon by Guilt, so that I wonder if courage has a limit somewhere or whether it is an organically dividing substance, for ever regrowing, that can never fail me. I wonder, as I wander past the tall delphiniums, to what extent it would support me against the current. If I could only be sure that it would, I would plunge right in and lift the lid from the infant room. Then the stillness of age and its regrets would no longer be something to take my life in advance about.

Sometimes I almost see this key. But feeling it near is the worst; the pressure of the idea that cannot achieve birth. Maybe the muscles and tissues of my mind are too set, or too tense, to deliver a child at my age. Perhaps I had better not prepare small clothes in a suit-case after all. I dig my hands into the pockets of my smock and, in my unrest, walk the length of the garden. Then I walk through the length of the house, go to the piano, go to the window, to another window, seeking some place in my small sphere where there is less discomfort.

But it wears off, wears off like any other labour pain and, returning through the garden to Selah, I step from the dark to the light. There I set my fire for the morning and cover my work for the night.

*"Wert thou my enemy, O thou, my friend,
How wouldst thou worse, I wonder, than thou dost
Defeat, thwart me?"*

I HAVE looked for Paul in town last Friday night but he wasn't there. I have crushed a moth in my irritation but when I open my palm I find despoiled delphinium petals. Yet he is so cheerful, a thing that racks me. But this Friday as I am resting a moment . . . I would never call it waiting a moment . . . here he comes down the street as drunk as ever. How painful it is to be forgiven! It's a minor department of hell . . . shall we say . . . a corridor.

Heavens, the way he leans his face through the window of my car in broad daylight! It might be all right in Latin America.

"Still that ravishing perfume of yours, Madame!"

"My dear Paul. This is only my second best. Wait till you hear my first."

"But you would be ravishing with or without scent, Madame!"

"Thank you, Paul. That is very gallant of you." All this is almost too hard on a lonely chaste woman.

He doesn't leave me. He has tea with me in the little Tip-Top where they have learnt how to make real milk-shakes (from the Americans when they were here during the war) and now the sweetest part of all comes. He comes shopping with me. He walks closely touching, as you see lovers do, being still well "primed," and we talk and laugh with each other in delight. He buys a pipe to look more mature and accompanies me into the shops. And the competence with which he argues with the shopgirls and men assistants makes me think he has been behind a counter before. He takes in his stride my lipstick, my powder, the curtains for the school and my nail-file. Indeed, at the cosmetic counter he even recites, *sotto voce,* a ditty he has sold for the face products once. Terrible, it is. "I wish," he says at length, easily, or his rum says easily (does it matter which for the moment?), "that we could have a holiday on the continent together."

"My dear Paul, forgive me for drawing your attention to my middle age."

And now comes the thing I have been waiting for; the sequel to his "if you were twenty years younger we could . . .":

"It doesn't make any difference."

"Our baby," writes Patu,
"she can laugh
in the morning
But not at
night."

I look up alarmed to find Parent Number One standing four-square in my precarious little dinghy. I shudder. When married women catch me alone they start on the unpoetic Facts of Life. But the usual doesn't come. Paul boards with Parent Number One, and she opens gamely enough. Also, although she's fat and redfaced and her eyes really belong to a fowl, she still handles the name of the Vorontosov with respect.

"He's got a cruel streak in him."

"Oh?" I've picked this of course but am concerned with the cause rather than the symptom. Hasn't she noticed his kindness to Patchy?

"You can tell by the oiyes, the oiyes. Haven't you noticed the oiyes?"

"Yes, I've noticed the eyes."

She hasn't come round to it yet though; Paul's appearance with me in town.

"He's got no friends, you know."

I try not to betray interest. "Hasn't he? Surely he's got some girls?"

"No, he hasn't got any girls."

"Oh."

"Why," she demands cuttingly, "doesn't he get friends of his own age?"

"Anyone who is lonely," I warm up, "may come to me. Old or young. Good or bad. Anyone, good or bad."

"But there's this cruel streak in him, Miss Vorontosov."

"There'll be a cause somewhere in the past."

"No one seems to cotton on to him. It would be better if he got his own establishment in town."

"He can come to see me. Anyone who needs to can come and see me."

"He'll make you pay for it. He always makes you pay for it!"

"I'll pay for it. I don't mind paying. He can still come to see me if he is lonely. I'll give him my time. He can have it. 'And whoso shall receive one such little child in my name receiveth me.' "

"Our baby," writes Patu, "is dead
When she got
to the *pa* they
cried in the
Meeting House.
They cried in
the Meeting
House."

"You disappoint me, Paul," I say, walking back from the basketball field where he has been watching us practise.

"Why?"

"I thought I had found a real live drunkard to play with. But you're nearly always sober now. I thought I told you I preferred my bohemians drunk. Isn't this your 'hour' at the pub?"

He reflects a moment over his pipe. "You have certainly been a distraction from the drink."

It is my turn to ponder. At length I test an adjective that has been alive in my mind for a week awaiting its turn.

"That is a very unfilial remark."

Back comes an answer smartly, wholly unexpected.

"It was due."

It takes me a few steps to get over this, although I asked for it, I suppose. For the time it takes Whareparita to pass us and walk just before us, every inch of her beautiful brown legs uncovered by her hip-high brown rompers, and black hair like the night against her yellow jersey, I think it over. Then I decide to extricate myself. "Nevertheless, my esteemed Paul, my feelings for you are strictly maternal." He must never know of the re-awakened woman.

He appraises the flowing body of Whareparita and does not reply for a moment. Then, "I know," he says absently.

"You are missing a great deal," I warm up, "by not being more filial." Pride joins determined battle with the rebel woman.

"I know," he says, even more absently still.

But when I arrive beneath the cabbage trees on my way to school in the morning I pause there to kneel unnecessarily to the Little Ones until his advancing steps turn my anxiety to something else.

Why does he seem so afraid when he looks down into my morning eyes? But why do I bother to ask myself? Surely I know the origin of fear between a man and a woman. But I must somehow pull myself out of his eyes. He must not see the treacherous woman within. It might frighten him in another way. He may fear it will leap and crush him to powder as Seven grinds his chalk. But he need not fear that. The gaoler of the woman in me is Habit: the habit of caring for the young. And he is young so he is safe. However close he stands.

But the woman will not come out of his eyes for all that. It must be the brandy. But all is well, however long this look. Here is no great soul, grand enough to leap the age barrier. As the age barrier can be leapt, since there is no age to the spirit.

The rain is falling softly beyond the cabbage trees.

"How are you, Madame?"

"Don't say, 'How are you?' I can never answer."

Where is his inattention of the afternoon before? What has happened to him during the night? At last I free myself from this look. "I can never answer," I repeat to my shoe.

"What shall I say?"

"Say, 'What are you thinking?' It's more likely to raise something."

"I won't say that."

66

I am thinking that my perfume has risen to him; by the twitching of that cheek, and the tremulous flickering of his eyelids. "Good gracious, don't tell me you are growing up. I apologize on behalf of the New Race."

"I don't have to be told what to say."

"Why, have you got something of your own to say?"

"I've only got one thing to say."

With my head lowered I feel that the blue, the ineffable, unlimited blue of his eyes is pouring over me like sky. It flashes to me that the classic "I love you," the routine declaration, is about to be spoken. Right here in the spring morning before school, with Little Ones clustering about us, with the yells and delights of the Big Ones encompassing and the cabbage trees and rain enclosing. Where is the dark mouth of the previous night now? Here is one of those shining moments of life that I "hoard from the Spring branches," in handfuls and armfuls of meaning: one of those moments that I use later when my spirit "droops deadly in its cell." I lay an ugly hand on the trunk of a tree. The rain is reaching through now. I look at the fallen leaf blades that so annoy my dear headmaster, then up above to the green. I feel the rain on my face like fingers of love. Like Paul's fingers could be if there were no keeper of the woman within. I am the chosen, I hear in my heart. Once more after the unlit frugal years I am the chosen. A courage and confidence, not wholly originating in the brandy, turn me towards him. Let him say it. Words won't hurt. Just let me hear him say it, then no more.

I smile and look up and whisper. "What is it, Handsome One?"

"What can I do for you, Madame."

"I mean, I mean, what is this only thing you've got to say?"

"Just that. What can I do for you, Madame."

"I saw," writes Twinnie, with much feeling forcing her pencil,
"Miss Vorontosov
at the coffin. She
brought some flowers.
She sat down
by Patu. He
started talking to

Miss Vorontosov."

This Friday I don't go shopping with God's lost child; it is our School Ball. And during the week, the fitting out of our hundred and a half children in fancy dresses, the dancing practices, the polishing of the orchestra work and the running of the infant room, all over and above my tired and desperate efforts to keep abreast of my work on the books in the evening hours, leave little left in me to wonder what this lost child is to me, or the Senior, the Canon, the Reverend, Rauhuia or even the photo of Eugene. In her never-ending contest with the teacher in me, during this pantomime week of work, the woman with her recurring and varied crises of the heart is all but routed, so that by the time the school rises to its climax and I at last arrive at the Meeting House in the early evening, even though I am wearing my dark-red ball gown, heavy with velvet and bishop's sleeves and memories, and the white fur jacket that so pulls men's fingers, I am not thinking of men at all. I am thoroughly and severely teacher.

Such a proud teacher too, in spite of my weariness, and soundly sober. True, I have not been unaware of the necessity to drink myself into a bravado where I can bear to spend an evening with Paul, but everyone knows that brandy does not mix with a keyboard, and work always came before men with me. So I reject the blessed crystal and remain all teacher.

Ah, so proud! Everyone needs me here. The Head can't do without my music and my touch on the children. Dozens of small brown hands feel the velvet of my skirts, a hundred tongues ask questions, big ones come to me ruefully to sort out their personal differences with their partners as Paul organizes them into their formation for the Grand March, until by the time I take my place at the piano for the two-hours' stretch of music ahead, no remembered words finger my heart, no recalled touch reminds me of the irrepressible inflammability of my person, and as my top-octave chords announcing the beginning of the Grand March summon my school to marry me for two hours, I forget my awareness of men.

But when supper is over and my orchestra takes the stage, when the children give up the floor to the adults and I look up from the sleepy brown eyes at my knee to find the lost child of God bowing extravagantly over me, my ugly hands, still alive from the keyboard,

68

suddenly reach to my throat to the unfamiliar pulsing there. Mercilessly the rush of hot blood betrays the evening; betrays my joy in children and fears of the Senior Inspector. All my steady and cool work in the infant room, all the unfolding of art in Selah, all are gone. As I follow one handsome rake out upon the floor, take his hand and shoulder and move to the hit tune, even though our dancing together turns out to be appallingly out of step, even though people without rhythm cannot be acceptable to me and even though his breath speaks of a quick visit to the pub across the bridge during supper, all I hear is the thunder and lightning of other music within me and all I see before me is the eternal, the demanding male. Secretly and poetically I count one more pure moment of fulfilment to my store.

But women don't show these things. . . .

But generations have distinctive rhythms. Is not this age of mine uncomfortable enough without its also being ridiculous? . . .

I follow Paul out into my garden. "That's the first cockcrow," he says.

"It's only Dawn's famous Left Hand hitting about in the Sky."

Some people leave you older.

I follow him in my ball gown through the difficult detaining trees that it does not occur to him to hold back for me. It is very cold outside after the warmth of the firelight but he doesn't share his coat. "I will end up a drunkard," he says.

"I hope so."

"In the gutter."

"Preferably."

"I will drink life to the lees."

"Have you any religion, Paul?"

"In my opinion the only religion is one's faith in another creature."

"Have you ever had that faith in another creature, Paul?"

"I have lately."

I join him near the dark outline of the gate. Within myself I am unstable; not with the emotion of an hour ago, nor with the clashing of our generations through the night, but with the compassion of the present. True, as he stands so near me in the darkness, I still mourn the kisses I have rejected, but it is the last stand of the woman against the teacher. I collect all the courage I have, to say something. Something that could well turn his inclination towards me away from me for ever. Yet the teacher demands that it be said. "In the gutter," he repeats, not without relish.

"I want," I begin, "to be your home."

He lifts his face in alarm. "But I am an impermanent person."

"Don't think that I, for myself, want anything from you. I don't mean a home socially, geographically or emotionally."

He forces open the difficult latch, goes through and out upon the road, but returns. "I've never had a home. I've never had a home of any kind. I've never had that said to me before."

At last we do not clash. Possibly it is the adjustment of the generations. We appear to be in step. After all, he could well have been the son that I refused Eugene one dawn in just such a way as this.

"If my wish to be your home embarrasses you in any way," I speak from my new, my real position, and now without any discomfort, "or disturbs you, then that is your misfortune."

No answer.

I continue with easy authority. "But since this is my dwelling, the standards of thinking and of behaviour will be mine."

His shoulders are rounded again. He is taking longer to adjust himself than me. He leaves me at the gate and once more walks away so that I can barely see him. There, he pauses while a cock crows and another answers, then he returns once more. "I am deeply touched."

"I don't believe it."

"Why not?"

"Because you are not used to it. You won't even know what I have said for about two years."

Restlessly he walks off again but as inexorably as before something brings him back. "If I had met a person like you," he says with no maudlin self-pity, "after I was turned out of the orphanage and before I went to sea, my life would have been different."

"I want you," I say with returning difficulty, "to come to me in thought. I want you, whenever the occasion arises, to know that there is one person who understands you; to whom you may speak at any time in any circumstances."

He gazes steadily out into the dawn and though I am old and cold and tired I repeat, "At any time and in any circumstances."

Silence, full of thinking . . .

70

"You must be cold."

"Paul, I am a hostess. And until you yourself choose to go, even though every bone in my body breaks separately and in sequence with rattling, I remain so."

He shouts with laughter, rolling out into the road with it, then returns as ever, as ever, to me. "Somehow," he whispers urgently, "I must tear myself away from you."

He closes the gate between us. "Goodnight," he whispers in my ear so that the warmth of his breath on me is the only part that is not cold, reminding me of what the warmth of his mouth could have been. "Goodnight . . . my dear."

I stand at the gate a little longer, watching the solitary form and hearing the solitary step of the son that might have been, had I been less enpoetried with Eugene one dawn wide years ago, and the father of a new son that could have been, had I not been so poetry-bound with Paul in this dawn today, fading away in the gloom. Yet am I not forsaken. I lift my chin. Birth and union and death of the person are not the whole concerns of my life. I traffic on a less prosaic level. No longer confused by the treasonable woman, I am able to see what Paul is essentially to me. And it is not the great male of yester evening. Neither is his mouth the only thing I want. I am no longer dreaming with Dawn's Left Hand in the Sky. Neither is Life's Liquor in its Cup yet dry. As the eastern light gives growing shape to the unintelligible, as the cocks answer each other across the scape, and as Paul's last footfall sounds, I can see outline at last. In spite of his fabulous face, in spite of his inclination towards me and because of the history of his wanderings over the ocean, and his possible faith in "this creature," he is no more than one of my Little Ones after all and once more I am proudly teacher.

"I saw," writes the other Twinnie, laboriously asking how to spell the words,
"Miss Vorontosov
at the grave.
Whareparita

sang by Patu's
baby."

Mark Cutter is on my mind. His mother, who hates us all conscientiously, won't buy him his book and pencil because, she says, he is
going too fast. Actually, my full Maori, Tame, is going faster. But
Mrs Cutter's little girl is at a private school in town to save her from
these "terrible Maoris," a school that is all Name and Clothes and
Fees, but with only one certificated teacher on the staff, so, understand-
ably, by comparison with her progress, Mark is going too fast. So is
Pussy probably and the Ginger Rooster who attends regularly.

But even though I know all this, up comes my rage because I can't
stand this phrase "not allowed" from a parent, and because all married
women are unacceptable to me in any capacity. They remind me of
sissy bachelors when it comes to prejudice. As Tame settles down with
his pencil and book, when writing time comes, and Mark looks on in
tension, it is as much as I can do to keep hold of my tongue. But I
do, believe it or not, and all I say is, "You'll have to keep to the blackboard and chalk, Little Mark."

He stands in bewilderment, his plain face searching mine for some
sort of solution. "I'll ask my mother again," he says. "She might buy
me one."

I touch his chin. "She might not."

He is deeply upset and, associatively, so am I myself, being a cas-
ualty with no top layer to my mind, and feel just about everything
all around me all the time whether I want to or not. So I blindly and
hurriedly and without counting the cost run over to the big school
and buy a book and pencil from the Head myself, as much to comfort
me as him, feeling enraged that someone should hurt one of my own
children, with the result that we both cheer up.

But returning through the trees to lunch I realize that I have not
closed the original division. A little boy, I tell the bread as I cut myself
a slice on the bench, should never be allowed to experience a conflict
of loyalties between his parent and his teacher. When I go back this
afternoon, I plan, plastering on nearly half an inch of butter, I'll say,
Your mother is right, Mark. It's best not to have a pencil and a book.
Just to save him, I conclude as I reach for my poetry, the payment of
my own appalling mistakes as a teacher.

72

But I forget and he is away for days.

. . . So is Paul Vercoe away for days. So I drove him from me after all. But I didn't dream he would leave school. Where is he? "Has your assistant returned to sea?" I tease the Head.

"Really, the least he could do is to send me word. But I'm jolly sure I'm not going to chase after him! But oh, the poor chap has had no chance to learn manners. But it's awkward with him away. Me trying to run both rooms and the school too."

"He's probably talking to the world. He told me on Friday night . . . or Saturday morning to be accurate . . . that his necessity was to talk to the world."

Mark reappears after several days with a cold. "My mother," he says with an air of crisis, "wants to see this book and pencil you bought me."

I shiver. I have been indiscreet. I have put his name on them. If that means anything in an infant room of Maoris where they still live by the community rule.

"And," he goes on in his mother's voice, "she wants to see them today."

"Why?" I ask, trying to loosen the legs of Guilt from around my throat with my fingers.

"I dunno."

"M-Mark," I say, I hasten to say, "your mother is quite right about you not buying this book and pencil. There's no need for them really."

He looks visibly relieved, poor little boy.

"There's no need to write at school," I go on. "You can talk instead."

"But Tame will beat me."

"Pouf, Tame!"

"Y-know," he says, striking his grown-up attitude that so racks me, "I like writing, you know, Miss Vorontosov."

"Oh."

"I think I'll do a little writing so Tame won't beat me."

All right then, I say to myself, let the conflict between mother and teacher move over on to mother and son. At least there will be some chance of reconciliation.

But I flush hot with rage. How a teacher hates this sort of thing!

Yet I've forgotten all about it when I run into town after school to pick up some more yellow blouse material for my girls' uniform making, so that when I meet Mrs. Cutter in the street too, and she looks in a shop window as I pass, and turns Mark's head away also so he won't see me, it hits me like a new thing all over again. I forget to buy Black Topsy. Indeed, when he runs into me the next morning and stands and holds both my hands for some time in pathetic silence, and in far too much emotion for an orderly Pakeha, I just have to make a trip over to the big school to ask the Head what to think. "Look, about this Cutter drama . . ."

"Heard anything of Paul?"

"No, have you?"

"No."

He seems too sad for me to go on about the Cutters.

I am sitting in my car this wet Friday evening holding an unlit cigarette. I sit with my back to the pavement since I can't bear to watch the bourgeois of a New Zealand town waddling its parochial and shabby way; I prefer the wheel. I sit and rest before I push on and buy Black Topsy and wish I had my lighter.

Paul won't come. I've frightened him away with my clumsy offer to be his home. I feared I might, but not from school too. Now look what I have done to the trainee the Head and the Senior were exercising themselves on! Has he gone back to sea? Pretty things in the shop window we have laughed over together pick up a load of pain, and here is memory again.

He can't come. Well, I'll survive without him. I've known a bigger loss than he. Also, which is more important, I have seen sufficiently often already the flashes of meaning that balance the nights of the soul; without looking greedily for more. "He can bear to die; he who has once been happy." All I need of life is a match.

A tap on the window behind me. Without warning, like a bolt of lightning through the rainlions, ecstasy strikes me and I see once again the meaning. He has come.

"What can I do for you, Madame?"

74

"You may light my cigarette, Paul."

I am late waking in the morning and the first thing I think of is tea. The next thing I think of is my precious work that has missed its early morning turn. I look out hurriedly my red taffeta housegown with all the vivid flowers, the heat being upon us, and pull it over my nightgown. I make the tea like lightning then taking my cup, set out down the back steps to Selah, my hair flipping, my gown flopping, and my feet bare, and here, without any warning whatsoever, I find Paul towering over me, pipe, eagerness, tobacco pouch and all. In a flash I cover my person. "How did you get in here?"

"I just walked in."

"I'm working. I'm not at home. I'm inaccessible!"

"But look at what I've brought you!"

"Go away! I'm not at home!"

He is standing an inch off and I have no powder. I step into the shade. I find I am in his eyes; my reflection there. I can't rescue myself from them. I must stop this. This look has to end some time.

"Look what I've brought you. Two bottles of Lager."

"I don't drink on Saturday morning!"

"You told me you would take me over my songs some time."

"I will later!"

Still the uninterrupted penetration of gaze. At length he looks slowly down the whole of me and dwells on the hem of my black nightgown. "I've brought you some Lager."

"I can't have it this morning. I'm not at home."

"But you are at home."

"How dare you intrude on my privacy at this hour in the morning! Leave my house immediately! Leave immediately!"

Silently he passes me, a twitch of appreciation on his mouth, walks into the kitchen, through the house, and I hear the gate. But when I come back in, flustered and shocked, I find his pouch and Lager on the table, and I remember what I said that dawn: "At any time, in any circumstance . . ."

"I don't know what to do with myself," says Paul, settling into my own private small chair in the pre-fab after the girls have finished cleaning. "Such a waste of life, teaching others. I'm at the end."

He knows exactly what chords to play to stop me going home. True, we have been through all his songs at the infant-room piano, and I have been startled by his tenor, but here he is, unbalancing my precious little dinghy still. Nevertheless I wait, my cheek against the door. I can't get it out of my head that he is one of my Little Ones.

"I'm going to take up singing," he says, biting his pipe in resolution.

"Professional singing is very hard."

"You stopped playing in rapture when I was doing the Tchaikovsky."

"That's another thing."

"I want to sing to the world."

There are times when I suspect that God doesn't want me to make my Maori books. And this is one of them. If He did, why doesn't He send this boy home? "Look, Paul, you'll have to excuse me. My legs won't hold me up any longer."

He rises. "Excuse me" means "Go home."

"I mean to sing to the world."

"Well go to that eminent singing teacher in the next town."

He studies me reflectively, smoking. "I'll need you for my practices."

The next morning, just as I am organizing my Little Ones for the day, here comes this most difficult of all my Little Ones dashing across the porch into my sacred pre-fab. I look up, alarmed and inadequate.

"He says in six months he will present me on the concert platform! He says I have a freak throat. He says I am the find of the year!" His face is flushed. "He gasped and stopped playing, just like you. I've paid a term in advance. I've bought all the music he listed. Here are my exercises. Listen to this scale!" A truly lovely scale soars up to the astonished inspector shade there. "But—" he turns his profile for me, and dropping his voice—"when I am on the concert platforms of the world it won't be only my voice that draws the women. It'll be my face! Now we'll get down to practice!"

Another week staggers by. . . .

76

"I'll have to go home, Mr Reardon," I say half an hour after I have arrived at school one sour morning.

He takes a look at me. "Another late night?" he asks nonchalantly. He closes his classroom door behind him, and I lean my head on it. It's always draping doorways lately.

"One of my heads."

"Another late night?" he repeats.

"Three o'clock."

"Three o'clock? What again?"

"That boy's killing me."

"Madame! I won't have it! I won't have you knocked up for school like this! He'll have to learn to leave earlier!"

"But it was all right," I murmur feebly. "I thoroughly enjoyed him."

"You know very well that you can't take it. This is almost a fortnight running you have told me he has kept you up. You will have to do something about it. He'll have to be told!"

My head is so horrible that I have to agree. "Yes," I groan, "I'll have to prepare some formula."

"Not to mention his own work!"

"Well, you see, it's his practices . . . his singing practices. I'm just copying off your own patience with him; that's all."

"I manage it without sitting up all night." He pockets his hands and takes to striding the corridor in a way I have never seen in him before. "I'll have no teacher of mine disturbed in this way! I know how much your work means to you, even if I don't understand it! That boy's got to keep out of your house! He'll know discipline when he's on my staff, inside and outside of the school! He'll do what I say, when I say, and how I say! I'll speak to him! You may have the rest of the day off!" And away he strides to Paul's classroom.

"The fire-engine," whispers Waiwini's little brother, "it burns me up dead."

I'm burning dead most of my material today: a Friday of flames. All the work of my youth. It's impressive to see it go up in smoke. If only my memories would go up too. It takes three hours. You should hear the roar! But teaching will be much simpler now, and there'll be more time for conversation. And whatever the past has or has not taught me I am satisfied that communication on any level, giving birth as it does to the new body, the new idea or the new heart, is the most that life can be.

And I don't forget to burn my workbook; this middleman of notes, intercepting some of my energy directed on the infant room. In the infant room I dream of, the question of a workbook could hardly arise.

Ah, dreams, dreams, dreams. But what's the use, I ask myself, standing up restlessly and checking on my Little Ones, of a dream without courage to give it birth? Courage . . . what kind of thing is it? Is it something that can wear out in time, or is it alive? And how can it not be alive when it belongs exclusively to the living?

I rise to my feet and stretch. It's time for work. But I've burnt my workbook anyway. And that's the finish. Never, never, never again will I accept this finer form of the many tortures of orthodox teaching. After all, what can I lose? As far as I know there's only the sack left.

I'm still full of bravado as I sit among my heaped pages in Selah in the evening. I paint a brilliant green pig with black spots that I have seen for myself on some small earnest blackboard, rooting away in the purple grass. Then I set about composing the most vivid blue I can lay my brush to for the fowls at the door. But mixing the brown for the Maori children is more trouble; not too orange, not too brown, not too yellow, not too red. If I'm not careful it goes bronze. I add some grains of black, and even blue, and when I've got it just right I put it carefully in a pot nearby; not too far away where I might lose it, and not too close where I might knock it over, or drink it instead of my coffee.

"The ghost," writes Rauhuia's Matawhero, in broken, shaky writing, since he uses his tongue for communication purposes, rather than a mere pencil,
"went in our kitchen
and frightened us.
It had big fat eyes.
It had a white sheet."

"What is it, what is it, Little One? What happened to your house?"

"Those kids bust it."

I've got two ways of bringing the Little Ones to sit on the mat together: One is to play the "Come and sit on the mat" music and the other is to whisper to the child nearest me, "It's time for story." The second is like magic. So I whisper it to Wiki. . . .

"The whole happiness of Fairyland," I read over my tea and cigarettes at lunch time, "hangs on one thread. Cinderella may have a dress woven on supernatural looms, blazing with unearthly brilliance, but she must be back when the clock strikes twelve. The king may invite fairies to the christening but he must invite all fairies or frightful results will follow. Bluebeard's wife may open all the doors but one. . . . This great idea is at the back of all folklore—the idea that all happiness hangs on one thin veto; all positive joy on one negative."

"Once upon a time." I set out cheerfully enough . . .
"Tell a story about a king!" suggests Mark.
"Now I once heard of a king who . . ."
"No, tell about Ihaka," says a brown one.
"One morning just as Ihaka was . . ."
"Sing about the ol' steam boat, Miss Top-off."
"Oh, going down the river in the old steam boat . . ."
"I like a story about a princess best."
"Ihaka, Ihaka!"
"Tell the B'ue Jug, Mitt Wottot."
"Shut up, all you kids!" cries Matawhero. "Go on, Miss Vorontosov, talk!"
"Why don't you talk?"
"She can' talks, ay."
I give up the idea of a formal beginning, also the intention of telling something new. Then Riti says, climbing up on my knee, "I like Wed Wideen Hook."
I take a leap beyond the beginning into the story. " 'Now,' said Little Red Riding Hood's mother, 'I want you to take these things to your grandmother. But don't talk to the wolf on the way. You must play with Wiki or Mark if you meet them in the forest, but if you see the

wolf, you just walk straight past. If only you don't talk to this wolf then all will be well.'

" 'But I like talking to the wolf,' says Little Red Riding Hood. 'He says funny things.'

" 'That's just it,' replied her mother."

Bleeding Heart giggles.

"Be quiet. Go on, Miss Vorontosov."

"Where was I?"

"But Red Rideen Hood she talk to those bad wolf," helps Tame. "Red Rideen Hood."

"Then the wolf," takes up someone else, "he run on to her grandmother and, and . . ."

"He knock at the door first," corrects someone else.

In no time I have lost the rights to the story. It is told emphatically and graphically and severally in different mediums of English and on various pitches, with argument and excitement and stand-up actions, and with vast appreciation from the large audience, far more vividly than I ever could, until, near the end, out of pride alone, I determine to battle my way back into it. After all it was my story and I had it first. "And then, and then," I cry above the other claimants, "as soon as the woodman slits open the wolf, out comes this grandmother. 'Where are my clothes?' she snapped. 'I had a nightgown and cap on before.' "

"Hell, she's naked," gasps Matawhero.

" 'Where are my clothes?' said the grandmother. 'I'm shivering.' "

"They's on the wolf," whispers Tame.

"Red Riding Hood," I push on, "took the clothes back off the wolf and helped Grandma to put them on again while the woodman modestly turned his back.

" 'My glasses, Red Riding Hood,' snapped Grandma, climbing irritably into bed again. 'And my comic.'

"She rammed on her glasses and snatched the comic that Red Riding Hood found the woodman reading. 'He's lost the place!' she accused. 'That's what I hate about a wolf: loses the place! Unlettered baboon!' "

A silence has fallen. At last I have won the attention. But Mark, with his orderly white brain is constrained to sum up. He strikes his grown-up pose and uses his mother's voice. "See, she shouldn't have spoken to the wolf in the first place," he says smugly.

"That's right," I remember. "If only she hadn't talked to the wolf."

But, looking back, I am aggrieved at the state of my story. It was my story. I had it first. But those kids bust it.

If only I had told something new. If only Wiki had not built her house in the doorway. If only Red Riding Hood had not talked to the wolf . . . all positive joy on one negative.

But those kids bust it. For notheen.

Our grading comes this week. The Head is marked high, Paul will have his later when he has been inspected, but me . . . I'm marked low. When I open the portentous envelope that I find in the box after school, I see that I am marked exceedingly low.

There can be no doubt about it: I'm a very low-ability teacher. For the whole of my teaching life inspectors have agreed on that. It's true that I have tried with everything I had in hand, giving far more of my life to my work than many a crack Infant Mistress in town, dancing upward on the grading list, but here it is. Plainly I am mistaken in all I do. The inspectors are right.

I turn from the gate into the garden and walk through the long grass to the delphiniums. They are as high as me now and in the way they change and lengthen and glow blue they are the nearest thing I know to an answer within these hedges. As I stand with my letter before them I wait for comments, but when I do hear them it turns out to be only sympathy, a thing I have learnt to do without long ago.

It's a disgrace, Anna, I hear, to be considered a good teacher. It is distinction to be marked low. "All rogues walk alone."

I walk back to the gate and padlock it; the gate that only the Reverend and Paul use; the one from compassion and the other from need. My catastrophic grading, I tell the untidy rose there, gives me less to lose. It rather widens the way to what I want to do. The level of this grading frees me somewhat. It's a big gain really, if only I could take it.

If only I could take it.

The spring rain comes over the hedge, ignoring the padlock, the only being I know that doesn't mind about my face, my name and my bad reputation, so I don't move indoors. He has a lovely gentle touch like no inspector I have met. He brings coolness to the rushing blood in my face, refreshment and inspiration as no inspector does. After all I have good friends: the flowers the Head has planted. How rich and blessed I am! True, they have little more than sympathy for me, but they all talk well and are the most cheerful company. And they love me: I know that. Why should I mourn? A little thing like bad grading? More mistakes? Heavens, I'm so accustomed to them that success would unnerve me.

I move over to the dahlias out of earshot of the road. I stand there, biting the inside of my mouth. Good God, I'm all right! The thing is not to go by those sympathetic delphiniums, I tell the dahlias. All their talk about it being a disgrace being a good teacher and a distinction to be marked low and about "all rogues walking alone"! Face the facts. I'm a poor teacher and all the inspectors to date have proved it. I'm a mass of mistakes, and all of life has proved that. I should have given myself to Eugene all those years ago, with or without marriage. Fancy mixing up orthodoxy with love! And I should have obeyed the inspectors all these years. Fancy teaching as though I knew more about children than they do. And I shouldn't have flouted an order from the Director of Education himself. It's time I fitted in and made myself useful. Come on, let's make some nice strong coffee and let loose some nice strong Beethoven . . . then take the padlock off the gate . . . I can take it. "Thou art indeed just, Lord."

. . . My fingers pause on the keyboard. If only Red Riding Hood had not spoken to the wolf; if only I had not spoken to him in mind. Then all would have been well with Red Riding Hood and me. . . .
. . . I wake and feel the fell of dark, not day.
What hours, O what black hours we have spent.
This night! what sights you, heart, saw; what ways you went!
. . . Courage is something that can run out, I reflect, as I walk down the street to the Steamship Company's Booking Office. And so is patience. The only thing that doesn't run out is mistakes. I'll leave teaching. I'll resign at once. I wish I could leave this very night, and if this new Senior Inspector arrives in the meantime I'll dismiss my Little Ones or absent myself. I'll never submit myself to this inspection again.

82

I'll never, never, never go through that again. They can sack me outright if they like but I'm finished. Courage is something that comes to an end after all.

"A first-class, single-berth, deck cabin on the *Monowai,* please."

"Name, please?"

"Fail, Anna Fail."

"Beg your pardon?"

"Sorry; Vorontosov, Anna Vorontosov."

"I didn't quite catch it."

"VO-RON-TO-SOV!"

"V-r . . ."

"V-O!"

"V-o-r-o . . . just let me have it again, will you?"

"V-O-R-O-N-T-O-S-O-V!"

"Thanks . . . destination?"

"Laundry!"

"Beg pardon Mrs . . . aa . . ."

"MISS!"

"Oh . . . so sorry! Destination Miss . . . aa . . . aa . . . Voron- . . ."

"Give-the-form-to me!" . . .

I'll find a country that has as many ugly faces as mine and where strange names and bad reputations are the rule; a country where gates are not built of respectability and where I will hear steps down my garden; where I can converse with wolves in the mind as much as I like and make any number of mistakes without Guilt strangling me. I'll get a job in a laundry where I can play with soap-suds all day and where the sound of water running is like Little Ones' voices and the eddying of it like children's dancing. Where, though my hands will be active, my mind will be free. Then all will be well with Red Riding Hood and me.

I wake in the dawn with the birds, and so does Guilt, and he is so uncomfortable that I get up and make the tea and sit in my favourite chair in the drawing room at my favourite window and look out into the garden.

I don't go out to work in Selah this morning; neither do I read; much less put in a couple of hours of Beethoven. It is my birthday.

I sit and look out into the garden and the steam from my tea rises. There are hours and hours of time left yet before washing and dressing for school and I settle down to peering through the shadows towards the gate as I can never help doing. It is my birthday so I don't even try to break this habit of mine of looking towards the gate and listening.

And sure enough they come. But it's not from the world beyond the gate that they come, but from the world behind my eyes. Neither is it through the gate in the garden but through the gate in my mind. They come to me, my memories, on my birthday and the tea goes cold in the cup . . .

The sun is well up before I move and there are concise shadows to the trees. At the sound of children's voices early at school the ghostly kisses and presences, the laughter, the hands and the love take leave and I see again only the world before my eyes; the rough-woven covers of the chairs, the floor-length curtains and the sober carpet. It is very cold too, this outer world, and I try to discipline myself to meet the washing and dressing and powdering and teaching, but I would rather stay here in my heavy battered red gown with the Past. My ghosts are better company than my realities for all their vanishing ways. I would care to sit here with my loves until nightfall, for the day, for the week, for ever.

But children's voices are very early at the end of spring and my mind shifts position a little. I see the ten-child easel with the paint dripping, the towers rising from the floor, the sand mountain with the steps on it, the clay bombers, the reading, the writing and the talk. Presently I rise and endeavour to make the difficult transition from the past to the present valid, and lifting the lengths of my gown I make my uncertain way down the hall to the kitchen and pour half a tumbler of brandy.

Yet all I achieve is half a tumbler of sobbing instead. Besides there being nothing left from the past for me other than the lessons I've learnt, neither with this grading is there anything left in the present. Why make the effort of a transition? I'm like the delphiniums with the blooms cut off except that there is no rain at my roots for a second blooming.

But you only need to give brandy time, like any other fire, and it's only a matter of an hour before I'm walking through the trees to school. Now, with this uproar inside me I am full of a loud courage. Too often have I been defeated; too long thwarted. The name, Vorontosov, I remind myself, tripping unsteadily in my high heels over the fallen leaf-blades, despised though it be here, has no history of resigning at the end of the year; no record of absence in the face of orthodoxy. I'll plough through Inspectors, Headmasters, Directors and Assistants as though I were the only one in the profession. Since I have nothing to lose I am free.

Moreover it is my birthday and as no one else has given me a present I'll give myself one. I'll give myself something worth while too; something to play with for years . . .

Soon I am singing.

With or without Inspectors, I determine, mounting the worn steps, with or without Guilt, I'll offer myself this infant room. And I'll take it too; even snatch it, in replacement of all that I've missed. I'll accept these seventy children to do with them as I wist.

A flushed face thrust in the window of my car one Friday evening. "Madame!"

I have nothing to say.

"You could be that woman!"

"What woman?"

"Balzac said there was nothing so beautiful as the first love of a man with the last love of a woman!"

My hand rises to my face and rests there. I find something to say. "It's true, Paul, that what you need is a middle-aged woman. Someone to take you over, and under. Someone to discipline you, praise you, comfort you, stroke your hair, applaud your profile, make you practise your singing and love you. On the other hand you yourself are by no means a light catch for that kind of woman; lonely, lost, poetic, pathetic, good-looking and homeless as you are."

He withdraws his head to roar with laughter in his old boyish way. "The trouble is that after a week of that she would find that she would have to do more; she would have to keep me."

I laugh aloud too. But again he leans precariously near in his characteristic way, his mouth twitching sensitively. "I wish," he whispers with a tremulousness and a desire, "that you would do all that!"

"Nevertheless I am not that woman."

"I wish you were that woman."

"I am not that woman."

"Balzac at twenty and his mistress at forty-five remained devoted for fifteen years."

I am silent for some time, then light a cigarette. At length I hear Paul, his words barely audible against the background of walking feet. "You could be that woman."

"I am not that woman."

I am longing for my tea and biscuit with the Head, a light let-up before the evening of work at home, but here is this young able-bodied man still in my infant room "at the end" again. Not knowing what to do with himself. He is clever enough to know just how to hold me and settles down comfortably in my own low chair. As for me, I lean against the door, looking upon him. After all, what is he but one of my Little Ones grown up?

"When are you going to prepare your school work?"

"I don't know. I might go to sea again and earn my passage home. I'm feeling a bit homesick." He knows to a brush stroke how to keep me. Paul can only take, and in armfuls at a time. Anything from six to twelve hours of me.

"I'm interested enough in you to care."

He lights his pipe. "I'm going to change my occupation. Or rather I'm going to, to . . . shall we say . . . select another. I'll choose employment talking to people. The Insurance Companies are possibly made for me. My vocation is to talk to the world."

"Have you finished singing to the world?"

"I can't wait as long as that. I must talk to the world at once."

Ah, communication, you manifest yourself in unlikely ways! But my feet and legs won't have anything more to do with me. The dreadful "Excuse me" will have to be said. Which means "Go away." How can I temper it? How can I do it gently with this most wretched of the young?

"Well . . . dear," the word comes very hard, "you'll have to excuse me."

One of the disadvantages of being on a good road is impromptu visitors. Important ones too. You know, big stuff.

"All of us at once," says the Secretary of the Teachers' Institute.

I pull my ugly hands from the keyboard out of sight. It has been the "Sylphides" of Chopin which Rongo in her sweet suppleness has been trying to put into body-talk. "I like you all at once," I reply. "After all, you're not inspectors or instructors."

I hope they have not seen my Little Ones at their classical dancing. It's too much part of myself.

"We couldn't go by without coming in to see you."

"I'll be getting to know you all yet."

But this can't go on. The past is too near. I turn to the piano for escape. I bring out my hidden ugly hands. Yet our private dancing must not be revealed before officialdom, for all my secret and desperate resolutions to ignore professional rules. Whatever is this I hear coming from the piano? "Big enough for Two," and in no time the whole room has joined in lustily. Next I hear, "If I'd known you were coming I'd have baked a cake." Then the Hula tune, and here are the whole lot to a man on their feet, some dancing and some clapping the rhythm and some finding room only on the tables. Completely given up. Jeni's hands, Lotus' tiny body and Wiki's rolling eyes. And here comes the real star, Waiwini, who prefers to be missed first before she is called, undulating through the converging children in a way that could only belong to my dream infant room after all.

But this Big Stuff doesn't know my dream infant room and after they have gone I realize that this is some of what has discredited me in the past. Ah well, I reflect, settling and cooling down after the strain of visitors, I've got nothing to lose. Act first and think last, is my motto. But whatever my motto, and whatever I have, or have not got to lose, I still feel the weight of Guilt, and his legs even tighter round my throat. What skinny merciless legs they are! Could I escape them somehow? I rise and take up a child and sit on my low chair. Would these legs follow me to another country into a laundry with soap-suds? Ah, my mistakes, my foolish ways! Ghastly soul that I am . . .

"I be your pet, ay," suggests Riti, climbing upon my knee as I sit on my low chair.

"But you're Daddy's pet."

"I'm tired of being Daddy's pet. I be your pet."

"All right, you can be my pet. But so are all the others."

"I be your pet over all them others."

"I don't have one pet over all the others."

Riti is four and a half and won't stay home and her hair is full of "those things," but she doesn't cry all the time now "for nutteen." She climbs a bit closer and the thin brown arms encompass my neck so that the nearness of her head to mine makes me wonder if I might not find myself scratching later in the day. But she wants what she wants and likes what she likes and what she wants and likes is a full measure of Thee and Me.

"You someone's pet?" she enquires.

"No."

"You be my pet, ay."

"Only over all those others," I contradict myself.

"I have you for my pet over all them others."

So I sigh and fall to dreaming. . . .

The nurse comes today to give mantu injections; T.B. tests. Four of my young Maoris refuse outright to go. One of them is the half-past-four Hinewaka who, after her experiences since birth with feet and white-gowned nurses, sets up such a hullabaloo of screaming that I hold her in my arms for the entire morning, including the morning tea interval. Also, the white children are left out, which they take as no small slight, so that Patchy comes to me with his sleeve rolled up. "Me want a pwick, Mitt Wottot. Me want a pwick." At which I laugh so loudly that he is at once embarrassed and away he runs to the blackboard where he makes strange impetuous marks with his chalk. Silly thing I am.

However there are still more than enough children to go on with and they are remarkably calm. True, when Little Brother sets out cheerfully across the grass to have his injection he is stung by a wasp and gets another injection instead, but he does arrive at the nurse according to schedule; considerably faster, of course, and not for the original reason, his screams keeping the rest of us up-to-date; but he preserves the sequence and the overall composure in the pre-fab remains intact. There is little of the uproar I have known elsewhere. Nevertheless on principle I see that they all draw both the nurse and her needle when they return, and we of course take time off to discuss the whole ordeal in detail, believing as I do that a lot of the nervousness is dissipated this way.

But the big ones are possessed with fear of it and take it progressively badly while the children from Paul's room are not as upset. Their new attitude of confidence in him deepens into a pitifully humble attitude of dependence, so that by playtime in the porch Paul is big with responsibility. "The child," he pronounces with profundity, "must be preserved as an individual. He must never be overlooked as no more than a part of a, of a . . . shall we say . . . an insensitive mass." He seems to be talking to the world through the Maori children. Can he hold this? I smile, maternally. It's good to see the young grow. But there's still a lot that I can't fathom about the differing progressions of fear. Especially in these big ones.

"Why, Sister?" I ask, looking around Hinewaka on my knee.

"I don't know. I haven't the slightest idea. They're always like that and I've done thousands."

"Why, Mr Reardon?"

"Well," he begins thoughtfully, "I suppose that . . ."

"Because," blows in Paul, "they have more grounds for anticipation. They know more of what's coming than the Little Ones do."

And you yourself, I observe privately, always know more than the rest of us do. I do weary of his intercepting my interchange with the Head. But I don't say these things aloud these days. There's always a possibility of another hurt and a backfire to the pub. Besides it's never too hard to realize when I see him in the school setting that he is young, and I am all concern for the young . . . at school.

I look up as I cross the grass to the pre-fab and note some big boys, Hori and Rameka. Rameka and Wero and . . . who's that, Tai? . . .

hiding in the shed, getting on with their "grounds for anticipation," exchanging and comparing their nervousness one with the other, until at last I begin to see for myself why the Little Ones take it better than the big ones. And I am moved to see these big creatures, larger than myself, in a torture of apprehension. I know this same torture sitting in the car outside church, trying to persuade myself to go in and afraid of the injection needle in there, held by a man in the pulpit . . . I know of course that a proportion of it is exaggerated emotion cultivated and honoured in the *pa,* and fed on almost necessitously. Yet it all adds up to suffering which I cannot help picking up associatively, so that I wonder if there is any end to suffering, mine and others'.

But we are all better next morning. Although the arms are very tender, just as my mind is very tender after church, the ordeal is behind.

"Look, Miss Vorontosov," claims Matawhero proudly, "I still got my prick on!"

I've still got my prick on too.

"Mitt Wottot," says Patchy, his sleeve up again, "my mutter she tay me to hab a pwick."

I keep my laughter inside this time, promising myself relief later on when I have my feet up on the table over lunch. "I don't think your mother said that, Patchy."

He rolls his sleeve down sadly, then he has an idea and jerks at my smock. "Mitt Wottot, wead the B'ue *Jug!*"

Crash comes the laughter after all. Bleeding Heart joins in, then the others not knowing why and I say, "Who will read 'The Blue Jug' to Patchy?"

Shouts of offers! Brown Maadi departs with "The Blue Jug," a bit worn by now, and Patchy, to the step. But Blossom observes disapprovingly. "We don wan the Blue Jug all day, an all day, an all day!"

So crash comes the laughter again; gales and storms of it. Indeed, Bleeding Heart rolls on the floor, bidding fair to end up in some kind of fit; until at length when the attack is over and we are able to speak we all carry on with comparing our sore pwicks.

"What is it, what is it, Little One?"
"My little brother he is crying."
"Bring Little Brother to me."

90

"Seven he bit my prick. Seven."
"Bring Seven to me."
"But Blossom punched it first."
"Bring Blossom to me."

I never quite know what's going to happen when I go to the piano. Sometimes they all get up and dance and sometimes only a few. Riti and Rongo always do. Riti rids herself of volumes of her vast Maori emotion this way and we don't have these long-drawn-out wails of hers now, rubbing her eyes enough to tear them right out. But it all depends on how deeply they are engrossed in what they are doing, on the mood of the room, and on whether it is a tune that means something to them. But there's never no one. There are some like Rongo and Riti and Waiwini and Little Brother and the Twinnies who dance whatever the tune, the mood or the occupation, composing freely; there are some who dance only to certain tunes and don't appear to hear the rest; and some, mostly Europeans, who don't dance at all unless it is suggested to them. And I do suggest it to Dennis, thinking that in some obscure way it may heal his nervous state a little; the motion of expressive dancing being the only unbroken course of the spirit right through the mind to the body; thinking that for the brief moment he is at the command of the music he will know integration. Poor little boy. All told, however, I'm ashamed of my own race's representation in this particular infant room. My own sons, had I submitted to Eugene, indulged the urgencies of the lost child of God, could I jettison the whole of my teacher's morality and abandon my obsession with the beautiful that keeps my chastity intact from the men about me who lure, my sons would have been better than these. . . .

No, I can never be quite sure what's going to happen. This morning I try out an idea from *Peer Gynt* from "The Hall of the Mountain King"; I like the eeriness of the bass quavers. A sudden silence falls on the room and, turning, I see that Mohi, my fair-haired Maori, bred from a wandering English circus man, has risen from his dreaming on the mat. He pulls his jersey half over his head, leaving his eyes alone looking out from the neck hole, his head hooded, his elbows withdrawn so that the ends of his sleeves flap emptily, and he is dancing out these eight quavers to the bar, these eerie bass quavers, so that Lo! here is real ghost amongst us!

The silence strikes like a blast of sound. As the passion of the rising music takes him up upon the tables he follows fastidiously with hastening feet each split beat until at length, when the Grieg falls in pitch and slows down to the last chords, Mohi also falls in pitch and slows down to his own last steps and is on his mat again, dreaming.

Here is an emergence of my own dream infant room. But how did it come out? Has it anything to do with me? Was it coming anyway, or is it I giving birth? I scratch my head absently, never knowing that there is something walking about with big feet in my hair. . . .

. . . It's part of the answer though. It brings that *key* nearer. I'm absolutely certain there is a key now. And I would have had my hands on it already if only I had brains instead of a poetic sentimental heart, and if only men did not disturb my equilibrium. There's got to be a "still centre" for vision. Oh, but it's hard feeling it so near. I leave the pre-fab in distress and stalk over to the elm tree that is giving birth too. Ah, even a virgin can know a labour ward. What a long-drawn-out spring this is. . . .

"No, no, I'm not at home!"

It is after school and I am deep in line and colour.

"But look what I have brought you!"

How dare any man open the door of Selah! "I'm working, Paul," raves the artist. "Go!"

"But I've got this Vermouth from the Vineyard."

"I can't drink! I've got to be clear for my illustrations! I've made an appointment to have this book bound."

He doesn't go to the pub when I give him my afternoons. Now he'll go. What hellish decision is this I've got to make? But artists in heat have no trouble making decisions. They just flash. "You must go away. I'm working."

He does; but he leaves his pouch and Vermouth on the kitchen table. "I shall come back later," he says, looking in upon me once more. "Shall we say . . . very much later."

These interruptions are almost physically sore.

After six he comes running through the garden beneath the trees and bursts in the open door of Selah. I look up and see the red flush all round his eyes. "Are you drunk?" I ask unnecessarily.

"A little."

"Have you been to the pub?"

"As from . . . shall we say . . . four on."

It is the first time he has returned to the pub since I have resumed giving him my afternoons and evenings. Today I have driven him there. He is rolling. A very ordinary remorse creeps into my heart. I rise and, shoulder to shoulder, we walk through the house to the drawing room. Very sadly I pick up the Rembrandt volume. "What have you been thinking?" I ask.

"Last night before I slept I was reading. Anthony Trollope."

We both sink upon the couch. He begins packing his pipe.

"What did he say?" Perhaps Trollope managed to say to him what I am too inadequate to.

"He said that women must remember that their breasts are for the suckling of the young mainly, and not for exhibition only."

I take this. For one thing he is drunk and for another I am beginning to develop a strange awareness that everything I say and do about this boy is being weighed. As though every word I choose is of moment; fatal or vital. Last night I dreamt that Paul was sitting on the mat in the infant room and I was helping him to build a castle but a dark figure with big boots and a shirt hanging out kept knocking it down. He looks openly and without his usual discretion at my breasts and although I try to suffer it I can't and lift my hands over them. He bumps me in drunken intimacy. "That garment of yours," he says with authority, "is better without the collar after all."

I reply coolly but with inward fright. "I couldn't wear the bow in front as you wanted. It made me impossibly pompous."

"Pomposity," he replies with drunken emphasis, "and you are irreconcilable."

I choose carefully. "Paul. I judge a man by his conversation when drunk." I try to put approval in my voice.

He smiles in flushed gratification. How little he has to smile about! I must have achieved approval in my voice. Surely I have some more. I have. "Paul. You have three assets: your voice, your face, and your love of words. . . . Of the three I like most the last."

He bows profoundly. "Praise," he observes. "How simple a thing to so, so . . . shall we say . . . exalt!"

I'm wide awake to it now. I'm playing for Paul's future. "What," I ask lightly, "do you judge a woman by, Paul?" I know the stake, but what's the coin? Myself?

He takes his time, not looking at me. "I judge a woman by the colour of her eyes."

. . . When the "Excuse me" time comes I wonder as usual how to temper it. He fills his glass with the remainder of the Vermouth and raises it. "My dear," he whispers, "to you."

"Paul," I say in the dark doorway as he leaves me, "do me a small favour."

"What can I do for you, Madame?"

"Before you go to sleep please think of me."

"That, my dear," he whispers, grasping my shoulder, "has become a, a . . . shall we say . . . necessity."

But it all seems no more than a woman's emotional phantasy after school the next day in the pre-fab; in the broad daylight of sanity. Here is just a young man dissatisfied with his job and looking for a little normal comfort. Just another Little One wailing that somebodies they tread his sore leg for notheen. But I daren't send him away to the pub. My tea with the Head must be skipped and my precious work at home wait.

"I have rejected the Insurance people," he says loftily. "They will have to get along without me."

"Why?" Sadly I lock the piano.

"Organized robbery."

I drape the doorway of the storeroom while Paul settles more comfortably in my little low chair where I am disposed to comfort the hurt and the wailing, and where I do my thinking.

"I'm going to take a correspondence course in English and take up writing."

"But . . .!"

"I want to talk to the world."

"Writing is very hard." If I keep him here he won't drink.

"I can talk. I don't see why I can't write."

"It's because you can talk that writing will be all the harder. What you portray in facial expression, gesture and intonation, all somehow must be conveyed in the character of your sentences. Written sentences carry so much more burden than spoken ones."

He seems to understand and appears relieved not to have a work of writing before him after all. "Anyway," I continue, "that decision to take English was not mine."

"No, it was my own." We never laugh these days.

"I want you to keep a diary for me."

"All right!" Eagerly.

"Write your thoughts whenever you have the occasion and bring them to me."

"I will."

Here is a man with a dream: to talk to the world. That he is writhing this way and that to express. Why have I not seen long ago this thing right under my nose? . . .

Thoughtfully I turn within the storeroom to hide my pre-war chalk and suddenly, catastrophically, here he is behind me. "Do you believe there is a beast in every man?"

"What are you doing in here!"

"This light is kinder to you."

"If you can't see my wrinkles in here we'd better go out again!"

"Oh, I love this mood!"

"Keep your compassion for your own generation!"

"You're ravishing like this!"

"Take a closer look!"

"It's all right: I can see your wrinkles. I like them. Those fine ones around your eyes . . ."

"Leave this storeroom at once!"

He whispers, "You're exquisite like this! With or without your wrinkles you are! This is what enslaves me . . . your rages. Your smocks, your high hair . . . your perfume . . ."

"Don't touch me!"

"Madame," whisper, "you're beautiful . . . you're . . ."

"Don't touch me! I'm inflammable!"

"I have no control. They told me at the Naval Psychological Hospital in England."

I scream with laughter. I stagger out into the better light with it. See? This is how you don't conceive sons.

Generation trouble.

"Why," he asks later, moving towards the trees as the rain falls, "do you want me to write for you?"

"Because I can see that you are a very nervous person and I want to find out why." Only utter truth will do in a crisis.

"I am," he supplements proudly, "a very nervous person."

I should laugh aloud at this but there doesn't seem to be any more laughter in me. *Anyway,* he hasn't been to the pub and he hasn't had a drink today. He has even read a line of Trollope. Moreover, since that blast from the Head, he releases me faithfully each night before nine, so that I see my bed, and am able at least to preserve my early morning hours in Selah; my precious indispensable incomparable communions with truth in the dawn, so that now there are no longer any more of my "heads" disturbing my work at school. My word, there's much to be said for a blast from a headmaster.

Oh, but I do listen for the steps running round my house, and how the traitorous woman longs for her own unpoetic way. But that's just one thing that cannot be. It's a full-out job of the care of the young now, whatever the woman in me clamours for. It's very hard, almost too hard, and there are times when I feel I may split in two over it for ever.

I'm still thinking of this as I arrive at my back step and rest there. Here is a man with a dream to express; to talk to the world. One of these days he's going to realize that he can't. Not that he is short of media. He has a voice, a tongue and his life before him. But he hasn't got the drive. His work at school, which is improving admirably, is all the Head's drive, as far as I can see. What is going to happen when he discovers this? Is he going to come to me as a last resort? To devour me; to feed off me? Is there any way out? There may be. What if he married some young person, or didn't marry some young person . . . does it matter? . . . and conceived a child? Would that be enough? I wonder. It could well be a postponement of the crisis when he knows at last that he cannot talk to the world. I wonder if the Head and the Senior and I can make a . . . No. We cannot make a true success of him as a teacher; it's that matter of drive; personal individual drive. And of charity too; that's missing. . . . Ah, well! I'm too tired to work

It out now. . . . It's time to break off the seeding tops of the delphiniums, to prepare for a second blooming.

Spring is thinking about handing everything over to summer, and the elm tree outside the staff-room window, the walnut tree beyond the pre-fab and the poplars along the river bank are taking their greening up more seriously by the time the new Senior Inspector of Primary Schools, Mr W. W. J. Abercrombie, calls in to make our acquaintance. He is as big and tall and elegant as his name and his office, with sedate grey clothes, groomed grey hair and an austere grey top lip, so that our poor rough corridor, worse now, what with the gear of the carpenters about, for once really looks ashamed of itself. Indeed, when we gather here at morning interval, it doesn't seem to be able to accommodate this large immaculate man, and when he sits, or tries to sit, on the ridiculously low form, he appears not to know what on earth to do with his long legs. Paul trips over them, I trip over them, and when the Head carries out the chair from his room for me, he and the chair fall right over them, so that we feel there has been quite enough to remind him of our conditions, as the Head has wished, without filling the basin with lost shoes and inviting him to wash his hands. Moreover, we all turn on our very best behaviour, as though we were sitting in some posh lounge in a boulevard hotel. The Head clears his throat carefully, Paul drives the children out, and I, forgetting my appointment with the elm tree, rejecting my resolutions to plough through Senior Inspectors, and skipping the leg-crossing act for Paul, carefully remember that I am the hostess of this school and pour the tea. "All of us new," I say youthfully, "like the spring. Gay, isn't it?" I've said this before.

The Senior collects up all his legs and considers what to do with them. He decides to bend the knees, lift one over the other, and fold his hands upon them. "It promises well for the school," he replies neatly. True, through the strength and decision of his voice, a note of boyishness reveals something else in him, but the answer is severely correct; full stop, ruled-off red lines and all. Back comes the constriction in my bowels, immobilizing me. Here is the past with me again, face to face in a draughty corridor. I don't answer because I can't. These are the exact words that passed between the Chairman and me a few weeks ago, yet, instead of opening up in gaiety as I did at that time, I am as one . . . shall we say . . . anaesthetized.

But he seems to know. He trains his efficient grey eyes upon me. "The spring must have been cold for you though, Miss Vorontosov—" he accomplishes my name like a practised hurdler—"in this corridor."

I light up and forget not to look gladly in his face. Here is a man, another man, who is concerned because I have been cold. Plainly, he is married. Yet for all the smile that breaks on my face I hear my unpredictable infant-room answer. "The spring is never other than cold for me."

Oh, if I could only keep these things to myself! Here is my spinster heart laid bare at once! God in Heaven, I am worse than Little Brother! A wise woman never lets a man know what she is thinking, or feeling; you practise mystery all the way. What confounded quality do some men have that beckons the soul to the surface immediately? Yet, even in the face of my dismay at myself, I want, just like Riti, just like Little Brother, just as Paul wants of me, to run into his arms, his big orderly arms, climb up upon his large orderly knees and rest there. How old am I . . . fifty or five! I complete the pouring and passing out of the cups, then sit on the Head's big chair, my back slightly turned from the Senior. You mustn't give this man any more clues to what you are thinking this time.

But elegant gentlemen in corridors are not the same thing as Senior Inspectors in revolutionary infant rooms and when Mr W. W. J. Abercrombie comes over to us afterwards he is no longer a charming and considerate married man but my nightmare. The shade in the rafters materializes into a man on the floor. Waking and sleeping I have dreaded this. In spite of my alcoholic resolutions to ignore Inspectors, Directors and all officialdom, in spite of the counter-attraction, counter-horror of the reverend man of God, in spite of the freedoms of my spirit in the early mornings in Selah, I am defeated. My contracting stomach proves that I am. I'm no brilliant innovator, no courageous champion of the young mind after all! I'm no more now, standing so small before him, than a manless woman. A woman with no background. No defences, no backing or protection whatever. Ah, return to the rafters, Phantom! Before these strangling legs of Guilt stifle my breath! Can I run away? Can a mother desert her children?

Yet, as he stands here, hands clasped discreetly behind him, huge in the doorway, there's a kind of violent radiance in the pre-fab for any who can feel it. I have been aware of it myself before I went over to tea. You can feel anything anywhere, when there is no covering epidermis to your mind, whether you are meant to or not. Working within this raftered shell of pinex you come to a place where you no longer miss it. On my own I forget my affliction. But now, seeing him standing, the living nightmare, calm and grey and tall, and orderly, efficient and correct, within my rocking dinghy, I am all vulnerability. I am reminded, at the melancholy sight of an Inspector within my doorway, once and for all, that I am indeed without covering, either of the mind or in the profession. Without epidermis. Somewhere back along the inspectored track I have lost it. Maybe it came off when my illusions came off, like skin separating with the sticking plaster. I am as uncovered as any other naïve soul in the infant room. Ah, what mortal calamity has befallen us! How I fear those hands clasped behind him!

But meaning, as well as fear, flashes more vividly without a top layer. The heart is immediately addressed. With Matawhero's kitten purring loudly on my shoulder, sweeping my face with her tail, I begin to allow that this may be less a visitation of evil than I had at first felt. For one thing, an unerring barometer, the children approach him, and for another, he doesn't appear to mind. As they stare up at his immaculate height I begin to suspect, not nightmare, but six feet or more of goodwill. After all, I decide agitatedly, you've got to allow for miracles. They happen every day. The edge of the agony leaves me and, as wide-eyed as Mark or Seven or Blossom, I stand staring upward too, and it is only because One-Pint gets in first that I don't blurt out something myself. . . .

"What you fulla come for?" he asks cheerfully.

"I came to see Miss Vorontosov."

"You her boy-friend?" inquires Matawhero delicately.

"He got the grey whisker," observes Seven.

"Who's your name?" asks Tame.

"How old are you?" asks Waiwini.

"Do you gets drunk?" checks up Bleeding Heart.

"Wead the B'ue Jug," suggests Patchy.

"He might be an Inspector," warns Mark. "My mother said you've got to look out for Inspectors."

"I read to you, ay," Wiki nestles up to a leg-pillar.

"Miss Vottot she haved her shoes off before play. She walked on her feets," reports some tell-tit most unfairly.

"Yeah. Ay. An she got a cootie in her hairs. I sawed her get it out I did. Miss Vontopopp."

"Oooh! Miss Vottacock she got cooties in her hairs! Miss Vottacock!"

Ah, well. All is lost before I've started. If only he would kneel to our level! The rest of us are at a disadvantage down here. I would pick up a child for comfort if it wasn't insulting the kitten. The ginger rooster peers combily in the door to see what's going on and the Tamati dog slinks from behind the piano in case there's going to be any food dropped from the visitor. As a matter of fact, the Senior is having the honour of a representative reception if only he could see it as such.

"Yeah ay! An' she wear hair-oil ay!"

"I don't wear hair-oil!" I defend myself indignantly. "It's just the smell of . . . of . . . handkerchief, Blossom!"

"I smelled it!" accuses Bleeding Heart.

"That's just the smell of . . . that's the . . . it's the disinfectant I put in the clay . . . on my hands! Shirt, Matawhero!"

"I see'd her pull the cootie out her hair!"

"That was Riti's cootie! It jumped out of her hair into mine last week! And I couldn't find it till this morning!"

Oh, well, all is lost now, I should say.

The Little Ones and stock eddy about his feet like wavelets on a shore; some move off to their work and some stay to listen in. Waiwini takes the opportunity to step a little nearer, her big eyes lakes of inquiry.

"You don't have to push in," reproves Matawhero, who values courtesy like his grandfather and doesn't want to be disgraced before a stranger.

I've had enough. All my mistakes as a teacher and all my professional sins rise like a tidal wave over my head. The dinghy has struck bad weather. I turn to my low chair with a sense of hanging on to the side. "Blow your nose, Blossom. Tuck in your shirt, Mr Abercro . . . I mean, I mean One-Pint!"

"We dance, ay!" calls Rongo with zest, with the confidence of one who dances regularly and at any time at all. "Play the piano, Miss Vontopoff. We do our works after, ay."

My constricted stomach thinks it would be a good time to vomit now and I feel my way to my chair in case it does. I think of the crack Infant Mistresses in town with all their dignities and their restrained greetings. . . . If I could reach the door now I would run away.

But, here he is pulling up a low chair too and sitting beside me. I lift Little Brother who is bawling professionally and artistically and hold him to me, saying aloud to him, and in mind to myself, "There . . . there . . . look at my pretty girl. Boy I mean."

Little Brother is dressed most beautifully in shantung brown and yellow and in one of those flash-changes of mind so developed in the infant room I am full of pride to hold in my arms so lovely an example of the New Race. My tears of failure lose their footing. "Look at this," I say proudly to the big man beside me.

He does, but he doesn't say anything. I don't know why he doesn't, since I sense in him any amount to say. He is remarkably quiet and unassuming for an Inspector, especially a senior. I can't make it out. Indeed, so open does he leave the field that I am constrained, uncontrollably, to talk myself. And, outrageously, that's what I do.

"I burnt my workbook," I hear. Oh my God, how this man does wrench my soul to the surface!

"Oh?" He lifts his grey eyebrows. "Why?"

"Because I can't stand it any longer!"

"Why?"

"I'm not that kind of person!"

"No?"

"I can't do what I say I'm going to do! And that's what a workbook is. Saying what I'm going to do!"

"Oh?"

"I can't stand the planning of it. The clockwork detail. I can't bear the domination of it. I hate the interference of it between myself and the children, and I resent the compulsion. Sack me if you like! Sack me."

"We are not thinking of sacking you, Miss Vorontosov."

I am trembling and red in the neck, if not everywhere, and I turn to the pouting brown face on my shoulder for refuge. I have a refuge after all, I realize: other people's children. There is stability in the boy body against mine which I have lost in my own, and communion in the up-gazing eyes. This borrowing from a body so small! Ah, this secret that mothers have never told! Gradually the horror, expelled from the crater of me, smokes away to nothing, while, with this boy in my arms, I forget I am a spinster and a teacher and am only woman. By right of need, if not by right of birth, he is mine.

Then suddenly and harshly I remember that no less than Mr W. W. J. Abercrombie, Senior Inspector of Primary Schools, is sitting beside me. What a way for a teacher to be caught! Sitting on a low chair holding a child like a woman! Why aren't I standing at the blackboard like other teachers with a pointer, telling the children to be quiet and to listen to me? Why aren't I raising my voice above the room in authority? Ah, what a din in here! There are Waiwini and Wiki dancing on the tables to the piano music of Hori, come in to practise. What a characteristic failure I am! Ah, Guilt, you are killing me!

But for some reason Mr Abercrombie has stopped right there and does not go railing on. Whatever is this miracle of a listening Inspector? Don't tell me I am going to be permitted to speak again! What in heaven will I hear myself saying next! I look up at his face in bewilderment and here he is, still sitting with his elbows on his knees and his hands hanging down between them, just like a man thinking. The lines on his face are hard and compressed and his grey eyes are too alert and alive to be kind, yet, in spite of the insistent feeling of a withheld forcefulness, I do still sense again the kindness in the corridor. I don't know how I get it but I do. I calm down even more, even more, and cool down too, and in a voice, unrecognizable as the violent one of a moment ago, I am speaking again.

"I keep a diary," I confide softly, passionlessly. "I am able to say what I *have* done. Waiwini," I say to my brown shadow beside me, "bring me that big black book in the drawer with the picture of Ihaka on it."

I judge a man by the way he holds a book. At length he speaks, his fingers laid upon the pages. "You must admit," he says reluctantly, "that this is the irreducible."

"I am irreducible."

"Apparently."

I smile and a few Little Ones copy, so I laugh and the whole seventy join in, fanatically, until the Tamati dog takes his leave. And when the gale is over I look round at the face so near. It is still a stern face and at variance with the general impression of relaxation his presence has brought, but more than ever I don't want to have to suspect this humane general impression. So I look away from his face, and bank on the impression.

He reaches over about two tables with one arm easily and takes from Tame the book he is reading. It is one of my reading books, still in the experimental stage, crude and bound with cloth. The printing and the pictures are all but worn away with the hundreds of little brown fingers that have quarrelled over it and the corners are chewed into dog's ears. "I—I bring them up on Maori work first," I explain. "They can't bridge the gap between the *pa* and the European school without it. They learn to read from books about themselves first, coming to love reading early. Then they go on to the imported books. Waiwini, bring me that big white book with the picture of Ihaka on it. These are the notes of my reading scheme."

He spends some time looking into this while I wait. "How refreshing," he says quietly at last, "to find someone really thinking."

I manage to say nothing for once; with other Inspectors I have learnt to be ashamed of these books. Nor does he say anything further. He looks at the big elegant watch on the big elegant hand, rubs the big elegant face as though he is trying to remember something, smiles at Little Brother in my arms, pulls his nose, and is gone. It's over. I put down the child, collapse back on my chair, my legs pointing to separate points of the compass, my arms to the other two, and my head falling backwards like one dead.

"Oh, Miss Vorontosov." My God, he's back again! I recall all my limbs. "The workbook. We'll have to make a special case of you. But be so kind as not to mention it to other teachers. Imagine what would happen in the Board if all the teachers turned irreducible." Once more he's gone.

I don't relax so smartly this time. Matawhero checks up on his car leaving. But I'm excused from the curse of my teaching life. True, he said nothing about my Maori books, but I'm used to that. I pick up the child again and stare at him until I see him. Then I smile at him and say in Maori, *"He mea nui rawa atu ki te ako i aku tamariki . . . tamariki maori."* Then "Look at my boy with the brown, brown eyes and the long, long legs!"

He laughs, and his sister Waiwini, keeping guard over him beside me, laughs too, and in no time a few more nearby catch it, like singing or crying, not knowing why, and Lo! here is the fantastic situation of an Inspector just gone, the teacher and children laughing behind him, with no flicker of bitterness whatever. . . .

"What did he . . .?"
"What did he say to . . .?"
"What did he say to you?"
"He said . . ."
"He said that . . ."
"He said that I don't have to do a workbook. But he said I wasn't to tell any other teachers. So I promised I wouldn't. You two won't tell anyone will you? Or if you do, get them to promise they won't tell either."
"I found him exceedingly gracious and charming," says the Head.
"I remain unconvinced," says Paul loftily.
"I told him to tuck his shirt in."

But there was no acknowledgment of my books, I remind myself as I trip over the fallen cabbage-tree blades on my way homeward. Still no one can see, apparently, with me, the wrench that occurs when a young coloured mind meets the respectable European book. All these years of experiment and effort again, like those constructing the Maori Art Scheme. Are these going to end up in flames too? All right, let the books die and we'll have a death in my one-woman family. And thousands of young Maoris can keep the vigil.

It's plain that my books are just one more of my monumental mistakes. My word, I'm getting on with my mistakes. I'm a master at them.

Just one more mighty mistake; these books.

In the evening, however, when I take my coffee out in the garden, I'm by no means as desolate as I should be. . . .

I smile. What reason I have to smile I cannot fathom. It's true of course that there is a new picture in the world behind my eyes of a grey-haired, grey-clothed Inspector, standing within the door of my pre-fab, his hands clasped ominously behind him; but for teachers to smile at the memory of an Inspector cannot be professional ethics. Also I have abandoned the work on my books which, I endeavour to persuade myself, is no small catastrophe; a disaster really; holocaust actually. If only I could behave in character and weep industriously on it.

Efficiently, elegantly and correctly, his hands contained behind him, Mr W. W. J. Abercrombie, Senior Inspector of Primary Schools, stands within the door of my mind. Other men, the Head, Paul, and Eugene, step back. There's plenty of room. Plenty of room for all in the mind of prolonged spinsterhood. In the chronicle of faithfully encloistered virginity. I answer positively to them all. It's a very low score, looked at mathematically. In fact I'm not so sure that it is not a disgrace that there are not more. Only aware of five men . . . six . . . no five. . . . Yes, five.

When the evening has darkened my flowers, I by-pass Selah where my work awaits its appointment, grope within the silent house, up the hall through the bedrooms where my shadow sons laugh and squabble over their homework, to the piano in the drawing room. And as I sit down before my keyboard in the darkness I am happy in the way my Little Ones are; by some mysterious and illegal right. Wilfully I refuse to search my heart for the reason; to examine its secret strata. Like a child I forget what engaged me in hours of solid sonata. . . .

Summer

". . . birds build—but not I build,"

SUMMER has taken over officially in my garden. You can tell by the conversations of the flowers. They're all chatter and flash. And the funny thing is that you never hear them talk about the spring before, much less the autumn to come. And as for winter! They wouldn't know how to say the word. Or recognize it if they heard it. And that's what makes a garden so sad to a solitary woman who can't see summer without its glorious lead-up, then its violent-coloured regrets, and finally the posthumous-minded winter. It makes me want to stride out there and tell them to be quiet, my flowers. To be quiet and pick up a few things like perspective; about before-and-afters; even about life, birth and death. It makes me avoid them in the evening when they can only compare their scents and their tints and discuss the love-affairs of the birds in the creeper. I don't know what people see in summer, myself.

Yes, summer has taken over in my garden and the thing is to rejoice. But where can I find the heart to, and where can I raise the voice?

Patchy's mother comes raging in at playtime as I am pouring the tea for the men in the new staff-room. She is red-faced and loud-mouthed and fat, but she is the Head's stand-by on many a school occasion and is important to him. Parent Number One.

"Look," she says, "Oi don't want to hurt your feelings, Miss Vorontosov."

"I haven't got any. I haven't got any."

Anyway she can say my name and I'm prepared to humour her.

"Sit down," says the Head, applying his technique to angry parents and standing himself. It makes a difference, he taught us once.

"No, Oi won't sit down."

"Have some tea," I say, the only technique I know.

"No, thanks."

"Good gracious."

"Well, look, it's about Patchy. Poor little tyke."

"Don't tell me something happened when I was away yesterday. I had to take my A and B teams into town for the competitions."

"Look, without a word of a loi, Oi got two dozen loive things out of the little tyke's hair! Two dozen!"

"That'll be my Riti." I scratch my own head reminiscently.

"The nurse," begins the Head, "cleans up the whole school regularly but they collect a new supply from the *pa* each night."

Paul does not crash in. He boards with Parent Number One. He does no more than feel through his own head, furtively.

"All you can do," I say, expanding in this unexpected chance to talk in peace, "is to buy a tooth-comb and keep watch."

Patchy's mother attacks in another direction. "What about Mark's mother? Oi was thinking about Mark's mother. If her Mark! . . ."

"I remember the time," I say, passing round the tea to the men, I always pour and pass the tea now, I don't know why, "when I was giving an Inspector a cup of tea just like this and a great thing jumped from my own hair and clattered round the saucer."

"But two dozen! Oi . . ."

Mr Vercoe, for some reason, has gone out on playground duty. Not, however, that the corridor outside is any the quieter for that.

"Two dozen?" says the Head. "What about the hundred and forty-four my wife found in our little girl's hair when we were not watching?"

I'll find out for myself about the lice, I reflect, as I drive into town after school on Friday. So Paul and I buy a tooth-comb, but what we call in the *pa,* euphoniously, a "cootie comb" and on Monday I walk into the Head's room and say, "I want someone to come down to the infant room and put this comb through the hair."

There is a hundred per cent response and I choose the cleanest and sweetest of them all, Whareparita, and we swing into action among the Little Ones.

"Do him first," I say, indicating Mark, and thinking of his mother who is sure to conclude that the comb went through his hair after all the others. "In fact," I continue, quite overlooking that Whareparita is a Maori herself, "do all the white ones first."

Whareparita is not as beautiful as she was, for some reason, I reflect, as I watch her under way with the little fair heads. Where are those flowing lines of her body? She seems heavier, duller, and less shapely than before. This must be the reason that I no longer find her and Paul trying to get together. She's lost her charm for him. For a moment I sense some conclusion right under my nose . . . but I can't put my finger on it. . . .

Of course they are all as innocent as the day, the little fair heads. Then we get down to business.

"Do Riti," hint the children. "Do Riti."

"All right. Do Riti."

Patchy is vastly taken with this performance after his own score of two dozen last week. He stands by me for support and points an accusing finger. "Tee," he charges, "Tee gived them to moi head!"

Riti runs up cheerfully enough, however, to Whareparita to be unmasked. She's a mass of smiles and affection with bare feet to match. She is thrilled with the first catch and so are the others. They cluster round to speculate on its length.

"Put it on the stove," I tell Whareparita. That's what I did with mine.

"See?" she cries delightedly. "They die on the stove!" How babyish she is for so developed a figure.

Zestfully they all watch the louse in its last hours on earth, then Whareparita returns to the hunt. It is in full swing when Twinnie calls out, "Miss Vontof, one felled outa Mere's hair!"

I take offence at this since I consider Mere, who has no mother, slightly mine. She is slim, dark, musical, emotional and beautiful as phantasy. But she has an illness about which they won't engage a doctor. "It diden fall outa my hairs, Miss Vontop," she defends. "I found it on the mat." She fondles it anxiously.

"Put it on the stove. Put it on the stove."

The corpses are mounting there now. Matawhero takes a quick personal glance at Mere's hair. "Hell! Mere's she's got plenty."

"Have a look at Mere, Whareparita." I'm feeling disgraced about Mere. I should have seen to this before.

Mere comes willingly enough, although not joyfully like Riti, and Whareparita has a look. "Ooh, Miss Vorontosov, Mere's got plenty!"

"She's got no mother!" I defend. "Let's clear up that head, Whareparita."

She sets to with zeal and the Little Ones and I get on with our conversation. We are very heavy on conversation in the morning; especially Monday. Towards playtime, however, Whareparita sighs and goes wearily to the piano for a rest. I look back at Mere. Here she is sitting on a low chair by the stove, her black hair sticking up high all over her head, from the intensive hunt, and as Matawhero, the natural master of ceremonies, assesses the score on the stove, her face is drooping and despondent and she doesn't look up when the boy avers, "Ooh, Mere's she's sure got plenty of cooties!"

From the piano, playing "Big Enough for Two, My Darling, Big Enough for Two," Whareparita explains hotly, "She's got no mother, that's why!"

I look at her. How strong is the maternal instinct in so sweet and innocent a child. But where has all that glow of beauty gone, I wonder? She has the greyness of a blossom despoiled. Sickening for something maybe. She has fainted more than once in the heat of a basketball match.

Something under my nose . . . something under my nose.

However I've always believed in rhythm and when things at school are looking their cootiest I cheer up and think there'll be a change soon. So after the girls have been mentioned at the Town Council for skating on the bridge on Sunday, and the boys have been to court for climbing the power poles, and both have been talked about at Traffic Headquarters for riding their bikes across the walking place of the bridge, and walking on the motor-vehicle place, and after we have dealt gently but firmly with every "thing" in every head in the school, I sit back for a little good behaviour.

But as I am picking up my pen-box after school and locking the piano for the day I hear the Head's step. I can tell by this step that he has something to tell me, and I can tell by the way he turns the handle of the door that it is bad, so by the time he has come in and sunk down on a small table, I have reorientated myself.

"I've just been up to see Mrs Rameka."

"That's right. She asked you up."

"It was about Whareparita being away."

"That's right. I've missed the lovely thing. Cooties?"

"Whareparita's pregnant."

My eyes pop out and bounce about. I have to go after them. When I've recovered and replaced them I ask, "How old is she?"

"Thirteen."

"No, Mr Reardon! She must be fourteen. I noticed her developed little figure in here just the other day."

"No, she's thirteen."

"Well, I would have said she was fourteen."

"Neither thirteen nor fourteen is sixteen, is it? And sixteen is the low water mark where the law is concerned."

"Who was it?"

"Oh, she was very loth to tell, of course. So I gathered it was some relation. I said, 'Is it some relation?' But she said, 'No.' Then suddenly she said it was a relation, eagerly. So I see plainly that it wasn't and that she was using the idea to shield somebody. Of course she was very distressed so I didn't press the matter."

I don't answer. It looks as though the Head is going to shield them all. Whereas I feel very much the other way. Not that it will hurt Whareparita. If she is ready to mate, and the Maori girls really are ready to mate earlier than the white ones, or so we like to think, well, why not? It's just that I am allergic to smug men using women and then cruising off; women from thirteen on. I'm so allergic that I sent Eugene cruising off without using me. I never mellow on the matter of men taking their pleasure from women, however noble their ideals of personal freedom, and leaving them to clean up. And this is just what this Whareparita story means to me. Some great hulk, some lofty Eugene, helping himself to a lovely child and bequeathing her the consequences. I hold myself very quiet, as I always do when my temper is involved on a deep level.

"I won't be doing anything about it until I have talked it over with

Rau. Of course I'll have to report the matter to the Education Board. What do you think?"

"Well, there are two issues as far as I can see. It all depends on whether you want your roll-number to drop. If men are to be allowed a free run through your schoolgirls there are a few more ripe. On the other hand there is the law of the land you live in."

"Anyway I'll go over and check up on her age."

Presently he returns. I gather by his step that Whareparita is actually only thirteen. "I've made up my mind about this," he says, putting his head in the door. "She's only turned thirteen last month."

"She was twelve at the time then."

"My word, old Rau is going to take a knock over this."

"I can't see that he will. I should think that he himself mated early. And hard ever since. Which is probably why he's out now. I can tell by the violence of the expression of his dream over this school. But you might as well die over the expression of a dream. Better than no dream. His life, what there has been of it, is just one flash of meaning."

"It might have been one of the big boys, you know."

"Might have been too: co-education."

"I'm going to report this to the Board."

"Just send them a telegram: 'Co-education de luxe.'"

It's in the paper about Whareparita. Reverse for the Head's school. Reverse for the re-establishment of the white children who pass. Reverse for his dream of a meeting-place of the races. He takes it harder than when the skating and the power pole incidents were published. I visit him in his room after school the next day and wish that Paul wasn't singing so loudly over the preparation of his work in the next room. What in heaven is he so disgracefully happy about?

"Never mind, Mr Reardon. I'm going to make an appointment with the Broadcasting Studio for the orchestra. And we'll have it written up in the paper in six-inch headlines. Have you written up how we won the basketball competition too, recently? Just make our headlines bigger than theirs, that's all."

Oh, don't I hate to see dreams atrophied! Away down within me I feel the continued rumblings of rage. However I keep it out of my voice. "Look," I say softly, "look what I've made you. I've designed a banner for the school. Look! Here's the Maori *teko teko*,* here's a book to indicate learning and I've got this rafter pattern from corner to corner. And here's the motto. *Utaina.* Maori for 'build.'. See? I'll get the big girls on to making them in wool for their pockets. See? This will knit the school together and stop them climbing power poles and skating on the bridge on Sunday and riding their bikes on the footway and getting pregnant. This is all that we wanted. We'll do it in yellow and brown and some red for the *teko teko*. . . . Oh, I wish that boy would stop that noise in there!"

"What you don't know, Madame, is that the police have just called. The two Tamati boys and Tai broke into the store last night. So the school will be featuring in the Police Court news today again. Also they had reason to suspect that the father of Whareparita's child is a white man."

I open my mouth to speak but nothing comes. So I swallow and try again. But all I achieve is, "Oh, that wretched boy in there!"

"Let him sing, Madame. Let him sing. He's only a boy."

"Oh, you spoil him!" I swing round and out the door and up the corridor and into Paul's room. "Stop that infernal bellowing!"

He turns from the blackboard where he is working. "Madame, there is one, and only one time in a man's life, when it is his obligation to sing; his privilege, his, his . . . shall we say . . . glory." He bows so elaborately that his fountain-pen falls out of his top pocket.

"And your time is when the school is in public disgrace!"

He smiles widely in appreciation. There are some able sketches on the board, the artist in me has time to note, and his writing is copperplate. "I love this mood of yours!" he whispers.

But I hate men laughing at my rages. "Why don't you set an example to the big boys? Why haven't you got a club, or tennis teams? What else do you do besides sing and mop the floor on Friday? You wandering ne'er-do-well! You spineless apology of life! You crowning example of synthetic manhood!"

"Madame!" he whispers coming forward, his arms lifting to me. "You're beautiful! You're exquisite like this! You thrill me . . . you thrill me . . . don't stop . . ."

"Go to Hell!"

* Maori figurehead on meeting house.

But the next thing I know he is down on one knee, his arms reaching. "Madame, you are for me. No one else, nothing else, matters. You are for me . . . like this, just like this . . ."

The Head appears at the door. I hear his step behind me.

"Here," I rage at him, "is this assistant of yours on his knees! Relieve me of this melodramatic ardour! Is this the way to prepare work after school? Are these the relations you cultivate on your staff? God in Heaven if . . . if I . . .!"

"Let him kneel, Madame. Let him sing. He's only a boy. At least he is happy."

"Oh you spoil him utterly! You ruin young staff!" I get out and fast.

It's time to let my fearfully noisy youngest ones go so that I can work seriously with my older ones. True, the bell hasn't said so, but it's matter for comment how this lordly bell is being flouted these days. Without any reference to me, seemingly, emotional time is taking over from bell time, and it turns out to be an exciting kind of time too. For one thing, less and less do I find the Little Ones whining to get outside, and for another, my pride doesn't get hurt as it used to. But the essential thing about this kind of time is, however, a headmaster who exercises his sympathies where a guilty teacher is concerned and where small children are. How much happiness and how much strain may stem from this one thing!

So I go to the door and turn and open my arms wide and call, "All my little new ones, come to me!" And Lo! Here they all come, a crowd of other people's children, running into my open arms. Fifteen or so. Brown, white and yellow, and beautiful as a woman going to her lover.

But the impact of them makes me step back and I feel my high heel go on somebody's toe behind me, the worst disgrace I know in an infant room, and I turn in great trouble. But all I can find is a bank of grey behind me, which turns out to be the waistcoat of a man. Curiously I follow this clue upward as far as some shoulders, feeling I have seen all this before. But before I have arrived at a clipped grey top lip I'm sure of it. I have seen all this before. I quite overlook the toe still beneath my heel.

But the pain on this stern face towering above me reminds me and I let the children loose in a flood and get off it. Then I turn and find my hand in his . . . but only my hand.

"I've got a typewriter, Miss Vorontosov, that types the size and the kind of printing that you want in your Maori reading books. I can get my typist to print your texts now." Correctly his hands meet behind him.

"Where did you get it?"

"It belongs to a friend of mine," he replies quietly, composedly. "I asked him to sell it to me, but he said it was left to him by a friend who is dead. He values it."

He shows me some samples of this printing. It is large printing for the very young. Simple and big. "Are you sure," he says with uninspectorlike humility, "it is what you want? Of course, he is only lending it to me."

"This is today's miracle!" I cry, flinging my hands. "I just can't get any further. I can make one model each of the four books, but I can't multiply them by six as I used to do. I'm getting old. I'm fused. I'm worked out. Today's miracle!" I look up at him suddenly. "I expect you know them, these miracles?"

He moves to my table where I keep my Maori books in a wooden box. The table is madly untidy but he knows exactly where to find them. He reaches out an elegant hand and takes one, fastidiously, like taking a "thing" out of someone's hair. "It has," he says, "been a lot of work. In any case I've come out to go into the matter of these books. I've always believed there should be some kind of bridge between the *pa* and the European infant room."

But for some reason, his calm manner only makes me more violent. This delicate touch he has on a room is disastrous in drawing me out. I don't know why, but I'm talking. Just like the Reverend talks to me, and as Paul does. I'm talking on my books with everything I've got in diction, intelligence, sensibility and passion. No mother recommended a child with more conviction and no parent pleaded so for the life of her firstborn. Waiwini, the Queen of Communication, stands with me at the table the full time, her whole self wholly given up. And I feel her sympathy, even though she is only six. However wild my expositions, still her face leans on its elbow, two ribbons on one plait and none on the other, her large brown eyes open to their fullest and her mouth too.

She can't possibly understand our words, but she reads everything else. Faces, voices, hands and actions. And here she stands from ten till eleven, until the head on the hand begins to droop, sharing with me every hysteria that swings me about. She accompanies me until I run to the storeroom and bring out all the other heaps and boxes and dozens of books I have made by hand; until I bring them faster, pouring them over the table, mountains of them, and until my august visitor groans and covers his face with his hands.

"I have always believed," he insists, "that there is a bridge needed between the *pa* and the European environment. I believe you have got something here: a transition."

"Congratulations, Mr Abercrombie, for rescuing this from its death-bed."

"May I take one with me?"

I hesitate. I can't possibly do this. Then I go on. "I'm going to begin a fourth lot. There's many a thing that, in the wear and tear of usage, has proved itself wrong. I'll make you a new one. With the typewriter everything will be different."

"Thank you, Miss Vorontosov."

"Now," he says later, changing his tone, and touching lightly, easily, my arm, "come and get some tea."

I accompany him across the grass. So severely big beside me! So foolishly small I am! So obviously out of step are our feet! My guilt sneaks back to me, that has had to leave me in his presence for one blessed hour. I'm full of shame. I've talked too much. I've let too much of myself escape. As I pour out the tea in our new staff room suddenly I burst out. "You come here and make me talk and I talk you down and say too much and I'm sorry after!"

He considers this, standing, large legs astride. "I always find," he says reflectively, "that if I keep quiet I learn something."

But I remain confused and ashamed in the afterwash of detumescence throughout the day and it is not till I am in the laundry, working on a large heap of frightfully dirty clothes belonging to Wi, One-Pint, Ani, Hine and Riti, that I realize that my books have been approved. And it is not until the evening, when I am ironing the clothes that are dry, that I can see the size of the thing. Then I forget to turn off the iron and make my way down the back steps across the garden to Selah once more, and here I sit with an untouched page before me and a poised brush in my fingers, deep into the night; going over again everything that was said, over and over, and living once more the scene of the morning.

Over and over again, even when I wake in the dawn, so that by brandy time, remembering fearfully the light touch on my arm . . . can a smart Infant Mistress in town brag of a touch on the arm? . . . remembering romantically the touch on the arm calling me to tea, I feel the occasion for celebration cannot be overlooked. Indeed so festive do I feel filling the crystal glass before school that I tip it all back in the bottle.

My beautiful little La comes through the door before school as I am combing Hine's hair for the day, shining from head to foot, yellow ribbons on black hair, and looking lovely in her new brown and yellow uniform. She gives me sixpence. I kneel to her level.

"Is this for your pencil, Little One?"

"It is for you."

I stifle the obligation to return it at once.

"F—for me?"

"It jiss for you."

"Thank you, thank you, La. What for?"

"Jiss for you to buy."

"What shall I buy?" I ask tenderly.

"A beer. Jiss a beer."

I put down Paul's diary I have completed reading on my table in Selah and pick up my brush. Saturday.

"What do you think," he asks from the old arm-chair here, "of my style, my, my . . . shall we say . . . my choice of epithet, my vagaries of English, my . . ." He flourishes a cigarette in finish. He is sober as always now and cheerful.

I put down my brush again, turn to him, cross my legs and take a cigarette. "I like what we must call your style. It's entirely you. All those words, unheard of before, some may deplore, but not me. Every time you supply yourself with a word you're in good company. Hopkins composed words right and left. I do myself. The more they're not found in the dictionary, the more I honour them. I wouldn't change one."

"But my punctuation."

"That's so. But as long as you put in a full stop now and again. Just as a kind of signpost . . ."

He springs to his feet, roaring with laughter, strides to the door and back and sits down again.

"You know," I go on, "just as a personal gesture to me."

He rises and looks down upon me from across the table. "I must find a farm where I can retire and write a book. Somewhere not too far away. So that I can come and see you . . . shall we say . . . once a week."

"There are times," I say, meeting his wonderful eyes with difficulty, "when I think that you remember what I said to you at the gate one morning with Dawn's Straight Left in the Sky." I find my brush.

"I do," he whispers.

I fall silent and my brush slows. One of these telling visionary moments that register the meaning of life is winging by. For an unmeasured span of time he gazes down upon me as I drag a brush. Then his voice comes above my head once more and his tone is one of profound discovery. "Love," he utters simply, "breaks all bounds."

Then he is gone again back to his chair and cigarette. "What do you think of the title, 'Frustration'?"

"It'll do for a while, but it will change."

"Then there's the dedication to fix up."

I take an appreciative draw at my cigarette and go on painting. I've had poems dedicated to me before. And novels too.

"Do you think I'll have my book finished by Christmas?"

"It all depends on school."

Back he strides again before my table. "Madame, you must be very careful not to overlook anything in me. The Meynells found a young man once in the slums of London, dying, and took him home and nursed him. That was Francis Thompson. You've got to be so careful. Tell me. What do you think? Is there anything in me worth bothering about?"

I look up bravely into the clear young eyes, gazing tremendously, the lamplight revealing the full beauty of his face, and the red shade hiding the age in mine. "I don't know," I say, counting the stakes, "I don't know."

Here I am at school faced with the real thing; no brandy softening the morning. True, I have a feeling of firmness as though at least my feet were on solid ground these strictly sober nine-o'clocks but I've aged easily five years over the effort.

Also I am faced with Mark's mother. I keep her out on the grass. Drunk or sober, I would never let anyone like her into my precious precarious craft.

"Mark said you wanted to see me," she says.

"I want you to buy a tooth-comb, Mrs. Cutter."

Up she blows! "Mark told me you went through his head with a comb! I said, 'I hope she didn't do you last. You would have caught them by then!'"

"Now, what would you think, Mrs. Cutter?"

Little Ones cluster round me. Brown Reremoana encircles me with her arms in protection. I feel the better for it too. I watch Mark's mother steadily. I don't like her face, this face of a married woman who has borne children. From the reckoning of a spinster her eyes should be soft with fulfilment. But they're hard and accusing and full of suspicion, as though there were no dear little boy to make her thoughts shine and no dear little girl. But then, what is a spinster's reckoning on such matters as these?

"He said you did him first. But he said it was a Maori girl doing them!" She is slightly hysterical. But I'm having trouble with my laughter again, just as I do with my crying. One of these days I'll be carried away to the hospital for a surgical operation to have all my accumulated laughter discharged. Fearing this, I try to keep my face in control and try not to see a Maori girl going through white Mark's hair for cooties. Why didn't I laugh at the time and get it over? Silly thing I am.

"Fancy having a Maori to clean a white child's head, Miss Vorontosov!"

Ah, she can say my name! I swing over to her side at once. I'm full

of extravagant sympathy that I didn't know existed. No trouble! I sort
out one of my voices to match.

"I know it is a shock to hear this," I say. "It's outrageous to find
'these things' in your own child's hair. You'll never get over it, finding
them in your own child's hair. What you want to do is buy a cootie
comb . . . I mean a tooth-comb."

"That's why all the white children left this school, Miss Vorontosov!
Before you and Mr Reardon came. And went away to the next school.
They found these live things in their children's hair and they said,
'Well, it's just no place for white children!' And they took them all
away. I took my little girl away."

"I understand," I say. "But there's no need for you to have this
shock. Just buy a little comb and run through that hair every night.
They jump, these things." Ah, if only the Head could see me in brilliant action trying to save his school!

"Oh . . . oh!" she gasps, hiding her face with her hand.

"He'll be all right when he is older," I comfort. "It's when they are
little that they have no idea of looking after themselves."

"Oh . . . oh!" I don't seem to be saying the right thing.

"His head could be full before you know anything about it. They
breed in eight days. Mrs Reardon found a hundred and forty-four."

"Oh . . .!"

"However, the nurse will be here again next week and will clean
them all up again."

"Mrs. Cutter," I tell the Head in his room after school, as he stands
and offers me his chair, "says it was the lice that drove the white children away. I thought it was the T.B."

"It was. But it was the wrong reason. There's no T.B. allowed in the
school now, with the regular mantu tests."

"Isn't it a relief to get out this word 'lice'! I can never use it when
talking it over with parents. I always say 'These Things.' But 'cooties'
is the answer. Pally sort of. Intimate. 'My Cootie and I,' and so on."

"I recall the day," says the Head reflectively, "when Mr Cutter first
brought Mark to this school. We were all standing outside in assembly
when in he strode with Mark by the hand. 'I attended this school when
I was a boy,' he said, 'and what's good enough for me is good enough
for my son!' Plonk! Here was Mark!"

I shake quietly and ridiculously with laughter. You can in here, thank God. "Well now, look, this orchestra practice. They're all over there waiting for me."

"Really I don't like seeing you still on the job after school, Madame!"

"Why, what do you call 'after school'?"

"Well, you're only paid until three."

"I didn't know school ever to stop at all since I began in my youth. Anyway, what about you? Whom did I see sneaking out the gate last night after five? Not Mr Reardon! Oh no, not the Headmaster!"

"What happened to that louse you had in your head?"

"Well, I made it welcome. After all, I was the hostess. Made it some tea and so on. Got it to talk about itself. Helped it with its perversions. Received its dreams. It turned out that it was a social outcast and wanted to be alone."

"Did it breed?"

"How could it when it was only one?"

"Man . . . man!" warns Matawhero, his eyes never wholly on his work.

Waiwini glances up swiftly to see if there is going to be anything worth listening to, Reremoana runs to me hard, skipping over Mohi dreaming on the mat, and holds me tightly to protect me from goodness knows what, and several pairs of brown eyes, from Little Ones near enough to hear Matawhero's war cry, focus upward. I straighten my stiff back from over a low table where four small hands are writing, and here he comes stepping long-legged over everything in his way, castles, trucks, clay-boards and children, just as I would like to step long-legged over everything in my way in the profession, his large hand outstretched. "Good morning, Miss Vorontosov, and how are you?"

They should all stand, I think hastily and nervously, like the crack infant rooms in town that he so likes, and say "Good morning, Mr Abercrombie," too. I urgently try to rub the coloured chalk off a hand, with the fullness of my smock, to give to him. In dismay I see the purple and black I have left on his.

"Leaving your mark on me, Miss Vorontosov?"

"It's hard to get off."

"Beg your pardon?" It's hard to hear, what with the orchestra tuning up in the far corner, Hirani at the machine, Hori simply thundering on the piano, a few big girls chattering over their work on the pockets nearby, and the yells of the C and D basketball teams waiting through the window on the basketball court for me; all on top of the tremendously rocking infant room.

"It's hard to get off, that chalk."

"I don't mind my teachers leaving their mark on me."

He has come to collect some of my reading-book text for the magic typewriter . . .

"The lady supervisor . . ." I begin some time later.

"I beg your pardon?"

"Take off the loud pedal, Hori! Can't you see," I call to the orchestra in the corner, "that I am speaking to a man? Tune softly! The lady supervisor never comes near me. Handkerchief, Blossom."

"That's my work. I asked her not to. I told her you were just working out something on your own. But if you wish it I'll let her come."

"No, no. Leave it that way. Leave it that way, thank you."

He reaches almost two small tables away and picks up Wiri's paper on which he is writing some desperate secret about Grandpa killing his sister's illegitimate baby with the potato knife and hiding it under the mattress, and reads it. "I'd like to have this."

"You can . . . you can. Laugh more softly, Bleeding Heart!"

"I'll pay him for his paper." A hand goes seeking down into a grey pocket and I hear silver rattling.

"Don't talk money to me!"

"But I'm taking his property. It's . . ."

"I beg your pardon? You big girls will have to be more courteous! You can see that I'm speaking to a visitor. I haven't been so rude as to interrupt you. But now it's your turn to let me speak."

"It's only reasonable . . ."

"But why be reasonable?"

A reluctant smile changes the stern face and the hand comes out empty. He moves to the end of the piano and leans his elbow on it and surveys the room, stroking his chin. "You could do with something better than this."

My eyes and mouth both open wide in protest. "We've got a roof! We've got a roof!"

The Head comes in after he has gone, to collect my Rolls to do the totals himself. "He told me," he says, "that he is going to send me a Junior 'to help Miss Vorontosov in all she is attempting to do.' "

I look ruefully round this holocaust that goes under the name of "infant room" and smile . . .

"He had a look at Paul too," he goes on. "He seemed to be very pleased with Paul. He was right in seeing something in Paul in the first place, to select him. I wouldn't have."

"I still wouldn't have accepted Paul. On the surface, I know, he is making marvellous strides. But I . . . aa . . . sense a . . . an instability in him. For one thing, it's these irrational things he does. He's got no respect for law and order and custom. He doesn't care what other people think. I know he's just right at school but I wonder how much of it is you, rather than Paul. He has to have someone else's drive in him. I don't overlook all that wandering. I wonder at times if this job is not just another stop-gap in his life, like the navy. Something to hide in from himself, for the time being."

"W. W. praised him."

"That might be fatal, you know. I don't know why. Or perhaps I do know. It might make him believe he is sincere. Whereas if you withdrew your energy from him he'd fall. I'd rather he knew it was yours. As it is, at school, he is far too sincere to be trusted. I can't believe that, on his own, he actually has the capacity to carry a thing through." The Head and the Senior know as little of Paul's private life as they do of mine.

"What I really came to see you about . . ." Ah, yes, I should have remembered that the Head would be thinking about something else.

"Now I'll just take your Rolls."

"Oh I haven't got them marked yet . . .!"

"Give them to me and I'll mark them now."

"It's a good thing that W. W. doesn't ask to see my Rolls . . ."

The Head laughs like anything.

"No one," I go on seriously, "stood up when he came in, you know."

The Head laughs harder than ever . . . I don't know why. Then he says in afterthought, "But you know as well as I do that Paul's improvement is not all my work. You yourself have taken many a demonstration lesson for him; both in his room and your own."

"Yes, but do you know what he says at the end? Not some acute inquiry on method, not some keen question on the work I've covered, but some question like, 'Do you know that line from Spender, "The grave evening demand for love"?' "

The Head sits down on a small table and laughs in a way that starts off the whole dinghy. At length he says, "I hope he had his shirt tucked in this time."

Strange how this Inspector leaves us laughing . . .

I find W. W. J. Abercrombie a very different kind of man when I visit him at his office in town to collect some of my reading-book text. Gone is the self-effacing listening attitude he wears in the classroom and I encounter a man of action. I'm astounded. The quick movement, the alert speech and the air of control. I meet an utter stranger. True, he is waiting at the top of the stairs for me with a handshake of re-assurance, but the main impression I receive, besides the courtesy and elegance, is of implacability. Who would have thought it? I whine to take the typewriter home but he tries me out on it first, standing behind me. I don't overlook my only weapon of scent to wring it from him, moving my head strategically, but there's no visible result. It's only because I prove myself proficient on it, and God knows it's hard enough to be efficient at anything, even talking, with his presence so immobilizing, that he decides to let it go, and not without a firm re-minder that it belongs to another man who values it for sentimental reasons. Sheer surprise carries me through all this. And it has to do more. It has to hurry me up when he carries this instrument across the road beside me to my car. What a fantastic performance a simple crossing of a street turns out to be! Strolling from the pre-fab to the big school was never like this. He spurts ahead, then pulls up suddenly to wait. I spurt to catch him and find myself ahead. We start off again together and in a flash I'm left behind. Start, stop; fits, starts. Where is the romance in this? We're hopelessly out of step. Maybe this is what marriage must be like. But from it all I see just to the extent that he adapts himself to a teacher in the classroom. It's a classic of orienta-tion: a masterpiece in change.

On the way home, however, driving slowly through the summer countryside, I work it all out. He has cultivated this deliberate self-effacement in order to bring out the teacher. God knows it brought me out! All that talking of mine; all that listening of his! Technique, my dear, only technique. Hell!

Ah well, I reflect as I brew the coffee, I might as well try to enjoy my errors since I make so many of them; since I do little else but make them. I'm just one thundering errata: Miss Anna Mistake is my name.

I don't think I'll waste good weeping over this. It's true that I have had to eject from the world behind my eyes all that romantic sentiment about the Senior being aware of me, other than as a teacher, whereas he is doing no more than a thorough job, but I can take it. In any case there's always others. There's plenty of men. Indeed there will be one running round this very house shortly. I'll just take this coffee out into Selah and lose myself in colour before he comes.

$\mathcal{H}$*AVE* you seen that work in Paul's room?"

I appear in the Head's classroom after school.

"Look at that now!" The Head is as excited as a boy. "By Gee, I'm proud of that work! The poor old chap had something in him after all! Oh, but have you seen him taking tennis, Madame; really it's laughable!"

"I really can't believe it." We stroll back down the corridor to the other classroom. "He's done what I said about getting in the easel, and the new mats on the floor, and Hirani hemmed those curtains this afternoon. He bought the material himself, you know. He chose it last . . ."

"You know he's not so bad with a bit of chalk. Look at those drawings on the board. I'd like to see what he's like with a . . ."

"He's got an eye for line all right. But look how tidy the room is for a young man. It's like the deck of a ship."

"And yet he doesn't seem to be happy." We move into the staff room. "He seems to be trying too hard. He's not happy."

"It's because the children don't love him. They obey him but they don't love him. It's plain that they do not love him."

"They're obedient and orderly and turn out magnificent work."

"Well, I wonder if that's the measure of a good teacher!"

"You can hardly call it the measure of a bad teacher."

But I see ahead that the Head and I are going to diverge here, which I don't like. So I change the subject. "He doesn't drink now, that boy."

"He's come a long way in half a year. Put on the jug, Madame."

"There was a time," I say, feeling confidential over the cups, "when I had some bad moments over Paul." We seldom, the Head and I, think along the same track together.

"How is the choir going for the music festival?"

"I dreamt once that I was playing for Paul's life."

"I heard last night at the Headmasters' meeting that half the town has entered choirs for the festival."

"But I can see now that it was just a woman's phantasy."

"The conductor was telling me on the phone last night that she was particularly keen to have a Maori representation."

"I used to tease myself with a theory about a man's dream: either he expressed it or died. And that's what it seemed to be with Paul: that he had outsize dreams but couldn't get them out. Remember that time he used to drink all over me at my place? He used to rave then about wanting to talk to the world. And I knew that he couldn't. And that's why I used to think I was playing for his life. And that's why I used to stay up all night with him, and drink with him too. I felt that it all depended on me." I sigh deeply. "But I can see now that it was just my ideas running away with me again, as you like to put it. We seem to have negotiated that corner all right."

There is silence while the Head stirs his tea. "The conductor," he says, "can allow you no more than eight minutes on the programme."

"I'm not a drinker, you know, Mr Reardon."

"Of course you're not. You wouldn't be in the position you are, if you were."

"I used to drink myself to school until W. W. put me at my ease about Inspectors, and I still drink myself to church, and I like sherry with my Schubert on Saturday night. But all that extra with Paul was out of character. I felt I could keep him company that way. I felt I was accompanying him through the dark labyrinthine dungeons of alcohol, believing that I could not hope to understand his tortures without experiencing them myself. I thought that either he was accompanied or he perished. Drink seemed to lessen the pressure of his inexpressible dreams. But oh, I can see now it was just, as you say, another instance of my ideas running away with me."

I lay a hand on my cheek, trusting that the Head's mind is still turned away. I couldn't speak like this if I knew it were turned towards me.

A guttural cough and a shuffling step sound outside the staff room window. He rises. "Here's old Rau," he says cheerfully. "By Gee, the old chap is looking well this weather!"

"I think that teaching may be Paul's medium after all. Perhaps he can do his talking to the world through the children. I—I feel so happy and relaxed about him now."

Rauhuia comes puffing up the corridor into the staff room.

"It's a funny thing, Mr Chairman," I say, "how you invariably appear when the tea has just been made."

"Don't read my mind aloud, lady." His hands flick unnecessarily.

"We heard the *pa* bell toll in the night, Rau," says the Head.

"You heard right, Bill. And someone has gone who is better gone. . . ." Whoever could be better gone?

I'm not thinking of the death in the *pa* as I make my way homeward on my high heels through the cabbage trees. I'm still thinking of Paul. It's that book he had on his mind to write that holds me. It has been a symbol. A symbol of his last effort to talk to the world. If he attempted that and failed I believe it would be the end of Paul as any kind of an effective living being. As long as he doesn't try to do that and find out that he can't he could remain a functioning being. As long as he does not find out that his dream of talking to the world, too big to accommodate, has no outlet, he might find expression in teaching after all. I do. But if ever he did leave teaching, the only thing which he is qualified for, and in which he is achieving some success, and try to find realization in a book, and sees himself for what he is, a man of potency without the medium, then he would be as good as dead. Worse than dead, really. A deceased spirit in a still functioning body is worse than whole death. And from what I know of him he wouldn't endure that state long. He'd just pick up a gun like any other wise young failure and complete the end of himself. It would be the right and brave thing to do when one's ill is "not for mending." The thing is to keep him carefully teaching. And keep on postponing the book; the last attempt, the last convulsion to talk to the world; to deliver himself. And pray that there is no shattering shock to dislodge him. Yes, I conclude, putting my pen-box and my Maori books down on the table and changing my shoes for low ones to do my afternoon jobs, the thing is to keep him teaching, and preserve for him the only stability in his directionless life that he has apparently ever known. And who knows . . . I set out down the back garden to the wood-heap . . . that the art in him, those words and compulsions in him, may trickle out on the blackboard and through the children and he would find equipoise at last. . . .

But it just needs some shock to start him drinking again and the Head and the Senior and I would lose the game.

So would Paul.

"I frighteen of those skellingtons," says Mohi. "He got plenty bones."

I go down to the *pa* when I hear that Whareparita's twin sons have miscarried. I go down round about the time of the funeral because that's when you get the singing. And I go down because there is something of a burial within myself since I refused the conception of my own son, many chaste dawns back now, and I feel a claim on the ceremony, and also because I sense the working of that other underneath will that so frightens me, driving me down to these babies. So I pick the last bloom of the delphiniums as I crack off their tall seeding spikes for a second blooming, taller than myself as all men seem to be, and I walk down there with a few of my Little Ones after school.

And sure enough here on the verandah of the Meeting House are two small white boxes holding two pale brown babies, in whom have met, in the New Race, the brown blood and the white. And as I look finally upon their faces I feel the beat of a knowledge that isn't mine. For some inscrutable reason, although the sixpenny countenances are not in the least like Whareparita, nevertheless they are familiar to me. And although they are very dead yet do they speak to me in a loud hollow voice. But all I am able to conclude in the confusion of my tears is that I have known their father some time; some white man whom I have since forgotten.

However, here is the singing that I have allegedly come down about and I dry my face. An inturned ring of young people, brown youths and maidens from the *pa* about Paul's age, singing the sleep song, the song of the long, long sleep.

The two coffins lie side by side beneath the window. It is a low window that looks out from the Meeting House upon the *roro*.* My six-year-old Waiwini creeps barefoot inside and leans out above the two tiny bodies below. She leans on her elbows, her black hair falling forward over her face and her large brown eyes exquisite in self-forgetfulness; attending them in their departure in the way that she attended me for an hour when the Senior delivered my books; in the same rapt absorption. I'll always see Waiwini hanging out the window over these twins; giving herself as utterly in death as in birth. I'll remember her when I myself have one to entomb.

There are clusters of flowers and children round the coffins and the grandmother is here lamenting. There are a few other Old Ones too nearby and on this side stand the ring of the young ones, inturned to each other singing. It occurs to me, through my unreasonable turmoil, that there are better groupings for delivering the voice, but the song still rises, and there is none of the strain of facing an audience. I even manage to take a careful note of this unlikely concert formation for the Head's functions at school.

Yes, I'll recall Waiwini hanging out this window, and I'll remember the sight of the two brown maidens carrying in their arms a little white box each, leading the humble funeral of children across the road from the *pa* to Rauhuia's nightmare, the churchyard. I'll remember Twinnie and Twinnie, chief mourners, the babies lowered into the flowers and the grandmother softly lamenting. I'll remember this tenderness for me.

I do. I carry it all the way back from the grave to the piano the next morning, and while I am playing for some summer dancing I change from Schubert to the Brahms A Flat. It is my own private epitaph for my son that no one need know about. Yet, glancing up, I find that someone does know about it. Twinnie is composing a dance of grief; a weird simple thing, swinging the hands on high and fluttering them down to the toes, like some elaborated beating of the branches in winter. Twinnie gets up and copies, and Rongo and Matawhero; Hine

* Verandah.

132

snatches a jersey and makes for herself a pall, until my epitaph belongs to everyone and is no longer private at all.

"I saw," writes Waiwini, laboriously asking how to spell the words, "Miss Vorontosov
at the
grave. They put
the babies
away."

I glance up alarmed from my table in Selah in the evening. Paul bursts in drunk. "Look what I've brought you!"

Something has happened. Sharp claws grip my stomach.

"French Vermouth," he says, approaching. "And it's good for Vermouth." He has been away from school today.

"Is it?"

"Good, not very good." He circles the table and faces me across it. "If only I could get you to come to the Vineyards and taste their Hock!"

"Bring me some then." Something has destroyed his equilibrium. Have I to go through these dark labyrinthine caverns again? . . . Has this dreadful game begun again? . . .

"The Hock can't be taken away. It's not for sale. You've got to go there to taste it."

"You wouldn't take me." What last thing can I do? Myself . . . is it time for myself? Is this truly "not an ill for mending"? I have a conviction that he has come to rest on his religion: his "faith in another creature." I lower my eyes over my colour.

"I . . ." he leans over the table, shaking it and spoiling a curve of indigo, "I would be proud to be seen with you!"

I look up. His face is flushed from his afternoon in the Vineyard; his heavy eyelids flickering, the cheek twitching a little from the sheer stress of feeling, the perfect brow and the wonderful lower jaw excuse any intoxication of the skin. He leans lower, searching unwaveringly into my eyes. "I talk like a young lover," he whispers.

I'm ill with the claws on my stomach and I'm still emotionally unstable from the funeral of the twins this morning. I'm silly with his beauty and his desire and worn wild from the sustained battle over the months with the woman in me. Suddenly and disastrously I cave in. Say just once, Will you marry me, and I'll rise and "be that woman."

But he wheels and strides to the old arm-chair. "Have a cigarette?"

Have a cigarette. Not Will you marry me. I resume my painting. Working with a brush is an harmonious accompaniment to madness. I wash on a vivid background for the next illustration while he sits gazing at me and smoking. At length he rises again in his restless way, as he does when he loses my attention for a moment, circles the table, fingertips it, and faces me again. "Cousin Bette," he says, "was a spinster of about your age in one of Balzac's novels. She found a young Polish Count in the Paris slums. She took him to herself. She made him her lover, she disciplined him, watched over him, fed him, clothed him and, and . . . shall we say . . . organized him. He began producing one masterpiece of art after another."

He takes a glass from his coat pocket, fills it before me, raises it in his dramatic way. "My dear," he whispers and drinks it all.

"Balzac," he continues, pressing on the table in a way that stays my brush, "was younger than me when he took a married woman with a grown-up family about her as his first love. She was his friend, adviser, companion, mother and mistress to him. He never once looked at a younger woman, to whom he had access in every stage of dress and undress in the theatre world. He found them self-centred and depthless whereas he found simply everything in his woman of forty-five. They remained faithful and together for fifteen years. He wrote about her, 'There is nothing to compare with the first love of a man with the last love of a woman.'" He pours the French again clumsily into his glass and pours it with equal clumsiness down his throat. Then he raises it, empty. "My dear," he whispers, "to you!"

I flash to my feet. I knock the water over my work and kick over my chair. "I will not supply your drive as the Head and the Senior do! I have supplied the opportunity! I have sent you to an eminent singing teacher and taken your practices. I have begun you on a diary and criticized your style. I have stopped your drinking and kept you at school. But if you can't talk to the world in your own way and under your own power, then I won't do it for you! If what you've got cannot come out on its own then it's no wonderful thing to honour! As for giving myself to you to devour . . ." I begin to shake and my voice hoarsens. "I refused myself to a leader of men; who had everything to give in return. He brought the wood in for me and set the fires. He had a concern for what I was thinking and feeling. He was wrapped up in me rather than in himself. *He* gave *me* understanding. Do I change my ways for a dreg? Do I give up all I am and was and can be to others for a selfish useless drifter? Am I going to drag myself through drink again for a ship's cook? I am the Vorontosov! My father's home was on the steppes of Kazakhstan. He broke in that wilderness. By God I'll break in your wilderness!" I reach over the table and crash my hand over his cheek. "If you've got the guts of a serf!" Crash on the other cheek. "Get on with your teaching!" I fling the empty water jar after the retreating shape. I flounder to the door and throw my paints after him. "You God-forgotten sot!" I rush after him and beat him with the flowing Vermouth bottle. "You stranger-within-the-gate!"

"And if you can't, and if you can't," I whisper as he vanishes through the trees, "get hold of a gun and blow your carrion inside out!"

It is not unusual for the Head to cross the grass to meet me in the morning. He often does when he wants to discuss something with me before school. The only thing he hasn't done before is to turn his back on the assembly before the Leaders have taken over. He doesn't like disorder in the lines. . . .

"Paul has resigned."

Flash of a hand to my face.

"He came up to the house last night."

There's a noise in the lines of children.

"He said, 'I'm going to banish myself to a farm to write my book; to the still spaces.'"

What a noise! Where are the leaders in the lines?

"He said, 'I'm going away. I'm going to a farm about ten miles up. I won't be back till my book is finished. I've four big hard-backed notebooks, a dozen scribbling pads and half a dozen pencils and a rubber. And a bottle of ink and even a tray so that if my ink tips over it won't run far. I'm being picked up some time this evening.'"

The noise in the lines is a roar. I've never heard the children like that. It's sore beneath my nails in my cheek.

"He'd been drinking but he was all right. I just couldn't bring myself to discuss the matter with him. I was too disappointed for words. He'd been making such progress! Why only last week he . . . but oh, what's the use. It's the waste that hurts me. I can't stand waste. Waste of all his effort and mine. Waste of all his training. And apart from teaching altogether, the waste of his pathetic life. Yet I feel that the fault is neither his nor ours. Nor the Senior's for selecting him. It's something out of our hands. He's got this obsession about talking to the world. Yet I still believe that patience and firmness pay. Of course it is I who have to send in his resignation to the Board. He has done nothing about that. But by God, I'm sure that W. W. isn't going to take this lying down. I wonder if it was the rumours that upset him. Oh I suppose we can find it in us to forgive the poor chap. He's got . . ."

The roar from the lines is a thunder, deafening me . . .

". . . his own life to live. At least we've done what . . ."

"I'm sick!"

A grip on my arm.

A bump . . .

I decide to stop grieving by Friday. For one thing my legs do me the favour of holding me up. One foot consents to step before the other. It's just like walking. And for another I have work to do. My work has waited too long and has been interrupted too often. I have that set of books to complete for the Senior Inspector and the big ones to take to the Broadcasting Studio and the festival to prepare for. Above all is this unresolved method in the infant room. I want to find out, before I'm too old to find out anything, the real way to teach infants. If it's humanly possible to find out anything on the high seas I sail. And finally, the Head is holding down a hundred and a quarter children on his own. Yes, I'll stop grieving now. I'll have a bath first and put on a cream smock with a scarlet collar and a narrow tube scarlet skirt. And I'll put my mother's scent on my hair. Yes it's time to stop grieving now. After all the soul of one of us was due for the sacrificial altar and it's too late to sort out which. I need a very good hot bath with a lot of soap and some fresh silky lingerie. . . . I'll wash my grief away as the Maoris do after a *tangi*.* . . . Life is too short to pause on the way.

. . . What's this pretty shine in my hair? It looks as though I have silver dust on it. Hullo . . . I'm going grey! I'd like to spend a while admiring it; but life is too short to pause on the way.

"I hope," I say to the Head when I return, "that you kept Seven and Blossom in your room with you."

"Seven and Blossom were well taken care of, I assure you."

"And Hinewaka? Her feet?"

"She spent the entire time sitting on my table, drawing little girls with their feet turned in." He looks away and I know something is coming. "Madame, tell me. What is worrying you?"

My hand rises to my cheek. "Thank you for asking, Mr Reardon. But forgive me. There are three things I never disclose. One is my age, one is my bank account and one is the thing that is worrying me."

"I give him one more week up there," says the Head as we sit forlornly together at morning interval, "and then he may be back. I haven't informed the Board. I think that I may have been too stiff with him. It's a very awkward position though because I can't even ask for a reliever. But I feel sure that W. W. would agree with me in giving him one last chance. His incredible lack of consideration for others! He knows I've got to run two rooms of close on a hundred children on my own! However, when he comes back, if he comes back, we'll make a fresh start. Perhaps I could be . . . could be gentler with him. I'm not a man beyond trying to correct any mistake of my own. We'll see what we can do for him when he comes back. See if we can fix him up."

I refer to my elm tree through the window, preparing to say something tender. But for once it does not soothe me, compose me. Violently I burst out. "I'm utterly sick of the sacrifices I see you make for others! But you're taking it too far this time, Mr Reardon! Who am I

* Maori funeral.

if not the Infant Mistress of this school? Have I no say in matters of staff? I tell you, Sir, I have! I will not stand by while another member of the staff, headmaster or no, takes over a hundred children in two rooms on his own to shield the indulgences of another! Let the weak fall by the wayside! Many fell by the wayside on the migration to Kazakhstan and the strong went on. My father went on! The Vorontosov does not halt progress for the unequipped. It's only fair to notify the Senior Inspector. It's only fair to him, and the children as well. I hate this disorganization! I'll complain to the Board of this disorganization if you don't notify them! I'm not just a cog! I'm the Infant Mistress here!"

All at once I fall into deep crying. I'm just lost in it. I feel the Head patting me helplessly on the shoulder. "My little mother fell by the wayside," I tell him, "but not from lack of courage."

"I'll notify the Board, Madame Vorontosov."

The bell has well gone and the assembly waits noisily unattended. Then we hear the leaders take over and silence.

"I'm terribly sorry you have been upset over this business."

"I want to go to Kazakhstan," I cry harder: my cream smock is drenched with handkerchief duty, "where her little person lies. My father took her on with him in the cart with me."

"Don't cry, Madame. Don't cry."

"I want to go to Kazakhstan. Her black hair won't be dead yet." Marvellous things are happening in the lines. We hear the smart orders of the leaders, the tread of orderly feet and the leaders take over in both classrooms.

"You take the day off." He pats my shoulder diligently. "I'll notify the Board. We'll get a reliever at once. I'm beginning to think differently about that boy after his causing such an upset. Now stop crying, Madame. Do you know what Seven said when they hauled him in to me for climbing the tree? 'Sir, I didn' climb the tree, Sir! Sir, I only climbed down, Sir!' "

I dry my face with another area of smock. There's a smile on it. "Now," continues the Head, "I want you to go home and make yourself a cup of tea. I'll keep Hirani over in the infant room."

"I didn't mean to say all that. I was only going to say that his 'is not an ill for mending.' "

My own heart let me have more pity on; let
Me live to my sad self hereafter kind,
Charitable; not live this tormented mind
With this tormented mind tormenting yet. . . .

. . . Soul, self; come, poor Jackself, I do advise
You, jaded, let be; call off thoughts awhile
Elsewhere; . . .

I don't take the day off. I just wait till my face is right. Cold water
and several layers of face-pack and powder, and a safety-pin in my
scarlet skirt before it falls off. Thank God for children. I go over and
bury my head and my heart in them. I'm right again in no time . . .

Someone has bathed the three little Tamati girls this week, Hine,
Ani and Riti, and washed their hair and even tied it. I am furious.
How dare anyone take off my children's clothes and wash them and
put them back on again! How dare anyone comb their hair!

"Who washed you!" I accuse.

"Mummie."

"Is she back?"

"Yea. She camed back. She doed our hairs."

"Well, you don't look as clean as I had you."

I'm flicked with jealousy. I'm sorry the bathing and washing is over.
I realize all at once that I actually look forward to the shearing season
when both parents in many cases leave the children to an elder child
and their dirt to me. I do miss my little game of mother. But the thing
I miss most is the stink. . . .

. . . Me take the day off! What more heinous crime against herself
can a teacher commit than take the day off when she can still manipu-
late her legs? Take the day off indeed!

The day I take off in self-indulgence will be the day I take my life
off.

"Gimme little bit dance," sighs Rongo.

"Jussa little bit dance!"

White Boy reappears this morning, a mass of tears. They concentrate
on keeping him at school until I arrive. They take him into the infant

room and sit him by the fire and read him "The Blue Jug" at which he is hard put to maintain the supply of tears.

I wash his face and hands and take off his filthy jersey to wash at home, and mention the whole matter to my friend Seven, who sent him home with a hiding in the first place. I have a ghost to lay.

And he comes back in the afternoon . . . Boy, I mean . . . seeming to have forgotten Seven's blows. Dirt and soap; grief and joy; and so the soul grows.

A tiny little red-haired brown-eyed fat-tummied boy from Nanny's across the road drops into our over-crowded dinghy and I show him his unlikely name; Nigel. From another background, white father, I presume. Some more exciting New Race. It sends my thoughts back to the twins. . . . After play I show him this name again to check up.

"What's this word, Little One?"

"That's why I tol' you afore." Irritably.

"Tell me," I ask Nanny when the tattooed wrinkled barefooted old Maori Kuia comes over in person at noon to lovingly collect him. "How did Whareparita come to lose her babies?"

"Tha's why when Whareparita she was walking pas' the church-yard after dark those ghost they frightens her; those ghost. An' she trip over."

"Did they breathe at all?"

" 'Course! Those baby they were alive. The hospital they rings up my ol' man. 'Come an' christen these kid,' they say. 'An' hurry.' Then the firs' he die in the morning and the secon' he dies in the af'ernoon. But they got christen."

She stoops suddenly in all her dark unnecessary clothing and kisses the red head beside her.

The grass is growing a bit now over Whareparita's twin babies in the little cemetery on the Corner and I think it is growing a bit too on her sorrow. But it makes me sad to see her across the road taking up duties about a house instead of helping me at school. Sometimes in the afternoon when I take my daily walk out to the gate to see if a letter from Eugene has come I see her leaning in the front door on a remarkably idle broom. Just looking. At what? What kind of face does she see in her mind? Does she see a face at all, as I do in mine? And how long is it going to endure; for a lifetime? I remember someone at school saying to me, "Whareparita was down at the cemetery yesterday crying over her little grave."

But on Friday night, walking through the crowds in town, I meet this same Whareparita all painted up and ready for more action. And you'd never know by the look of her that there are two darling little babies at the bottom of a deep grave at home, and a white man lurking in the background somewhere, reflecting maybe or even grieving, unless by the advance of her skin and figure into an exercise of glamour; unless by her eyes, eloquent with the unsayable. It makes me think. Has she rid herself of the obsession of a face through conception out into her babies? Maybe, had I indulged Eugene when I was as young and as exquisite as she, I would not have carried him so indivisibly with me until now. Have I made a mistake in killing the moment of love for a rule? . . . "Often a man's own angry pride is cap and bells for a fool."

Then watering my blue garden one evening to refresh the white lips of my cut delphiniums, I see a truck pull up across the road, back with its shearing gang from the shed, and Whareparita get out. She has overalls rolled up beneath her knees and bare feet. What a pretty sight! How could men leave her alone? How could a young man like Paul, tuned up with want, possibly pass by a loveliness like that, day by day at school, to hound a witch like me? How can he not have desired her? Has his inclination for me been the reason he hasn't required her?

Yes, the grass is growing, the grass is growing, as it does over some people's grief; yet the vigil is not unkept. It is I who keep the vigil over the New Race in the churchyard. I dwell on how much bigger they would have been by now and how their sixpenny faces would have filled out. Their eyes would have been wide open and two more voices would have joined with those of all the other love-children in Nanny's house: Hinewaka, Blossom and Nigel. They were conceived, miscarried and buried from there.

But it's I who keep the vigil.

"Nanny," writes Wiki,

"called out to me to
get a marshmallow
lollie. For Hinewaka and
me. The marshmallow had
some coconuts
and some walnuts."

Here comes Paul up the street; the Lost Child, the "stranger within
the gate." For some inscrutable reason the Reverend chose to preach
a sermon on Sunday evening on "thy stranger within thy gates." One
of the sentences I overheard, quite inadvertently, was, "We are all
strangers within the gate; within the gate of life." And the drive of it
was, from what I could hazily gather, that, under the circumstances,
one could do worse than be hospitable to another, as long as that other
was within the gate of life. That's a point too, I remember observing to
myself, before I slunk out the door. *Anyway,* here's Paul coming up the
aisle, I mean street, and thank God for fickleness: there's much in
favour of this side of forty.

But oh! in the lights and shadows, how glamorous he is! He looks
like some wonderful futuristic painting of himself. It's hard enough
on any woman without the tragedy in his face. One glance is enough
to show me the resignation in his bearing and walk. But compassion
has no hope against pride this time. He's my failure. Something else
comes back to me too: a dream of some recent night in which I saw
Paul going out of the door of the pre-fab into the dark night of eternity,
and slamming it loudly behind him. Possibly I can find it in myself to
be hospitable to this Little One of mine through the remainder of his
sojourn.

Later at home he says, "I've no work. I can't do the work that is available. And I'm not educated enough to do the work I would wish. I'm
lost. A child. That's what I am. I'm a lost child. Why must I have this
fate? Will these blows never cease raining on me?"

"You know that what I said to you one dawn is true. But you don't
realize it."

I feel that I have not understood Paul enough. Just as I do not understand my Little Ones enough. I think that the *key* which hovers over me when I am not disturbed might have been the answer, whatever it is. Because it has some relation to the deep frightening force that makes me do things I don't mean to. But how can I find, reach it in the unevenly swinging life I lead? You need the "still centre" for vision. And here is one of my Little Ones in front of me, bawling like Little Brother, in heart.

"I wanted to talk to the world."

"I understand." There . . . there . . . look at my pretty boy. I'll look after you.

"I feel I must talk to the world, or, or . . . shall we say . . . perish."

"I understand."

I make him an extra big sandwich with cold potato and meat in it, and anything else I can find in my inconsequent safe that is thoroughly unhealthy, no vitamins or anything. "What are you using for money?"

"I've been selling my things."

"Have you anything left?"

"Only my bike."

I try not to laugh; my ruinous laugh. "Whom are you going to sell that to?"

"You."

Roars of laughter in the old style. "Who, me? A man's bike?" Suddenly I pull up. "All right, I'll buy it. How much do you want for it?"

"Eight pounds."

"I trust," I reply severely, "that its accessories are complete? Bell, carrier, tail-light and such?"

But he is too sad for me to go on. I tackle something else that has been on my mind. "Now look, dear, I want you to do something for me."

"What can I do for you, Madame."

"I want you, tomorrow morning, first thing, to ring the Senior Inspector at his home and resign formally and courteously, giving reasons. And thank him for the opportunity he gave you."

He considers this, looking down like a bad boy. "He doesn't understand that I must talk to the world." Suddenly he glances up, a flick of hope in his eyes. "Is there anyone in my room at school?"

"There is." I don't know whether to go on or not. Then I realize the unbearableness of looking forward. "There is. A senior teacher. Man, of course. Being no board in the district for a woman and the travelling arrangements in the bus unsuitable. About thirty-five. A long way above the position but he is relieving until he lands the job he wants in the city. Gay. Tall again. Another set of neck exercises for me. With all the outer appearances and appurtenances of a Galahad." Can I tease him any further? I cannot. "But he's a woman in everything else, Percy Girlgrace; instinct, ways, conversation, name. In fact," I warm up, "he would have been married by now had he met the right man."

But he has lost interest before I have done and looks drearily out through the kitchen window into the night. Fearfully. "No one," he repeats, "understands that I must talk to the world."

I am silent. Because that's just it. I don't understand him enough. I haven't worked hard enough and thought hard enough. My searchings are nebulous these days. Blurred by passions and enthusiasms. Too much loud laughing and far too much voluptuous crying. Where is the austerity, the simplicity, the purity and the sanctity of the engaged artist? Relationships. I'm as side-tracked as my Little Ones.

"I'll be round tomorrow afternoon," he says, making the very first arrangement with me I can remember.

"You can bring the bike."

"I slew him! I slew him!"

"Who?"

"The Right Honourable the Senior Inspector of Primary Schools, Mr W. W. Abercrombie! He came over and I graciously acceded him an audience in the bar. He requested me to, to . . . shall we say . . . reconsider my decision. I slew him with words!"

"I don't believe it," I remember my afternoon at his office.

"It's true!"

"I mean, I don't believe you slew any W. W. with words. He's unslayable. Least of all with words."

" 'Six tweed feet of administration!' I opened up with. 'Six grey feet of efficiency! The ritual of human kindness! Only the ritual left after the inspiration has died away! There's nothing in that chalice you hold high above our heads!' I told him. 'I grant there must have been at one time. I grant that all the kindness of which your teachers speak did once inform your technique. But the chalice is now empty. The inspiration has dried away in the dust of administration. Empty! *Empty!*' I told him. 'There's only the ritual left!' ''

"And how much did that cost you in courage?"

"Seven beers and four gins! Oh, I'm happy! I'm happy!"

"And what did he say?"

"He had nothing to say. The whole large dried-up length of grey material, ten yards of grey tweed, the whole six-foot-two tower of administration, efficiency, elegance, technique and token kindness tottered and crumbled, and I had to give the barman a hand to shovel up the rubble!"

I don't believe it.

"Three cheers for the ginny exaltation!" He gets out the Claret. Eagerly he overfills my glass, swaying admirably like a sailor on a deck in a storm. "Here," he whispers, holding it high, "is to an evening of, of . . . shall we say . . . understanding!"

So we take Claret and Van Gogh in the drawing room. This lad has a marvellous capacity for obliterating the past, even the recent past like a death. His own. I'm only too glad to peruse all the oils and drawings of the wonderful artist with the wonderful drive in his life; who died young from the heat of his passion. What an immeasurable distance from the aborted passion beside me! But soon my work begins its clawing. I must get to my paint! Paul picks up his own French Vermouth he has left here a fortnight ago. . . .

"What did W. W. say tonight?" I ask when we settle down. Only truth exists among the cobwebs of Selah.

"He slew me."

"Not after that marvellous exposition of yours?"

"He simply said, 'I trust you enjoyed that, Mr Vercoe.' "

Evening embraces more closely, and at this too-late date I at last see what Paul means by talking to the world. Complete relaxation gives his intellect full and brilliant play. As the released mind revolves, flashing different colours like a *paua,** I witness the very best in a man; a man fighting for something.

* Iridescent shell.

Yet to me, from the distance of generation, his exaltation is sadder than despair. This glow of transitory glory makes the night about him darker. Sepulchral almost to one who has already mourned him. Evening embraces deeply and long, but there's no question of my "being that woman" now. The sooner this is over the better. There has been a reshuffling in the world behind my eyes; dating from his break-away from school. It will not be this man who will devour me. This "Thee and Me" is dead.

In the middle of a sentence of his, about passion being the source of inspiration, I move over to him and stand there. For once I am not gazing upward. Easily I'm teacher once more. Lounging in the old chair he is looking up at me. I tip his chin; the only time I have touched voluntarily his person. "What is it, what is it, Little One?"

He stops, and is silent; ceasing his exposition.

"What are you going to do tomorrow?"

I know what he is not going to do tomorrow. He is not going to wreck my day. He's not going to delay my work. He's not going to keep me from church and he's not going to keep me from my bed until four or five in the morning. In all, he is not going to make me "that woman." In short, he is not going to devour me. Has he realized these things? I think he does realize these things. He was never one not to be able to read "faint indirections." He must know by now that I am not his last sanctuary. That for him there is no sanctuary. He must read by now the failure of his "faith in another creature."

He looks beyond me through the window out into the darkness of the night, out into the endless night. . . . Now at last he has nothing to say. Neither have I. A silence comes to Selah like a presence. I don't restoke the fire but move over to the door and lean against it. What words have I got for him? What would the Reverend say? He would say what he so aptly says to me on occasion: "Bless you." But I'm not qualified to use that. Indeed I have nothing to say of value. At last I begin to see, at least, my mistakes over Paul, if not the remedy. My thinking has not been pure enough to have guided him well. All those hours of music and drink and talk and laughter were not the answer, at the expense of my work. Art and work should not be put aside, since from them comes vision. I should have put Paul aside for my brushes and reading and then what little was left of my time for him would have been of more value. I have given him quantities of time, but not quality. I'm nothing at the moment.

"I mean," he says simply, at length, "to board the morning rail-car to Wellington. There I will work on the wharf until I can get a job on a boat. My uncle has a partnership for me in his window-cleaning business." He tips the remainder of the French in his glass back into the bottle.

"You'll go home in the morning?"

"Home?" he says looking up.

I am a chalice that is empty also.

The eyelids flicker and he examines his empty glass.

"I think I will get you off home now; you'll need sleep."

"Home?" he repeats, looking up at me again.

I run my fingers through my hair, already greyed over him. At length he raises his empty glass. "Here," he says without melodrama and without self-pity, but with the resignation of the aged, "here is to my home." Then he turns it down on the table.

I run all my fingers through my hair, trying once more to find something, to find something wonderful, something just right, to say. But all that happens is that my hair falls down. I swing round to the door behind me, open it, run through the dark garden, stumbling, to the house. I run through the unlit kitchen and up the hall and into the bedroom and shut the door and crouch on the bed and pull the quilt over my head. But even that is not enough to blot out the sound of his steps walking away beneath the trees. I can hear every footfall distinctly, then the sound of the gate. Do you hear that, God? I say. That's because I was unfaithful to my work. I gave him quantity.

But not quality.

As his steps echo back to me, fainter and fainter into the receiving boundless night, I remember those words of mine months ago: "at any time, in any circumstance." Does he remember them too? Ah, the shadows those words have cast. . . .

*W*E'VE been the whole morning," cries Parent Number One sensationally at my back door, the next afternoon, Sunday afternoon, "cleaning the ceiling! Been through buckets of water! And we've burnt the scrubbing brushes! Really Oi never knew a man had so much blood in him! Look, without a word of a loi, Miss Vorontosov, there were bits of heart on that ceiling! You can ask the others!"

"What are you going to do with him?" No one ever loved Paul; not even me.

"Oi dunno. He doesn't belong to nobody."

"As a matter of fact he belongs to me. You can bring him here. Would you mind seeing the . . . I suppose Mr Reardon is . . ."

"It's all fixed up about the undertaker. It's just that we had nowhere to loi him."

"My drawing room would take a coffin all right." I've done my grieving over Paul. No mortal can go through that twice . . .

. . . I stand and look at Paul lying in my drawing room. His face is intact. But it's different in death. It looks just like some other face I've seen dead. Small dead faces. Now who am I thinking of? But

I've attended so many funerals in the *pa*. I suppose all dead faces really have a likeness. My word though, there's something remarkably . . . but I've been through a lot lately.

I couldn't save you, Paul, I say, moving to the window and lifting the blinds the others have pulled down, letting in the cool sweet dawn. I didn't understand you enough, Little One. I didn't have my *key*. And really, I move back to the still beauty in the coffin, you must admit that you didn't give me much of a chance to find it.

I sigh very, very deeply. Not just for Paul. But for all the others that we don't understand soon enough. I'm dreadfully tired, if that means anything to anybody. Which I can't see. My legs! I sink upon the arm of my big chair where I can still see his face. There . . . there . . . look at my sweet boy. "That was right, lad, that was brave." A nice clean ending . . . well, clean in decision. Don't fret. I'll talk to the world for you. You cheer up now. You were right. "Yours was not an ill for mending."

. . . I just can't make out why Whareparita screams so at the grave the next morning at the *pa*. Canon Maui has to stay his burial service to help stop her throwing herself in. Now who would have thought a schoolgirl could be so devoted to Paul? Someone must have loved him after all! And why in heaven are they burying him in an already inhabited grave? What? With Whareparita's twins? I suppose it's because he has no money. My word, I forgot to pay for that bike! Only Whareparita and her Nanny and Canon Maui here. And Waiwini. I should be standing at the head of this grave. I'm the chief mourner. That's not Whareparita's place. Here comes the Chairman. That's better. Quite a crowd now. He's come to represent the school, since the Head is holding down a hundred and a quarter children on his own until I come back. Where have the men gone who fill in the grave? We'll have to do it ourselves. Whareparita's no good; she's trying to get in. Nanny can't; she's trying to keep her out. Rauhuia couldn't hold the weight of a shovel let alone wield it. Canon Maui and I will have to. My word, what magnificent screaming of Whareparita's! She must be enjoying that. . . . The Canon ploughs through it with his burial service in full warrior style. "Waiwini, hold the book while Canon Maui takes a shovel. . . ."

I give Rauhuia a kiss on his brownish cheek for coming and standing by me and Maui and I take up a shovel each. It's easier to fill in than dig out. Thud goes the first clay on the coffin. There you are, Little One, you settle down. Thud, thud. Now you go to sleep and be a good boy. Thud. You did the right thing. We're making good progress, brown Canon and I. Thud, thud. His white surplice will have to be washed again after this. Scoop, grunt, thud. There . . . there . . . look at my sweet boy. I'll look after you. Puff, puff. Why ever didn't you comfort yourself with Whareparita, the loveliest thing this side of the . . . puff . . . river. "So quick, so clean an ending." Filling up "O that was right, lad . . ." thuff, thuff . . . "that was brave." Thuff, thuff. "Yours was not an ill . . ." scoop . . . "for mending"; . . . lift, strain. "T'was best . . ." spread, spread . . . "to take it . . ." smooth, smooth . . . "to the . . ." sigh, rest . . . "grave."

"You should be on your bike, Mr Chairman," I say as I slow myself down to his shuffling gait on the way up the road to school. The tea may still be hot in the pot in the staff room. Hullo, it's raining!

"No bike, Lady, lasts long with my young rascals about. The next one I get I'll lock in my room."

"There's one inside my gate you can have. Green. It's got all the fittings. Can you raise eight pounds?" How long has it been raining?

"There couldn't have been a thing between them," I hear women's low voices at the bus stop. "Miss Vorontosov did not drop one tear."

*A*N enormous smile awaits me on the doorstep of the pre-fab when I return from the churchyard in the rain. It is set in a flat freckly face with close-cropped sandy hair above and the body of an adolescent boy below. He is standing here easily with legs astride and hands in pockets, the Little Ones eddying about him, as though not only were there no such thing as death, but life itself were no more than one non-stop amusement.

He says nothing when I arrive beneath him; neither does he stand aside to let me pass; me, the august Infant Mistress. As I wait here in the rain observing him, he pays me no more homage than to broaden the smile a little.

"What, are you my new Junior?"

I think his head nods but I can't be sure. He remains wholly at home on the step above, his clothes as sandy freckled and easy as he is himself, smiling benignly down upon me in the rain.

"He camed on those bike," supplies Mohi, waiting in the rain also.

"I hope you didn't get wet," I remark, glancing at the dry cosy frame in the shelter of the gable.

His head definitely nods in negation, which I consider is an advance.

In fact the conversation is shooting along admirably. From the point of view of pauses. From the angle of thought being permitted to run comfortably along beneath. No railing voice hacking at one's innards here. No predatory personality pressing itself into one's secret recesses. One has time to think and to feel and to sort out what to say. Indeed, his attitude, his silence and his smile amount to a verbosity I didn't think possible. For a moment I wonder what the unfamiliar feeling is on my own face, then realize it is a smile.

"Oh well," I answer, "as long as you didn't get wet. That's the main thing." I brush the drips from my chin.

"He got plenty teef," notes Seven of the smile.

"Yeah, he got plenty teef, ay!" comes in the chorus.

The boy opens out in wonderful laughter. It's true about the plenty teef. Bleeding Heart joins in as heartily as ever, I join in, then the complete chorus. Really, the different ways people can arrive!

"What's your name?" checks up Matawhero.

"Guess," he replies slyly.

"Sandy," I try.

"Right."

"See?" I turn excitedly to the chorus. "I'm right, first go!"

"Somebodies they told you," accuses Wiki.

"Somebodies they did not," I defend. "Oh well, Sandy, if you don't mind letting me pass we'll get on with our teaching."

"All the same to me."

I almost laugh again, but something in the very recent past dries it up. I walk by him in sudden silence to get on with my teaching. I should be able to get on with it now all too well.

But it is not until after school when I am ironing Rauhuia's pale yellow shirt that I see behind it all: how the Senior Inspector has chosen the character and how he has chosen the time.

Unerringly.

I must burn that letter I wrote to him all last night; the chronicle of a spinster. I must pick up the permanent things in my life again: my pen-box, my piano, my paints, my reading, my scheme, my books, my woodbox, my garden, my Guilt, my memories, my "reverence for conscience," the gift that God has put in my hands, and my tears.

I must take up again my loneliness.

152

J UST only God," writes Mohi, then slams down his pencil for the morning and goes and dreams on the mat.

I can't help noticing all this strange writing they do. It must be the beginning of composition; the first wall between one being and another; the putting of thoughts for someone else into written words instead of speech or touch; the graduation of talkers and touchers into writers; the progress of mixers into hermits; the springs of loneliness.

But I didn't start it: they began themselves. I didn't tell Twinnie to write on the wall blackboard "My sister she can't draw for nuts." She asked me how to spell "sister," "draw" and "nuts," and I look up and see it. Then the other twin as always copies, and a few more copy until now among the sixes and sevens we have smart exercise books and it's all "Sharpen my pencil" and "Where's my rubber" and "How do you spell 'ghost.'" Plainly it is another medium of expression and another subject in the creative vent; two actually, writing as well as composition. But I didn't do it. I didn't do it. And I am far too removed from the good and real teacher to halt it. I can only say I'm sorry.

Not because it is an offence against current professional method but for another reason. I don't think it is fortunate to write. Or clever. It's cleverer to converse. To read the facial expression, to extend the voice, to interpret the intonation, to sense the temperature of the emotions and to reply in keeping. It's cleverer to make the physical conversation of love-making. For what does it require to sit alone at your little table and write what it is yourself? Not the hazards and glamour of communication itself but technique. Only technique.

Even reading a story rather than telling it is a step apart. Waiwini, anyway, can't take it. She rises in the middle of it and comes to me for the real thing. She touches me and examines the depths of my eyes and asks questions to which she insists that I reply. It reminds me of love: the encounter absolute.

It's like this in differing degrees with them all. They press as close as is humanly possible to whatever's happening and to whomever it is happening. Waiwini at the funeral, like Reremoana when a strange man visits me, and Matawhero at all times. Livers, all of them, in full measure. Not too much of what is commonly known as work, of course, but oh, the living they accomplish! Because of this preoccupation with the personal relationship the work of many of them doesn't get done. But I cultivate and honour it, not so unhappy about it now since I have come to know my new Inspector, and knowing it to be the stuff that Meaning is made of.

No, I didn't start off the writing; but I'll not stop it. They can get on with it. All told, even though the moment a man starts to write he ceases to live, it is a widening of the creative vent from the volcanic unconscious, and a blow, however infinitesimal, at the destruction of the future. All I do as an accomplice is to sharpen their pencils, spell the words they ask for, show them the bodily attitude most favourable to writing, suggest full-stops and capital letters and place it, necessarily and undoubtedly, in the morning output period.

But a nervousness, a vague discomfort, accompanies the recognition of it. It makes me think that the solution to infant teaching is near by; not near enough, and yet too near. If only I could put my finger on it; the finger of my mind. I want it and I don't want it. It both frightens and exhilarates me. It's like, like . . . shall we say . . . the fear-and-joy of birth; the imminence of the labour ward. What a long-drawn-out travail this is. . . .

"Just only you," writes Mohi on the next page with a borrowed pencil, then comes and dreams with his head on my knee.

"It's very pleasant to see you, Mr Abercrombie."

He has dropped in with the typewriter . . . my turn for it . . . just after nine. School is different in the morning without brandy. So is it different without an inspector shade in the rafters. Your thinking is clearer and your feeling more accurate. Moreover there is no longer any hazard about fingers on the mat. I can step my way through the fingers and toes without treading on them.

"It is pleasant to be here." The hands withdraw reasonably behind him.

I don't answer. I must not let him know just how much of a pleasure it is for him to be here. I take Nigel's fingers from the keyboard and put some blocks in them.

"And how are you keeping?" He frowns in concentration.

I wonder what has provoked the remark. Has he noticed the grey hairs behind my ears, "sad and stealing messengers of grey"? But when the subject is myself I try not to let men know what I am thinking.

"I'm on top of the world," I claim. "My usual place. How are all your teachers?" I don't say all your "other" teachers.

He thinks it over, looking down the long fall to his feet. Then he looks up at the rafters and out the window over the plains to my blue hill in the distance. I know another man who thinks carefully before he speaks. Even over such a simple question.

"There are many whom I have not seen for a while."

"Some of them too far away?"

"Hundreds of miles. I wish I could get away from the office more. Some Senior Inspectors don't get out at all. But I'm getting cunning. I'm putting more and more of my administrative work on to the other men. For a fortnight I have been sharing my mail with them."

I have steered the conversation off myself successfully, for the time being, and mean to keep it that way. Not that it's hard. He has no demands on me, Mr Abercrombie. He doesn't crave my person or my soul, although I flatter myself he is interested in what my mind contains. My usual violence in his presence seems to be wearing off. It's a rest; a great rest.

"I suppose," I say taking a low chair . . . my feet and legs don't hold me up for long these days, I don't know why . . . "that you have to train Inspectors just as you train teachers." I am thinking of that technique of self-effacement in a classroom of his own.

He draws up a small chair beside me.

"Train them? They come to me as green as any Junior. It's some time before I can work them into shape."

"I should think it would be." Sandy is doing lovely work in the writing group, I notice.

"Well, I must move off. There are two schools I want to see about twenty miles up."

"You will find the creative part of your job the most exhaustive."

"It's all like that at the moment. And how's the Junior turning out?"

"He's made for the job. He's just all receptivity and self-effacement and smiles. Thank you."

"Well—" out comes the alert elegant hand—"goodbye for the present, Miss Vorontosov. Take care of yourself."

I take the hand gladly enough. I can do with it. I step forward to follow him to the gate. "No, no," he says, "I've got to look in on Mr Reardon. This new infant block is coming up."

He's gone again. And he hasn't trodden on any fingers or toes, even though his going is as swift as his coming.

"Just only me," writes Mohi, then breaks his new pencil in two in order to give half each to Bleeding Heart and Blossom who have none, and the next thing I see is the highest and most balanced and most tapering and most beautiful tower I have ever seen in all my years of teaching. So beautiful that I leave it there for the day and chalk a message on the blackboard, before I pick up my pen-box to go home, for the big girls to sweep round it.

Working among my Little Ones and fingering continually the tender truths they show me, I come nearer to God. But peace still avoids me.

When will you ever, Peace, wild wood-dove, shy wings shut,

Your roaming round me end, and under be my boughs?

I need that you should soften my passions. When will my exercised heart, hourly tightened by the memory of Paul, unknot and curl down in the sun like Pussy? Yet "I yield you do come sometimes"; I am aware of a forgiveness for everyone, for myself also, and some tall perspective, like the lofty thought from a pulpit, takes over. I find tears resuming their sad routine in Selah as I think of these things over my brushes. Tears of resignation rather than rage at my passions with men. I even allow the ways of Inspectors. I see good intent in everyone as though a rainstorm has lifted. None of the turbulence and terror I knew seem for the moment authentic. I sink my head that I should so have misread my world. I sob most dearly over the many I have mis-understood. And a vision comes to me in the poetry of the summer evening of the loveliness in the worst. If only I could stay like this and go out from Selah in purity. But I know that I don't and I know that I can't, and all I can do is pick up my brush again. There's a season for tears as a season for love. I dip the marmot in the yellow and paint like Wiki with it. For there's a magic in the minds of Little Ones and my fingers get sticky with it.

"When I got up," writes Rongo, the light-toed, heavily on the black-board for all to see,
"I got ready
for school.
and I hurried
because Daddy
was wild
and he looked
cross."

The Senior Inspector stops a moment on the grass in a flash of sun-light on his way over to tea. The playground is brilliant with yellow. It's the only time I go over to tea now. When he's here.

He pockets his hands boyishly and stands astride. He changes outside the classroom. He changes in each situation he finds himself in. "There's a vitality here," he says.

I do follow him to the gate after tea, as he strides off with the typewriter; it being his turn. So do half a hundred Little Ones. Wiki says, "I go wif you, ay!"

So do I. In mind.

He has one last brief economical word for me as he gives me his unromantic business-like hand. "I trust you are keeping better?"

"Oh! I'm on top of the world, thank you, Mr Abercrombie."

I must not run away with the idea that these frequent visits, unrelated to professional matters, have got anything to do with a concern for me. The touch of compassion would bring down the battlements of my encloistered self to rubble, and all would be over with me.

"Just because," writes Rongo, whom I have been thinking the most adored child in Maoridom, until she took to writing,
"Daddy got wild
and so I got
wild because
Daddy was drunk.
Then he hit Rongo."

Yet for all the occasional moments of vision I sometimes find the writings of my Little Ones too jolly well hard to bear. Communication is so fiery. It's like flames leaping from one to another. The daily word-of-mouth kind, the emotional kind of Waiwini and Matawhero, the physical kind that conceives Whareparita's twins and hits Rongo's mother in the face, and the racial kind that forces the Mighty Birth of the New Race. But although I know it is life I can't bear one to strike another; even though I have done it myself. And I can't bear to know of lovers together when I myself am separate. Yet I suspect some universal power in communication if only I could put my finger on it and use it in my teaching and my books. Freed from orthodoxy, my Little Ones write of nothing else. And they are my arduous teachers. Wouldn't you think I could understand this endless lesson by now sufficiently to harness it?

This something that goes between one and another . . . how both tender and coarse it is. How inebriate and glamorous it is. It makes me tingle as though living in the pre-fab, in Selah, in the garden were all no more than facets of one vivid vast love-affair.

What kind of thing is it? Can you touch it? Has it got feet or wheels or wings? Why is it so magic? And so indispensable? Must a virgin really brace herself to accept the unpoetic Facts of Life to know it; to endure it? To "ease the greed that eats me day and night"?

Do others feel it as madly as I do? Or is this intensity exclusive to Thee alone? Is it from deprivation that flourishes the Thee and Me?

The mail must be here now. I leave the washing of Rauhuia's eloquent shirts in the laundry and make my way through the trees to the gate. Who knows, a letter from Eugene might be there; even from Thee. Who knows, communication might be there!

Even for Me.

"Mummie is crying," writes Rongo, who sets her whole school day by the "little bit dance; jussa a little bit dance," and who is exquisitely dressed in yellow with every black silken hair in place,
"because Daddy
hit her in the
face. Mummie is
going to Nanny's
today. Daddy is
angry."

There are times when I can't teach and this is one of them. There is a lot of creativity, colour, music, reading, singing and laughing; indeed, the dinghy swings over the waves in sun and sparkling sea. But "I droop deadly sometimes" in my cell.

Yet in Selah in the evening as the summer rain thunders on the low roof my brush works steadily enough. After all, I have seen the meaning of life, over and over again. And knew at the time that I saw it.

I cover my things carefully from the falling dust of the old woodwork and from the floating ash when I prepare my fire for the morning; I turn back from the door, from love and habit, and run through the pages I have done. Suddenly I recognize the violence creeping into Book Two, both implied and actual. In the colours, in the action and in the thought; inextricably woven with sympathy and love. What will the Senior think of this? These books are for him; indeed they are because of him. Will he understand? Does it matter anyway whether he does or not? The real point is made. The dawns and the evenings when I prepare for another the essential and best of myself are new times of meaning.

But the thought of a pillow inexorably takes over and I close the door once more. Yet the time spent with my dear work has not been without its subtle healing. As I pass through the scents of summer to the house I am not unaware of a surcease. "What is precious is never to forget."

When the birds in the creeper wake me in the dawn, I pull myself up on the pillows, stare through the curtains of the far window to check up on the pattern of the black tree against the new and tender sky, then turn to the window behind to look out upon the garden, and through the lace-work of the trees to the fields across the road, the hills in the distance and the shadowy brooding mountains. The day rising before me is a mountain too, with crests of effort, ravines of failure and the cold snows of loneliness; but I am still, amazingly, a part of all this shining living and there is yet another day.

"Daddy," writes Blossom, his ton-weight boots still for a blessed moment,
"went shearing on the truck.
He took
the blankets with
him and. He
took the
materess."

"Come, Little One," I say to tiny Hinewaka, the small head on my shoulder, as she cries away over some weighty untold matter, which I happen to know is the story of her feet. "Come, Little One." I sit down on my low chair, settle her on my knee and get on with my lesson with Tame. He is reading my Maori book about Ihaka, Book Two, which concerns another span in the life of this little Maori boy, and I'm looking into the usage like an eagle for the mistakes I've made. He comes to the line, "Kiss Mummie Goodbye, Ihaka."

"What's this word?" he asks.

" 'Kiss.' "

A strange excitement comes over him. He smirks, then laughs outright, says it again, then tugs at Patchy nearby and shows him. "That's 'kiss,' " he says emotionally. "K-I-S-S."

Patchy lights up too in an extraordinary way. They both spell it. The reading is held up while others are called and told and I feel something has happened although I don't know what.

The next morning Patchy runs in, his freckles all agog. "I can till pell kitt!" he cries. "K-i-et-et!"

Tame simply gallops in. He brushes past me, snatches the Ihaka book from the table, opens to the page and points out the word to others nearby. "Look," he says profoundly, "here's 'kiss.' "

Why this sudden impetus in the reading, I wonder, putting up the words from the imported books on the blackboard for the day? What's this power in a word like "kiss"?

But it is not until my mind is turned the other way and I am engaged in something else that the significance begins to unfold. Playing some Tchaikovsky for dancing I see that this word is related to some feeling within them; some feeling that I have so far not touched. . . .

I don't hear the steps coming in, since the music manages to continue. I don't know the Senior is standing here with the typewriter for my turn. I'm well on through the "Nutcracker Suite" before I feel a touch on my shoulder that is not from a small hand and I jump, throw up my hands, then cover my face. Too sudden a transition . . .

Later I say, "This word 'kiss.' Look what it does to them." I call Tame and Patchy and Reremoana and reach for the book.

"It's got some relation," I say, "to a big feeling. I can't put my finger on it."

"Do you mean it is a caption?"

Caption! Caption! . . . caption . . .

"I've got to drop in on Mr Reardon. We'll have to try to get hold of the Meeting House for an extra class and an extra teacher."

Caption . . . The whole question is floodlit. This word is the caption of a very big inner picture. "We've got plenty of room," I reply from the surface of my mind. "We've got two stories: the floor and the tops of the tables. Sandy uses the top story."

"Why not a third story? A few slats over the rafters?"

It's the caption of a huge emotional picture. "What I'm going to ask the Chairman to ask the Board for next is a rope from the roof with a seat on the end so that we can cross the room by air."

Indeed, I find, as the large grey form disappears through the door, it is the caption of a mighty instinct: sex.

But I'm so slow. You never saw anyone as slow as me when something is under my nose. It is a day or two further on before I see any more. I am bent double over the clay container in the storeroom working over the consistency of the clay when it comes to me that there must be other captions of a like nature. Other captions carrying their own pictures in the mind. . . . Fear, for instance, the only instinct I know that is bigger than sex. What is its caption, I wonder? I straighten and begin scraping the clay from my hands.

"Sandy," I say, taking some time to reach him at his work among the writing groups, "I'll be away for a minute. I'm going over to the big school to wash my hands."

He straightens from where he is bending over a small head, rubbing his back, "I'll drop my bat then and watch them."

"Not necessarily. Creativity is a better teacher than me. I can turn my back on creativity any time."

"But I've been bending for half an hour, Miss Vorontosov. If I bend once more I'll never straighten again."

"Do you think I don't know? 'The labour we long for, physics pain.'"

What, I wonder, as the water runs, are all the other captions and pictures? What terrible power there must be in words for little children if only we could tap it and harness it! At length I return slowly across the grass to the pre-fab and dry my hands on my own towel, in some distress, as though some unstemmable pressure had been let loose within. I hear a Little One crying wildly nearby but I don't pick it up. I go to a group of children writing their passionate and condensed accounts of themselves. "What are you frightened of, Tame?"

"The ghost," he says, his eyes changing.

"What are you frightened of, Patchy?"

"The alligator."

"What are you frightened of, Patu?"

"The ghost."

"What are you frightened of, Reremoana?"

"The ghost."

I try out "ghost" and "kiss" on the ones who can't learn to read. I print them on the low wall blackboard where they can touch them and

Lo! The next morning here are these non-readers recognizing these words from one look the day before; children who have stalled on the imported books for months; on the words, "come and look, see the boats." Wiki and Blossom and One-Pint "an' them." Lo, here are these stallers reading overnight!

I edge and dodge and manœuvre my way through the loud children towards the window to examine my favourite hill in the distance. It takes a while to get there, what with the castles, garages, picture-theatres and cannon on the floor, the ten-child easel, the stove, the piano, the sand, the water and the furniture, and freeing my finger-marked smock from demanding hands. But all I do when I arrive and lean over the open piano is not to wonder why this hill is blue on some days, grey on others and white today, but to bite at a finger-nail. Ghost . . . kiss; captions of the instincts. There must be many more words like this, analogous to these two; captions of other instincts, desires, resentments, horrors and passions. What are they? How do you get hold of them? How do your hands plunge into their heads and wrench them out?

I can't find them on my hill. I wander restlessly among the children clamorously putting their things away for play; thunderously dropping and packing the big blocks in the long chest in the porch. What are these powerful, self-chosen, self-illustrated words? Tame is having one last draw on the blackboard. A big ghost with white cloak and red eyes. And a wide-open black mouth; like the dark mouth of the night when despair is my guest. I push to the piano. I run my fingers through my hair, learning the full meaning of pressure. I try a difficult Beethoven. The Hundred and Eleven. Its tortuous composition serves for the screams of a mind in labour. . . .

Then suddenly there strikes a clanging and a clattering. It is the bell. The Great Lord of the school that arranges when one starts thinking and when one stops. The delicate structure of thought rising block by block in precarious balance like the castles I am always stepping round or over, is shattered as though Blossom had knocked it with his big boot, and my tower shivers and crumbles and is lost.

Where is my tower?

That bell bust it!

"When I went to sleep," writes Matawhero,

"I dreamt
about the ghost
The ghost went
in our kitchen.
and frightened
us. It had big
fat eyes. It had
a white sheet.

I'm meeting some diverse people this year, but not even the Senior
himself moves me as much as one other being. He is a grave soul who
governs not by self-effacement, but by outright fear: a soul of untold
psychic dimension and of universal power. Through my work at school
I've come to know him; day in, day out; thought in, thought out. In
all the seething young minds in my keeping I have learnt to recognize
him. Indeed, I have met the most singular personality in my professional life. I have met the ghost.

"Daddy's gone shearing," writes Blossom, warming to his theme,
"and he is not
coming back home
till
he's finished his
shearing and he
is going to bring
back the blankets
with him and our
matteress."

Yes, it's a funny thing all right that I never see any of the other
Inspectors . . . and a good thing too: the fewer the better.
"Sandy, bring my tea over, please. Pour it yourself. No Maori I
have met yet knows how to pour tea. And carry it over yourself. I don't
want a saucer full. And I don't want finger-marks round the rim.
And don't forget to pour the top milk into my cup. And make it
strong. And see that it's hot."
"Yes, Miss Vorontosov."
Sandy's easy ways are changing. All Yes, Miss Vorontosov, and No,

Miss Vorontosov. And why not? You won't find me mixing generations again.

"They said over there," he says when he returns smiling, "that they
haven't seen you for weeks. And that they miss you."

"There's a reason for everything," I reply curtly.

"Mr Reardon poured your tea himself."

They never speak to me the second time, these visitors. I shall men-
tion to the Headmaster the next time he comes over how these other
Inspectors never appear. The next time he comes over to mark my
Rolls.

"And Mr Girlgrace said . . ."

"Sandy. Be so kind as to send all those Little Ones out of the porch.
Right away outside."

I want peace.

I have a note during the morning from the Head. "Mr Jason is
here," it reads. "I've had a talk to him and he's not coming over to the
infant room." He is an itinerant instructor from my past.

On my way through the trees to lunch the Head strides after me.
. . . "I told him," he said, "that I didn't want him to go over to the
infant room. We had a good go over it too; believe me! But I managed it without playing the card I had. I didn't want to hurt the poor
chap."

"No. There was no need to hurt him. What was the card?"

But the Head goes on in that way he has of not listening to me,
although his whole attitude is one of attention. However, it never fails
to give that pleasant feeling of his mind looking the other way. He
continues, "I said, 'I don't want you to go over at all; in the interests
of harmony.'"

"Thank you, Mr Reardon. What was the card you did not wish to
play?"

"I've had this on my mind the whole week, you know. I didn't tell
you he was coming."

"Sandy told me."

"You knew?"

"Knew? I dreamt it out from start to finish."

"I expected him to slip over behind my back."

"He did in my dream. And you took off your coat to him. What was the card, Mr Reardon?" Now and again I require a direct answer from the Head, for all his mind on something else.

"Oh, didn't I tell you? W. W. said I was to keep him out of your room. But only to use his name as a last resort."

"Daddy came home," writes Blossom, a ponderous tear dropping on his dirty book,
"and he took our
last blanket off the
bed and we got
cold because he
took the blanket
because he was
cold too. That's
why we got cold
too and Daddy
put on dirty coats
and he got so hot
he jumped
out of bed."

Summer can materialize her dream all right.

Without any of the stress that some men have over it, and without ending up in a churchyard about it. Her flowers are beautifully dressed. All her trees are in full foliage and the elm tree I see as I make my furtive way around the rising foundations of the new infant block is her pride. It spills shade for the children with the largesse of one with the right to expect fulfilment, and with untiring reliability. Such a stirring sight, greening away here in the centre of the playground. Soothing too, in that she remains with me, pacifying me from the loss of the cabbage trees, slain to make room for the new block. And she is all too attractive for my little boys who are hard put not to climb up into her exciting branches. Also the poplars along the river's stopbank help to pull away the focus of the eye from the sapping trunk-butts of the cabbage trees, together with the walnut tree beyond the pre-fab and my own trees about the house. Yes, summer manages to express her dream safely. A season needs no midwife.

The school is winding up for the year. From the pre-fab windows when I look up and out from teaching, allowing some thought to stretch its limbs, I see that the big boys have made tennis courts for themselves and the girls out on the plain a little; with some tall umpire seats from which my little boys have to be lifted down regularly. All of which involves intense sewing of white clothes on the breathless machine in the infant room. Also there are our uniforms to be touched up for the Break-up and the piano Programme to be practised for. A class overflows from the big school into the Meeting House down at the *pa* across the road from the graveyard, including a fifth teacher, some fully trained and experienced young Maori, from what I can see from the windows of my self-cloistered pre-fab. There must be quite a crowd of men in the staff room by now. Indeed, peering out from my middle-aged encagement, through this window and that, I witness dream after dream breaking into birth like babies from the minds of men. The playground, now a clean-swept concrete, is alive with carpenters working on the new block, remarkably patient with my little boys touching their tools. From the new shower rooms and laundries, mopping up the surplus animal energy of the big ones, I hear the whistling of big boys and the singing away among the suds over rompers and towels and aprons of our big girls. Indeed, with all the additions and improvements and growth you'd think the Head and the Chairman would be mollified. But no. The Head ignores promotion to a school three times the size of this, explaining that he is busy, and Rauhuia, plying and perspiring to and from the Board in his best clothes, is more guttural than ever and his pace more and more ridiculously out of character with his health. But there you are. That's what dreams do to men. Yet you might as well forfeit position over them, or wittingly die over them: it's more like being alive.

As for the pre-fab, the numbers are so like a Walt Disney cartoon that one morning when W. W. calls to borrow the typewriter he can't get in at all. Plunging through the porch in his swift way in his urgent economy of time he is pulled up so suddenly in his stride at the door that he all but overbalances into the water-trough. A castle rears up before him big enough almost for himself to live in. And next to it is the sand-bin and the water. "Can't you put these things somewhere else," he complains, "and clear the right-of-way?"

"Where?" I reply in innocence.

The school is winding up, and the year. From what I hear from

Sandy and from the Head when he comes over, patiently and regularly, the staff is tired. Indeed, we are not even all still alive. No doubt the Headmaster is a slave-driver but there's no escape when men are possessed with dreams. Yet it's not all this. It's the drama, which is more exhausting than chopping wood. And it's teaching itself, which again is harder than drama. Oh my feet and legs! How many more days now until the six weeks' vacation at Christmas? I'll send a message down to the Store after school with a boy and get them to put a ring through to the Lodge, and tell them to hang on to that cabin for me on the Lake-shore.

Yes, just look at what dreams do to men. They are the serum of procreation. If men are impotent they live without knowing the meaning. And if they are fertile they express or die. And where is the man who would rather die from continence than from excess? Cursed is the mind that has the dream, unable to do the thing it must: "Dust's your wages, son of sorrow. But men may come to worse than dust."

Six weeks of barefoot way, complete possession of the days, and peace. I don't go to the lake. I don't go past Selah. I use up the whole of the time on what I want to do myself until here at last is the last Saturday of freedom before school.

I put a bucket of white clay in the shade of a tree where it will set away from the sun, just, I suppose, as a mother tucks her baby away for a sleep. And in no time, here are the irrelevant tears. But they no longer break harshly, dryly, shaking my attenuated body, in the way of half a year ago. They have a gentle legitimacy in them. After all it is some time since I remembered my unborn sons. Self-pity is best released. How blessed to weep in the sun.

But they go, they go. Just like the rain when it comes. It is worth another brew. I take my cup to Selah and become so frivolously involved in the intellectual birth of short three-word sentences of Book Two that I dip my brush into the tea while I'm speculating. Whatever is this new flavour, and the colour, for that matter? Turquoise tea . . . how fascinating!

By the time the six lovely simple weeks of the summer holiday have drawn to their conclusion, however, my arms have become itchy on the inside to hold children. From the wrists on the inner side along the skin right up to the shoulders and across the breast I know a physical discomfort. If ever flesh spoke mine does; for the communion of hands, the arms stretching round my waist and black heads bumping my breasts. It amounts to a deprivation and I realize as I hide in Selah away from my remembering garden on the eve of school how wild were my thoughts of resigning last year when the grading came out. The truth is that I am enslaved. I'm enslaved in one vast love affair with seventy children.

But as the summer beats more deeply and the year settles into its theme, like a sonata of Schubert, and the poplars parade more greenly along the river's stopbank, I find myself, even though the instructors for some reason no longer punish themselves by taking my room, not without visitors after all. Not strictly. It's just that they are, they are . . . shall we . . . no, no! that they are, that there is something different about them . . .

. . . I am sitting on the table where I sometimes sit bawlers and before me are the Senior and some glamorous exclusive gentleman from the Department of Education in Wellington. I haven't a doubt that he has a lot to say, and worth listening to also, but Mr Abercrombie takes the responsibility of pressing the button of my tongue and the visitor doesn't get the chance to say it. On occasion when I pause to draw breath he slips in a question or observation but it is so well-placed that it only sends me off harder and faster in another direction of all my new thinking until, when my lord the bell rings, I hear myself expounding, "You can find as much emotion in a schematic drawing as you can in a Rembrandt. You can find as much drama in a schematic writing as you can in a . . ."

"Come and have some tea," suggests the Senior touching my arm, and recovering the situation he has brought on himself anyway.

"The way you make me talk," I reprove as we cross the new concrete to the big school. I go over to tea when he takes me.

"I like it." What a crowd in the staff room! Times are changing.

"Anyway," I say, pouring the tea, "I approve your technique of dropping important people on us." What is this strange freedom now to talk in the staff room? "And I trust," I say, turning to Glamour, "that you are important." I haven't exchanged two words with the two new teachers, Percy Girlgrace and Rangi.

"Me?" he protests respectably and seriously. "No, no, I'm not important."

"It's just as well. *Anyway*," I continue to the Senior, sitting relaxed with his large legs crossed, "if I knew they were coming I, for one, would certainly not be here."

"But you've got something, Miss Vorontosov," remarks Glamour. "I'm quite satisfied that you've got something."

All of which may have something to do with the picture that flashes in the world behind my eyes as I walk with Reremoana to the gate with them. Somehow, with all the talk during the morning he has afforded me in the infant room, the destruction to my thinking from the bell last year has been repaired and I see again the tower, rising in all its precariousness and delicacy; the tower of thought that I had lost. And on top of this tower I see this shape that has been hovering above me, ungraspable for two seasons; this *key*. And it is no longer mysterious and nebulous. It is as simple as my Little Ones. The whole system of infant room vocabulary flashes before the inner eye as though floodlit. As I walk alongside the Senior, engaged in conversation on the surface of my mind about the regimentation in many schools, I am realizing what this captioning of the inner world is. It's the vocabulary I've been after. And as the two men seat themselves in the suave car and ease off down the road I christen it the Key Vocabulary.

Flowers, flowers . . . flowers. . . . Red flowers along the side of the house, flaring out above the long grass and from beneath the lace-bark tree; dahlia, geranium, gladioli and lily. Blue flowers, backed by the passion-fruit creeper upon the garden wall projecting from the house; canterbury bells, cornflower, gentian, lobelia. Yellow flowers, glowing from between the trees between the verandah and the gate; dahlia, daisy, marigold and canna. From the base of the hedges the hydrangea, and in corners and by walls the hollyhock. Sweet pea climbs beneath the window of Selah; at their feet are the phlox. While from under the tank near the door nasturtium running wild.

I am surprised at all these flowers as I walk alone in the dusk. They seem like a new garden. I have not enrolled them all yet. I pause and smell the new ones blossomed in my mind's absence and as I move from one to another among the shadows they put down their loads of pain; even the delphiniums, the most moody in the garden, with an escort of beetles zooming. Indeed, here are their first blue buds at the tip on the eve of a second blooming.

I know, I know. There's some kind of pact between the Senior and the Head to do with visitors for me. I cannot see why and I cannot prove it; but I sense it.

I sense in it, wrongly maybe, an aura of protection, giving me a faint idea of what it must feel like to be married and in the care of a good man. I even come to wonder whether in some unsuspected and indeliberate way I have not come to a kind of heaven-haven; "To fields where flies no sharp and sided hail. And a few lilies blow."

In any case I have stopped thinking about another country and soap-suds to play with all day long, and that my hands are ugly enough for a laundry anyway. For the frightening inspector shade in the rafters, limiting and aborting all I do, has materialized into a figure of good-will. It's worth weeping very loud crying about. But as I walk with my coffee in the garden in the evening I do not. As I brave the brilliance of the colours it is the last thing I want. What does this mean? I could only say it with Schubert.

It's true that outside school I am still not wholly unaware of men; four or five of them at a rough count; either in life or out; in spite of the padlock on my gate. But no man, dead or alive, can disturb the plot in the wild garden of myself where art grows, although mine is a self-sown personality, an enclosure of wilful wanton weeds, there is yet one dell of order. Inside of the pre-fab I know a precarious peace. The kind of peace in which the seed of art has time and composure enough to germinate. A peace which allows the roots of the heart to explore comfortably about in the soil to collect water. A peace which affords the shoots of thought light and elbow room above ground. A peace in which the foliage of the mind can breathe from the air around it. A peace from which my wintering soul draws inspiration to bloom again. Ah, the protection and care of men!

I am a flower reaching beyond the restraining grasses. I am a Little One piling up a tall tower in the doorway. I am a teacher cleaving a track through the undergrowth of method. I am a bird. . . .

Rebuilding.

Autumn

"The fine delight that fathers thought . . ."

S*UMMER* has just about had enough of it by now and seems relieved to hand over everything to autumn. She's covered the most of her curriculum. Well enough too. She has got a good percentage of her flowers through their exams and has kept their clothes nice. All her trees are in full dress and her birds loud with conversation. Indeed she may well retire in blazing colours and brilliant sound. It's time for autumn to take over now. It's time for autumn to turn the full capacity of her mind upon the question of fruiting.

It's time for me to take a plunge into the Key Vocabulary too. It's true that there is a swelling vein behind one knee and something different about my feet, but exercise of the mind has not been unknown to cost you something physical. Not that I am willing to pay it. I'm touchy about the welfare of my person, such as it is; but when I am caught up too closely with the underground stream of energy that does not seem wholly to be my own, I have little if any say in the pace I work, as a separate entity. Also, working with the Head you hardly have time to cultivate your separateness. A cell in a brain doesn't speak for itself alone. And when you are one cell in a school brain you speak and work for the school. Whether you like it or not. And when a school mind is geared to creativeness, so are you. It just comes normally, like Percy Girlgrace's club for boys in the *pa;* like Rangi's football organization and opening tournament and Sandy's hitching himself to everything around him.

But the days are heavy now. Becoming heavier and heavier like the autumn branches. What with the dressmaking going all day, the piano lessons at strategic points, given often by the more advanced players, the organization of four basketball teams among the girls, the making of motto pockets and team bands for inter-school visits, the teaching of manners and courtesies, the continuation of the Maori books in the early mornings, and the beginning of tentative notes on my new thinking on method in the evening—you would think it is already too much without, on top of it all, on top of the usual infant-room routine, the testing of words. I need to be free for this testing but I'm not and I can't be, yet I still must find out these things.

The reading is very much on my mind. All other concerns take second place. I must satisfy myself on this matter. Day by day I seek the most vital words for a child to begin with. So much hangs on the issue. The love of reading for a lifetime, for one. Day by day through the unrelenting testing these words sort themselves out. With alarming clarity they group themselves round the two main instincts. I'm thinking about it most of the time, either on the lower levels when attending to something else, or on the surface when I am actively experimenting. I cannot see that there will be any break until I have found out all I want and need to about the whole sad affair of infant reading.

Today I work on Rangi, a five-year-old Maori. Nothing will make him learn the first words of the imported books. Yet they seem normal enough words. "Come and look." "See the boats." "Little dog." "See my aeroplane." Words that I had taken for granted as having been chosen by adult educationalists for their emotional significance. Indeed, the glamorous visitor from the Department claimed that they were the mean. And it's all but impossible for a teacher to contest the rightness of anything from the Department.

But Wiki and Rangi and others like them, sit and smile and never recognize them again. All this toil, I think, trying to teach them something that doesn't interest them and trying to force them to like something they hate. Why must we? Why don't I teach them something that does interest them? Then they might develop like the flowers that are interested in the rain and the sun; in their own time and way. What does interest them?

"What is Rangi's background?" I ask the Head.

"His father is a pugilist who runs a gambling den at the pub."

"What are you frightened of, Rangi?" I ask as he sits in a knot of others.

"P'lice."

"Why?"

"P'lice they takes me to gaol and cuts me up with a butcher-knife."

I print these words on separate cards and give them to him. And Rangi, who lives on love and kisses and thrashings and fights and fear of the police and who took four months to learn "come," "look," "and" takes four minutes to learn:

butcher-knife	Daddy
gaol	Mummie
police	Rangi
sing	haka
cry	fight
kiss	

So I make a reading card for him: out of these words, which he reads at first sight, his first reading, and his face lights up with understanding. And from here he goes on to other reading, even the imported books. His mind is unlocked, some great fear is discharged, he understands at last and he can read.

The days are very heavy all right and so is Guilt. But so are the days of anyone else nursing a young and new thing. I've got two new things now, constantly needing attention, in my Maori books and the Key Vocabulary. There are times when I feel a little like Whareparita with her twins, except that mine, so far, survive.

"Mummie shut the window," writes Twinnie,
"The ghost
can't come in.

I saw his black
teeth."

Many things pass through my mind during the lessening occasions
when I sit on my low chair. Ideas and conclusions arrive erratically
in twos and threes, and in fours and even fives at times, so that it
seems that under pressure one can think on several levels at once. Invariably there is a Little One sitting on my knee, revealing in un-
restrained conversation the fastnesses of the world within while the
precariously over-crowded dinghy jerks and heaves along, or sometimes flows, without a quarter of my attention. Questions to be an-
swered Hirani on the making of yellow aprons for the infant room,
patterns to be laid, Tai's hand position to be corrected on the keyboard,
mistakes from his stumbling fingers to be endured, tears to be dried
on the lower levels, laughing, singing, dancing, the thunder of falling
blocks, the strange and piercing sounds connected with carpenters
building, the roar of the tractor on the plain outside the window and
the "How do you spell cowboy?" all over and above the testing of
words and all at once.

Really, the things I see and hear and feel and think when I'm sitting on this chair! I must get a cushion for this chair. . . .

Plainly there are private Key Vocabularies. They belong to children
with some emotional impediment blocking the creative channel and
twisting their living. What with Rangi's "butcher-knife" and "gaol,"
Wiki's "daddy, fight, broom," Blossom's "blankets, mattress, cold"
and Patu's "baby, dead, cried." Pussy or the ginger rooster could see it.
Even Sammy Snail hanging on the rafter. What are these imported
books imposed on the Maori infant room doing to the children in
them? Even the white children, for all their respectability and painfully
good manners and distressing concern with cleanliness, have their own
exciting vocabularies. What a big new strange uncharted ocean I find
myself floundering about in! For one thing the tone of the infant room
is changing. It's making a transition from a series of violent explosions
to something that feels like an artery rhythmically pumping blood.
Something with the same force, but more natural, more comely.

Of course I'm alone. The Senior doesn't come now. He has given
up the fetching and carrying of the typewriter at last and left it with

me; bringing me dolefully to realize that it actually was all typewriter, and not my irresistibility. I'm alone once more, not only professionally but ethically. Even more so now than ever before, what with this key in my hands. But, to the rigid silence of the orthodox infant room, I nevertheless prefer this frightening inspiring beating of the child-heart in the raftered pre-fab. With or without company; with or without professional status; with or without the return of Guilt on my shoulders, and with or without courage. For after all these yearfuls of mistakes I'm engaged in the grandest mistake of all; so encompassing, so irrevocable, that its effects can no longer matter.

Plainly there are private vocabularies. I suppose Pussy has one in her little furry heart, and wouldn't I like to know what makes the ginger rooster leave his own kind, and why Sammy Snail chooses our particular rafter? As for what Paul has buried disastrously within him . . . "that is bound in fixity that no repenting power can free."

"Miss Vorontosov," says one of the big boys, "d'you mind if I bring the axe in here. Seven is chopping my brother."

"Miss Vontof, Seven he hit Mohi on the head wit a post."

"Who's that crying?" I accuse, lifting my head like an old war-horse.

"Seven he's breaking Maadi's neck, Miss Foffofof."

I leave the lesson in reading style with the upper ones and go and collect Seven in person. How I respect all this force in him and how I understand his violence. I take his hand with particular gentleness and he comes with me like a lamb and sits in his desk hopefully. But although I'm an outcast and a fool, by both necessity and choice, I'm not a servant.

"Go and get your own clay," I say to the long mournful face, "and make something for a change. . . ."

"What are you frightened of, Seven?" I ask the next morning in the output period.

"I not frighteen of anysing."

"Aren't you?"

"No. I stick my knife into it all."

"What will you stick your knife into?"

"I stick my knife into the worms."

It surprises me but I don't accept it. It is a symbol for what really frightens him. I'm not satisfied. There can be so much in a child that we don't know. But I print him the word Worms which he fails to recognize the next time.

"Come in," cry the Little Ones to a knock at the door, but as no one does come in we all go out and here we find in the porch a barefooted tattoed Maori woman of much dignity.

"I see my little Seven," she asks huskily.

"Is Seven your little boy?"

"I bringed him up. Now he five. I take him home to hees real family for school eh. I see my little boy?"

The children willingly produce Seven and here we have in the porch, within a ring of sympathetic brown and blue eyes, a reunion.

"Where did you bring him up?" I ask over the many heads.

"Way back on those hill. All by heeself. You remember your ol' Mummie?" she begs Seven.

"I see, I see."

Later, watching Seven grinding his chalk to dust as usual I do see.

"Whom do you want, Seven," I ask, "your old Mummie or your new Mummie?"

"My ol' Mummie."

"Do you like your new brothers?"

"They all hits me."

During the output period the next morning I print these words on the big cards for him, "Old Mummie," "New Mummie," "brothers," "hit" and "hill" and they all turn out to be one-look words. And now and again, as the days beat by, I think I see some shape breaking through the chalk ravage.

"What's that, Little One?" I ask one day.

"Tha's your house. I burn it down."

"Why?"

"Because."

"For nothing?"

" 'Course. And here's you getteen burnded."

"Oh. But where will I live now. And who'll fix my sore burns?"

In a flash, like a *paua* turning in the sun, there's a new mood. The mournful face with its long features looks up at me in compassion.

"I—I fix your sore burns. And—and I make you a new house."

Clumsily he cleans off the chalk thickness and begins on another holocaust of colour.

My twins.

My Maori books and my Key Vocabulary. Whareparita was never more thrilled than me. But there's no little white boxes at the bottom of a deep grave for me to weep upon. As the little babies' should have done, the faces of my children are filling out and they're beginning to show real strength.

"Tell me," I say to Whareparita's Nanny one day when she comes over to the pre-fab to let off a lot of steam about all her many-sired grandchildren, "why did Whareparita lose her babies?"

"I tol you before, Miss Votov. Those ghos' in the dark they fright her and Whareparita she trip over."

"She tripped over in the dark?"

"Yes, like she trip over, see, in the dark."

I haven't tripped over in the dark. I stride forward in the light. I take this key vocabulary in the morning output period when nervous energy is at its peak, because it's a creative activity and as such is more important than anything else. I place it where I place all the media of creativity between nine and ten-thirty.

I take it the minute they come in before they touch any other medium because I don't like to interrupt them later when they are deep in blocks or dance or tears or clay. Also I want to catch the first freshness.

I have their known words on the mat, so that when they come running in from assembly they make straight for their own, not without discussion, concentration and satisfaction. And it's a gay performance this finding of their own words, taking time and involving noise and personal relations and actual reading, and above all communication with each other; the vital thing so often cut off in a schoolroom. Then they choose a mate and sit together, knee to knee, and hear each other their own words, making it more a matter of personal attention than one teacher could possibly do.

And it is at this stage that I call one at a time. I call white Dennis, a very obedient and clean little boy, who already at five has had a nervous illness.

"What are you going to have, Little One?"

But he's too disintegrated to have easy access to himself. He gazes about furtively and says the first thing he sees.

"Window."

But I know better than this. This is no caption in this case. It will be as unproductive as the "come" and "look" of the standard books.

"I had a dream last night," I say. "A bad dream too. I was frightened."

"I had a dream too!" he says with emotion. "I dreamt about the sky."

"That's funny. I dreamt about the sky too. I was frightened. Were you?"

"No, I'm not frightened of anything," he protests.

"Oh, I am!"

"Only the sky. I hate the sky! I don't want to go up in the sky when I die!"

"Who said you're going up in the sky when you die?"

"They said in Sunday school!"

I suppose they did.

I reach for my big black crayon and one of the large white cards I keep near at this time and write sky. He watches me.

"Say 'Sky,' Little One."

"Sky," he says with some feeling. Then he sits down and traces the letters with his fingers. I watch this little white trembling finger following these twisty black marks on the card that have such intense meaning to him. And I imagine the picture of horror within of which it is the caption. A moving, changing picture which he could never describe to us and which not one of us could possibly draw for him. Such a little thing with such a big unknown burden. But it will be this much less now.

"You're a dear little boy, Dennis," I say involuntarily.

But they're not all as hard as Dennis.

"What are you going to have, Maadi? Sit down, you others. I'll call you when I'm ready."

Of course they don't sit down because these new entrants from the *pa* don't know what obedience is. Only the white ones sit down, and smartly.

"House," whispers Maadi.

"Toast," says another with a fat stomach.

"Beer," says Little Brother.

"Piano," says the one that doesn't speak.

"Ghost," says another.

"Ice-cream," says my little Tamati rat, Riti, who never has one.

"Shearing shed," say several whose parents are away.

I often make mistakes over these words. It takes a little while to assess a newcomer. For the variety of character on the five-year-old level is as legion as nature itself. And then there are these pitfalls of copying, mood, repression, and crippling fears which block the organic expulsion of a word. . . . But I'm equal to this after a while as long as my own mood is right, by which I mean not tense. There comes a regular flow of organic words, captioning and pictures in the mind. And as long as I keep away from town, keep the padlock on my gate, and avoid poetry, my mood is usually right.

It's the easiest way I have ever begun reading. There's no driving to it. There's no teaching at all. There's no work to put up on a blackboard, no charts to make and no force required to marshal the little things into a teachable attentive group. The teaching and learning is in their own hands mixed up with all the natural concomitants of relationships. I just make sure of my big cards nearby and my big black crayon and the indispensable freedom and relaxation in the room.

After the morning output period up till playtime, there is what I call the intake and it is here that the words are brought out again and checked. The ones they remember they keep but the ones they don't I destroy. They can't be very important for them if they're forgotten. And only important captions qualify for the privilege of being written.

True there are some unlikely words lying about in the room, from the butcher-knife set, through ghosts, along to spiders, ol' Mummie, and sky. But I have nothing to lose. Although Guilt never lets me forget his legs on my throat during the operation of the Key Vocabulary, I still know that by professional standards if not by emotional, I am free.

There are two answers to the villain in my life: memory. One is to pick up *Education through Art* and lose myself in the underground of the mind and the other is to visit the little church in the graveyard on the Corner when the bell calls. It's not a place I'm anxious to see, this churchyard, knowing as I do more than one of its inhabitants. But I go, as, if there's one thing that can sometimes rout Memory, it is to look him in the face and stare him out.

I look towards the mountains as I return alone along the road. The mountains with their snow. The shadows in their ravines are full of blue as though the sky had spilled. Then I glance at the poplars along the stopbank. Just turning colour, with shadows of blue also. And look at the blue daisies along the roadside: good enough for a garden! My garden anyway. Willing bright creatures they are! Drops of autumn sky fallen. And as I walk back through my gate here are the delphiniums: eight feet worth of second blooming. The gardening notes in the paper say it is time for sowing delphinium. My word, we are off course!

But I'm not really seeing these bluenesses. I'm thinking of the gracious images the preacher has replaced in my mind. Both lofty and lowly. Continuity in living and humility. What an escape from temporal desire! Something immutable for the heart to feed on; that does not change or tire.

Wiki is small enough herself, but her little sister Hinewaka who cries so much is even smaller. She's about the lightest-weight little four-year-old tot that ever broke the five barrier to get to school. How can I say what I feel when I see them coming hand-in-hand through the gate, straggly-haired and barefooted, the whole of Hinewaka's little life trusted to the small hand of Wiki. It's this trust of one so small in another so small that racks me. That Hinewaka should feel that safety was in the head and hand of little Wiki is one of the things that wrench me out of myself so that my private life and awareness of myself are from nine till three completely obliterated.

When the nurse comes in, in her white overall, I play the attention chord in case she has something to say to them. But although the immediate silence at the attention chord that I have trained falls at once all over the infant room there are still voices and movement in the storeroom behind me. So I turn round surprised and I find Wiki in there with her little sister by the hand.

"Wiki," I say, "you know that when the piano calls you come where you can see me."

Wiki at once drops the tiny hand and does come where she can see me, leaving Hinewaka alone. As for the Very Little One she is so quiet anyway that I leave her there; besides she is learning by watching her sister.

I turn again to the nurse. "Have you got anything to say to them, Sister?" I ask.

Suddenly there is the sound of running feet and a burst of screaming and here is Hinewaka hurrying limping from the storeroom past the nurse to the door, shrieking as though a skellington was after her.

At once I see it all. The treatment since birth for her feet. I catch her and pick her up and walk up and down comforting her until the screams have subsided, and cursing my heavy-handedness in not seeing the issue of the storeroom in taking away the small protection of Wiki at Hinewaka's worst moment.

"The nurse won't get you," I say within earshot of the sister and feeling sorry about it. "It's the treatment of her feet she's had for years," I say. "It's not you yourself. The other children are not afraid of you."

"Yes," says the sister thoughtfully, "it's the treatment."

Wiki is standing nearby, her brown eyes looking up at Hinewaka in my arms with relief. Such a little girl understanding a thing so big. Even better than me. But the day will come when I shall understand Hinewaka too. I already see what her Key Vocabulary is going to begin with. Tomorrow in the output period I'll give her "nurse," then the next day, "feet." And we'll open up the whole dreadful festering of fear beneath the lid and let it discharge itself away through the channel of the Key Vocabulary.

Doubled down over my clay pot with my arms deep in it sorting out the soft from the dry I notice two big feet beside me. They're men's feet and for a moment I study them. They're not Mr Reardon's and they're not Sandy's and they don't belong to the other two men on the staff. I don't know whose they are so I go on with my clay.

But my Little Ones don't let me get away with this. "Man, man!" they cry. "Look, Miss Wottot! Look up wit you head!"

So I get my head to pivot upward. It's a long journey. You go up two long, long legs to a waistcoat. Then you sit back on your heels and put one hand back on the floor for balance until you arrive at the neck, but to find the face you just fall back on the children behind you. How public are my meetings with Mr Abercrombie!

". . . Sometimes," says another *name* from the educational world whom the Senior has brought to see my Maori books, "I think we are all wrong."

We have been talking about the illustrations of my books being schematic, which means that they are drawn in the strange way that five-year-olds draw, with all their arbitrary colouring and shaping. And often, to an adult, an incomprehensibility.

"Sometimes," he says with an humility out of place in one of his position, "I think that this schematic drawing of theirs is a private language of their own that we don't understand."

This is what the difference is between these selected visitors the Senior brings me and the ones he has kept away. It's an humility in them. The modesty associated with wisdom. And the more august the more humble. They are easy to speak to and listen to, and what knowledge they have is accessible. They belong to some aristocracy of the intellect.

"Yes," he goes on, "children's reading could well be illustrated in their own medium." He turns another page of Book Three where there is a little girl crying. "Sometimes I think we are all wrong."

"It's all very simple," I answer. "In the text and in the illustration I merely drop to their level. What they do, I convey. How they draw I draw, and how they speak I write. Their own mediums in meaning, line, colour and word. That's all there is to it. Simple."

He turns more pages. He is dressed in quiet worn clothes. He has a quiet worn voice. "Yes," is all he says.

"I want one of these books," says Mr Abercrombie in his economical way, "to take with me. The Director will be up next week."

I fling up my hands. The Director is one of the ogres from the past. "Oh no, no! Don't show the Director! You must not show my work to the Director!"

He does not reply but looks down in that way he has. It is early afternoon and we are expecting a smart town school to visit us any minute for an afternoon of competitive sport. My Little Ones are outside with Sandy. Yet some have crept back. As the three of us pause together I feel hands, tender small hands, entwining mine; hands of children born of other women. Reremoana's arms encircle me. They feel the disturbance in me and join me in it. I feel my short smock tugged. After all, the Director must have forgotten me by now.

"I want this set," says the Senior briefly.

"You don't have to ask," I charge with uncovered violence. "They've been made for you in the first place!"

"Thank you, Miss Vorontosov."

Although he is very tall he spends a portion of his time looking at the floor. Working out careful answers, I should say. Answers that must take quite a bit of working out; gentle enough not to wound, true in essentials to what he himself thinks, what he believes I really want to hear, inspiring enough to provoke a further step of thought and unpresuming enough to still leave the field for me. I appreciate all these sequences and give him time to cover them all. "I think," he says at length to the august *name,* "that the Director should see this."

"I think," replies the other softly, "that she's got something."

"I'll bring the Director out here next week."

I wish I could be as economical in words as they, but no. I fling them physically with my hands and verbally with my tongue in all sorts of unnecessary directions. "Oh no, no. I don't like being important! No, please don't bring the Director! He doesn't have to see this. He doesn't need to see me!"

They both observe me in quiet composed surprise. "Have you met him?" asks the visitor.

"No."

"He's a man of sensitive principle."

He is a man who has witnessed my worst mistakes. But I cannot let these men know what I am thinking; such an ugly rigmarole. Such a petty routine misfortune. So unrelated to thoughts of Continuity and Humility and cool truth and dignity. I'm ashamed to have such a mess in my memory. Is the Vorontosov going to whine to these men? The mistake was mine anyway. A good teacher does not break out from the curriculum, even when it is deficient. A worthy teacher does not defy an order of a Director. I feel very alarmed and unhappy that this disgrace from the past should suddenly take on new life.

I notice that the Senior has become quiet in a different way. It is no longer the silence of courtesy in accomplished conversation. In his enthusiasm over my books he has seemed like a man with a dream to fulfil, but now he is disappointed. But did I ever not support a man possessed by a dream? How I hate the killing of inspiration! Yet that's what I am doing with my objections. Because there is an ugly rigmarole in the past. In any case the Director cannot possibly remember the defection of one teacher among his thousands, years ago. A tide of faith in this large grey human of the present swamps me. I free my hands from Reremoana. I clasp them and find the face high above.

"What you say," I speak with difficult articulation, "Mr Abercrombie, I'll do."

"Thank you, Miss Vorontosov," he says for the second time this afternoon. Ah, the economy of it!

There is a commotion outside. The buses with the visiting school teams have arrived. The Head will be looking for his hostess. I touch his arm. "Look, I've got to go. I've got to go."

But there is more they wish to discuss and my yellow-jerseyed teams fight out their battles on their own. . . .

In town tonight, however, amid the clashing lights and shadows and the clattering of heels on the pavement I am not thinking wholly of the eruption of the past into the present during the visit of the afternoon; nor am I marvelling at the fine gift the Senior has brought me: the talking to my kind like other and normal people, forcing as it invariably does a progression in my thinking. I am concerned with the Inspector himself and when I see a tall man in grey crossing the street and for a moment believe it is he, then realize it is not, I steady the sudden uproar within, by consoling myself that at least I have learnt something: that, for all the resurrection of the past today, the present is even more present than ever.

So that as the days follow each other I no longer hound the letter-box at the gate for the communication that never comes, and as I sit over my books in the evenings I no longer see the inner picture of another country and of soap-suds; a place where ugly hands are an opportune thing; where my mistaken ways are no longer a burden of Guilt on my shoulders and where brandy answers all. I see only the present, the continuity of my work, the dignity of my function in the school, the gift of teaching that God has put in my hands, and another charming man. I see only the fruiting present and a very charming man.

Making these Ihaka books in the early mornings and evenings with the magic typewriter at hand brings me to dangerous heights. They are *for* someone: *for*. They are *because* of someone: *because*. What glamorous words these turn out to be in this text! for a spinster. Words show their souls when graciously enough set. These words, *for* and *because* of someone, lift the books to the responsibility of a message, however diluted, from me to another. However vague and impersonal this message is it is unmistakably communication. It's a tremendous step in my shadowy life. It's the biggest thing in it. This talking of all I feel through the medium of colour and line and children's language to one who is listening. I'm very important to myself. I'm precariously happy. I'm so happy that I put the teapot lid back on the milk jug instead of the teapot and it falls in. Music gives more and so does reading. I talk to the flowers again and take my meals walking among them. And it's all because my work temporarily holds the attention of someone and because I cannot help thinking that what I am doing is indispensable again. Indeed, there occur long hours when I don't know the presence of Guilt in my teaching and short ones released from men.

Yet even when I am not troubled with the images of these men I am still keyed up; aware. Not just with one, not with the several; not wholly with my infant room nor solely with work. I'm very much in love with breath itself. My small beat from the house to Selah, my beat from the house to the school; from the house to town for shopping and to the pathetic little church in the graveyard, become exciting romantic journeys. Meaning in my meagre life fruits like the branches of autumn. With or without Guilt on my shoulders, with or without sound reason; with or without a letter at the gate, I'm plainly, though temporarily, in season.

"I saw the ghost," writes Bleeding Heart,
"in the pictures.

Then I came
home and got
undressed and
went to bed.
I dreamt about
the ghost and
my brother
got frightened."

The leaves spilt about the garden from the trees are as pretty as the
paint my Little Ones drop about the easel. All colours. How careless
is autumn with his brush! Painting his passionate pictures from the
stopbank through the churchyard up to the garden, he takes no thought
whatever for the cleaning up afterwards. Hasn't he got any Inspector
to complain about the marks on the ground? Or is he as defiant as I
am?

It's pretty though. As I take my coffee out there in the cooling twilight I find myself thinking it is as pretty as the floor of the infant room
after the brushes have been let loose. You don't know which is prettiest
in the end; the floor or the pictures. But then it hardly matters what
children or autumn do with paint; whether they splash it on the
picture or on the floor. It's still lovely.

I find myself thinking how silly it is to remove oneself at will from
life when there is still colour in the paint pots. True, it is not what I
have thought at the time when I witnessed others actually doing it,
but it's what I think at the moment with the leaves beneath my feet.
But how can you think the same in two consecutive seasons? What
are seasons anyway, but change?

What a lot of thinking gets itself done in the garden over coffee! I
must get a bigger cup for this coffee.

My vast amorous ache for life has many facets. With no trouble at
all, and no brandy at all, I pick up my pen-box and books and make
my way across the paddock, manœuvring my way through the debris
of the carpenters about the rising new block to my infant-room passion. . . .

. . . At last I'm beginning to see what these surprising writings
are that the bigger ones indulge in during the morning output period.

They're captions too. Two-word captions: my shoes. Three-word captions: I want you. And story-length captions. I take up Matawhero's book. His letter formations are almost unintelligible, being a boy who does far more with his tongue than with his hands, and they are not made any clearer by frequent rubbings out and doubling. But I can read it. I can read him without writing at all if it comes to that.

"Yesterday I came home
late. My Daddy
gave me a hiding.
Then I start to cry.
Then I have to go to sleep.
When I went to sleep
the ghost went on our
kitchen. It had big fat
eyes. It had a
white sheet."

I take up the standard imported books and turn curiously to the page where he is reading.

"Mother went to a shop.
I want a cap, she said.
I want a cap for John.
She saw a brown cap.
She saw a blue cap.
I like the blue cap, she said."

I pick my way through the movement and the noise and look at some other writing from this new aspect.

Tame.
"I ran away from my
mother and I hid
away from my mother
I hid in The Shed and

I Went home and
got a hiding."

Waiwini.
"I went to the pictures and.
My brother went for a sleep
and then my next brother
hit my first brother and
woke he up and the
pictures start all over
again."

Ani.
"Jeni said to
Me Look here.
She saw a cake then Rosie
hit us mary.
said the kai is cooked
then she said
hurry up or you
will get late."

But Irini suddenly crumples hers up and puts it in the basket and
begins again. It is a long time before she is finished and the others have
gone to play. Her industry has plainly come from the Chinese half
of her and is unusual in a six. She asks me to spell several words and
writes with her hair falling forward making a curtain round her page.
How she can see I don't know, but finally she stands and shakes back
all this thick black hair and brings up her writing.

"Mummie said to Daddy
give me that money else I
will give you a hiding.
Daddy swear ta Mummie.
Daddy gave the money
to Mummie. We had

a party. My father
drank all the beer by
hisself. he was drunk."

I turn to the imported Book Two and find the passage on the
parents:

"Look at the green house.
Father is in it.
It is Father's home too.

There is Mother.
She is in the green house.
She can see us.
Let us run to Mother."

"Come and read, Little One," I say.

She smiles with her head cocked on one side looking at me like a
blackbird, then she tosses back all this hair and snatches the book from
me, in that vivid way children have who have not suffered too much
discipline, and reads the two pages.

Then I give her her own manhandled page and to see her read this,
her dug-in printing, her faulty spacing and childish lay-out, is to realize
that legibility and expert setting run nowhere in the race with meaning. Indeed, it is to realize something else and it comes to me with
the same relief from pressure with which the other realizations have
been emerging: primer children can write their own books. They
actually *are*.

Moreover we'll read these books. Every day. Think of it! New exciting books written every morning about the *pa,* with all the illustrations
vivid in the infant-room mind already!

Why am I so slow to see these things? This has been with me for
a year and I have not seen it until now. What a truly remarkable
capacity I have for not seeing the obvious beneath my nose! It amounts
to an infirmity, this blindness.

What else have I not seen beneath my nose?

Autumn beats on. I change my routine at home and begin on the writing up of the new work coming at school into a scheme. I write during the hours from dawn, leaving the evening for the books. Things like reading and music have a frugal time since the afternoon belongs to domesticity; ironing, Rauhuia's shirts, the Tamati clothes and sometimes One-Pint's and Bleeding Heart's, and setting the drawing-room fire. How I long for a rest in the afternoon, what with the heat and the roll number once more lapping under seventy, with or without Sandy's help. But I can't work it. I seem to have no say in it. After a cup of tea beneath the tree in the garden and a short think I get under way again. There's so much of urgency to do, and life looks short from my age.

I've got so much to say. I can't contain it. I sit up in bed with it. I stop on the way to school and stare unseeing at the hacked trunks of the cabbage trees that were, about it. Coffee grows cold over it and even my personal passion for men. I put the made tea in the teapot away in the cupboard instead of the tea tin and wonder what's the matter when I pour the dry tea leaves into my cup. Can't make it out for a while. And I find myself talking aloud to the flowers, the excited flowers, explaining passionately some new development in my thinking. How fortunate I am to have the flowers to talk to! How will I do without them when winter comes? But it is only when Mr Abercrombie brings into the infant room some new faces with exclusive tongues provoking me to further exposition and defence, starting my own tongue going, my hands flinging and my person trembling, that I know real release.

I work on the scheme and the books with all the blazing drive my father left in me and with all "the loving attention to the matter in hand" of the artist; banked up in the heart of a spinster. My work becomes so much like the presence of two people that I forget altogether to go to the gate in the afternoon for the letter that does not come and I stop listening for considerable periods for the sound of the latch and a heavy broad stride down the garden. Longer and longer stretches there are when, mixing colour for my pages, shaping a sentence for my scheme, or thinking through a new movement of Ravel, or over my coffee, I escape the villain in my life; I neglect the past: "a city in the twilight, dim and vast."

Like the finished stalks I broke from the delphiniums the past is gradually and surely changing from its characteristically vivid inner life to no more than humus for the mind to draw on, and in the wide, wide world behind my eyes, before so sodden and damned with memory, now concerns itself with the present. I'm madly in love with the present. I'm madly in love with everything and everybody in it.

There's so much to do and life looks short from my age. For here, quietly giving itself birth, right under my nose and without my having anticipated it, is my dream infant room. Oh how slow, how slow, how slow I have been! How many subjects in the creative vent now? Talking, dancing, the plastic arts, vocabulary, printing, writing and now reading.

"And not breed one work that wakes . . ."

Am I so irremediably sterile? Do I not breed too? True, my disappointed person clamours for its right to fulfilment but could a birth from the body possibly engender anything like this radiance of the mind? How can any photo beneath a mattress, any physical meeting with a male, compare with an engagement like this?

Voluptuous tears.

I retreat to the storeroom with them one day; edging between the stove and the overloaded easel, stepping over children and picture-theatres and manœuvring my person unscathed through some rich argument to get there. But they are no longer difficult tears of grief for the past: they are an easy joy for the present.

How blind were my thoughts of resigning; how trivial my passions for men! I'm enslaved by seventy children. I'm alive and alove again!

"Men, men!" shouts Matawhero, scattering in on his tiny bandy legs. "Mr Abercrombie and some men!"

"Heavens, where are my shoes?"

"They give you a hiding?" asks Seven hopefully.

"Maybe. Where are my shoes? Quick!"

195

"Go on!" repudiates Matawhero. "You won't get a hiding. He likes you. He's your boy-friend."

"Who said! Quick, my shoes. Sandy, Sandy! For God's sake!"

For the first time I have time to be nervous. He has always just appeared beside me at other times, or in the doorway. That's the worst of Matawhero. He knows too much. The organ that I call my heart is heaving about inside me and, to prove it to Sandy, I flutter the front of my scarlet smock. But I haven't timed it well for I hear laughter at the door and sure enough here he is upon me, taller and greyer and correcter than ever except that he is shaking with laughter.

"How are you, Miss Vorontosov!" He grasps my hand and holds it most authentically. I time it for future reference. He's still got hold of it. He is actually and openly, before Sandy and the two others, holding my hand. But it's far too public to be worth anything. I withdraw it myself. If only he would do this sort of thing in the storeroom!

"Are you going to make me talk?" I accuse.

But he only goes on laughing and introduces me to the others; Mr This and Mr That. They're both modestly dressed men like the others he has brought here. Indeed the smaller of the two might well have been some roadman who had just helped the larger out of a drain. But you've still got to be careful here on a good road near a town and within pouncing distance from the capital city. After all their names mean nothing to a hermit.

"Who are you?" I charge with my terrific infant-room bluntness.

"Oh, just a friend of Abercrombie's," answers the bigger one, laconically. It is an innocent enough answer but there's a loftiness in voice that doesn't get by. Also the meticulous enunciation is that of one with a concern for words. I plunge on suspiciously.

"Are you important?"

"Oh no. I'm a mere nobody."

Sincerity in the infant room is as holy as in Selah. I believe him. A mere nobody. Good. I overlook the Senior's increasing laughter and attack the smaller. "Who are you, then?"

"Me? I'm just a knock-about."

I've never seen the Senior laugh like it. He's just pure man, for the moment, without an ounce of Inspector. He joins his hands behind him out of the way.

"Important?"

"Who, me? I like children, that's all."

So I relax, and what I call my heart looks round for its place once more. I still can't make out the convulsions of the Senior, never being one to see what's under my nose. But I'm becoming accustomed to his large bulk mixed up with the turmoil of my Little Ones and suppose that all is well. For a moment I wait to see what I am going to do and I find myself stretching my neck to locate his eyes. "Are you going to make me talk again? Don't make me talk again."

The laughter cools off and he looks down at the floor in that way of his, sorting out the right thing to say, the safe thing and the constructive. For once I have a view of his stern face.

"I want to hear you talk."

A strange light feeling comes as though some weight is removed. It is Guilt that is removed. Pleasure diffuses my over-simple soul. So much so that I don't answer, violently or otherwise. I wait, wondering what has happened, seeing flashing the Meaning I am always hoarding. Then the weight descends to its normal position again on my small shoulders and the light goes out and I know only that I am nervous once more.

"I want you to take reading," he says briefly, he also returning to his normal inspectorhood.

"We—we've just had it. We have just this last hour had it."

"We'll have reading now," he repeats with all his classroom technique jettisoned and his self-effacement replaced by authority. "Call in the children." How ominous are those hands behind him!

A deadly realization all but knocks me over. I hold my breath for a moment, then let it go and gasp for more. Is this the Past returned? I grasp his grey sleeve and pull him aside. "This is not the Director?"

He looks at me, concentratedly, then answers, and for the first time since I have found him in my pre-fab, he is hesitant. More than hesitant. For the very first time he is not sincere. Sensing this is A.B.C. in the cold truth of the infant room. "No. But I did intend bringing him."

"You said you were going to bring him. Is one of these he?"

"We set out that day, I remember." He escapes me and looks out the window to my private hill. "But we were late for the plane and turned back."

I say nothing.

"Call in the children, Miss Vorontosov."

But I can't give Sandy so suicidal an order. I just can't do this thing. Here is a ruthless Inspector again, after two seasons of gentle adaptability, sickening my soul and pulverizing me to immobility. He moves to the unconscionably untidy table that Sandy has made even worse since his coming and finds the Maori books himself and in no time here are the three of them in discussion without any more talk of the children. Soon I am in the talk on the books too, trying hopelessly to control the violence so accessible in a mind without epidermis. But no, here is all the harsh voicing, the hand-flinging and the trembling that so shames me in the low places of the night. Irrelevantly I seek the face high above. "Must I take this reading?"

He pauses to work out his answer. "Bring in the children, Sandy."

I move to the doorway, pressing my fingers to my neck. I know all the discomforts of labour married women boast about. Except that in the mind it is a condition beyond sound. The spirit is white-lipped, close-lipped. As the Little Ones flood in about me, frothing and cresting like waves, I can do no more than stand here in the current, tugging at the throat-line of my smock, suddenly so unbearably tight. True, many of them, Reremoana, Hinewaka and Mohi, and others throw themselves upon me in embrace and the physical feel of them on my wretched person, and the lovely organic movement of them tiding in through the bottle-neck of the door is like some kind of ether, but it only tones down the periphery of feeling. Here is the Inspector—ogre of the past again with its cloudy height, its red eyes and its black mouth. God have mercy on me, a sinner.

"Sandy, put up those reading lessons again on the board we have just rubbed out. Matawhero, you teach the green children. Reremoana, teach the blue children; Tame, take the yellow children; Mark, teach the red children; Mohi, teach the purple children. Handkerchief, Blossom. Shirt, Bleeding Heart . . ."

Mr Abercrombie strides over to the piano and closes the lid upon Tai's melancholy octaves and sends him back to his room and here we are having reading all over again . . .

. . . After school, while the sweepers wait outside the door with their brooms, laconically challenging each other, the four of us sit on the low tables and thrash it out. Out comes the Key Vocabulary and all its implications and we call in a few Little Ones. The roadman turns out to be good at answers. I can't help noticing the clarity of his thought, the elasticity with which he is able to accommodate new data and the economy in his choice of words. Neither can I help noticing that when, in easing my position on the table and my knee accidentally, I assure you accidentally, communicates with the leg, the mighty leg, of the Senior, he does not move it. But I can still see in the two visitors a precision that is utterly incompatible with their appearance. Whatever they say, all through the examination of the children on the Key Vocabulary, the Very Little Ones, and all through my headstrong expositions on my own subject, their attention is alive with understanding and acutely to the point, until I find myself thinking, clearly these men should have better jobs. True, the final comment as they rise, "I think she has got something," is becoming a boring one to me, but I can take it just once more. I can also take the observation of the smaller and more untidy of the two when he trips over the duster box in the doorway, all but splitting his chin: "Tidiness kills education."

Because I like that kind of thinking and although I heard him quite well the first time I say, "Say that again."

"Tidiness," he repeats, fitting the two ends of his leg together, "kills education."

"Well," says Percy Girlgrace, catching me up as I make my way home through the carpenters, the debris, the rising infant block and the torn cabbage-tree trunks, "How did you get on with the big bugs, Madame?"

"What big bugs? Who were those men?"

"That was Professor Montifiore and Doctor Augustus from the University."

. . . I can't make it out, I say to the delphiniums blazing out of season and out of character well above my head, as I walk in the sudden wind storm in the evening. I just can't make out why he brings these people to see me. The work I do is so elemental, irreducible and inescapable. Surely they know already all about this. But there's one thing that I can make out. I know that in every discussion that takes place in the pre-fab, every time I find myself protesting and gesticulating to my visitors I take a major step forward in my thinking.

Then I go to Selah and, instead of doing Book Three, I write another exposition to my scheme.

For a while. Here is one of these sudden vicious storms out of bounds from the Pacific. What do they call them? Tornadoes . . . hurricanes? Anyway it doesn't belong here in New Zealand. Selah all but lifts from the garden. Hastily and fearfully I cover my work and take myself and my thoughts back into the shelter of the house . . . and put a match to the fire.

"Miss Vorontosov," says Hirani sweetly, making her supple barefoot way through my Little Ones, "Nanny told me to tell you that Rauhuia had a bad turn last night. Thursday."

I don't answer.

"Last night at the hospital after the lights were out."

I still don't answer.

"They put him on the verandah because he was a little better but after the lights were out some men came in to see the other patients on the verandah and they brought beer and they smoked. They made a lot of noise and smoke and it upset Rauhuia and in the night he had a heart attack. Then the Doctor moved him inside again to a room of his own."

"Did Nanny say he had a heart attack?"

"Yes, Miss Vorontosov. The hospital rang her up."

"Thanks, Hirani. That's good of you to come and tell me. Does Mr Reardon know?"

"Yes, Miss Vorontosov. I've just told him, Miss Vorontosov."

"Thanks, Hirani."

She turns and takes the long way back, brushing young Sandy accidentally on purpose. He glances up from where he is bending over the morning writing, blushing in every freckle.

"Matawhero, come here."

Here comes Rauhuia in miniature. "Here is some paper and find a pencil." I turn to my hill, grey today, until he returns.

"Sit here at my table and write a letter to your grandfather."

"Aw hell I hate writing."

"I'll go over to the house and bring you a real envelope and a stamp. You can put the stamp on yourself and fold your letter in the envelope by yourself and post it in my post-box. No. You can take your little bike and ride down to the store and post it there in the real letter-box."

"I can spell 'dear.' How do you spell 'grandfather'?"

"But you call him 'Nanny,' don't you?"

"That's right. 'Dear Nanny.' I can spell Nanny. You don't have to tell me."

"Dear Nanny.
  Daddy and Mummie
won't take me to
see you but I will
come on my bike.
I won't go in your
room and touch your
things. You might
give me a little
hit.
  Love from
Matawhero."

"And here are some little photos I took of you. Put them in the envelope too. So Nanny can see you. And here's a photo of your grand father I took on my back step not long ago. For you. So that you can see him. So you can see him for always."

It's not I of whom Rauhuia will be thinking in his last days.

"Was the Chairman conscious yesterday, Canon?" I ask the following day after the Head's funeral oration.

"Yeh. He was. Yeh."

"I was just wondering if he got a letter yesterday. Matawhero posted him a letter on Friday."

"I couldn't say. But he was conscious. Yeh."

"When I arrived," says the Head, "he asked me to wait outside a moment as he was reading a letter. He's never said that before."

"Did you find an opened letter from Matawhero among his things, Hirani?" I ask at the feast afterwards.

"There was one with photos in, Miss Vorontosov."

"Ah. . . . And it was opened?"

"Yes, it was opened."

"Ah. . . ."

"That Guard of Honour from the school it look smart, Miss Vorontosov."

Ah . . . so it was Matawhero who was with him when he went after all.

"Ai've bought a double ticket for the Cabaret on Saturday, Madame Exclusive," says Mr Girlgrace, idling about in my infant room before school. Percy says he is not forty. He always says it. Every time . . . so he can't be.

"How many in the party?"

"Twenty-faive, without you."

"Too many by twenty-four." He likes to be seen about and to be amused. He knows all the smart slang of the day and his ambition is to be Popular.

"But it's celebrating my new job in Auckland. How can you be gay without a crowd?"

"Why be gay? I like to be melancholy at a cabaret. What's the band?"

"Maori strings."

"Drinks?"

"Gin, whisky . . . brandy. All the talkie-water."

"Nothing less than champagne. Or vodka."

"You can't get vodka in this country, Woman!"

"Don't call me Woman!"

"Christ called Mary Magdalene Woman."

"Excellent answer. Congratulations."

"Have you a dress?"

"Seven and Blossom. Be so kind as to get the bucket and fill the water trough."

"It's got to be slinky."

"Matawhero, are you big enough to open the windows? Sandy, you do the clay this morning. There's a good boy."

"Ai requaire," goes on Percy suavely in the language of his set, "every one of those points of interest on your body to be accessible without too much strain on the imagination."

" 'Body,' Mr Girlgrace, is a word I do not include in my vocabulary. Reremoana, put Hinewaka up on my piano to stop her crying."

He laughs and settles down on the piano stool, reclining fashionably. "Too earthy?"

"Hirani, Sandy is able to do the clay by himself, thanks. You go and ask Mr Reardon if there is anything you can do for him." I'm over-sensitive to sex in its ubiquity. I'm terrified of the word itself, except when used academically. I cannot stand to witness the pulsing Thee and Me between these two children. I cannot endure the contemplation of two lovers together unless one of them is I. Besides I do not want any more miscarried twins. There are enough dead loves in the grave-yard as it is. I think Sandy may have to be removed from this school. Ah, it would be surcease to dance and drink the night away to Maori strings and champagne with the utterly sexless Percy . . .

Work or perish.

And there are still a few weeks of the autumn left to do one or the other. Before the winter comes.

They are due this week; the Inspectors. Not informally as have been the calls of the Senior over the year, fetching and taking the typewriter and bringing me converse with my kind, as a listener and constructive presence; but seriously. They are due for a full-scale inspection, as Inspectors and as nothing else.

I'm very nervous. It's twenty to nine on Wednesday morning and they have been due since the beginning of the week. I was full of con-fidence on Monday and not so bad on Tuesday, but now I'm a dead loss. I still wear my cream jersey in which I meet bad crises and it's been hard to keep clean these three days. I've cleaned my black shoes energetically for three mornings running, a thing I never do normally, and I've worn all my Maori belts. But it still doesn't bring them and it is still not over.

It's no good trying not to be nervous. My admirable list of failures and mistakes in the past rolls itself up into a ghoul of my own making; quite unrelated to the Inspectors as they actually were. Nothing at this moment can make me realize the faithfulness with which the Senior has cared for me over the year, his diligence in encouraging me and his determination to win my trust. Just as in the minds of the Little Ones all goes down before the Ghost, so in my mind all goes down before this, this . . . shall we say . . . this Phantom of the Profession.

I've forgotten all my secret hopes of being recognized as a crack Infant Mistress, of excellent grading that will catch me up with my group in one spectacular stride, and of taking my place at last in the community with honour. I'm sure I'm not a good teacher. I'm not even an appalling teacher. I'm not a teacher at all. I'm no more than a certified nit-wit let loose among children. If only I had kept workbooks and made routine schemes and used orthodox time-tables, and stood up and taught from the blackboard with a pointer, and insisted on silence like other teachers, then I should at least have had the confidence of numbers.

Ah, this price of walking alone! What will they think of the reading scheme I am making? And the design of the current rhythm on the blackboard in place of a time-table? Yet I must present them. I've got to do what I believe. And I believe in all I do. I'll go back into hell before I go back into orthodoxy.

What if the Little Ones get up and dance in the middle of it all as they sometimes do? What if they answer with the freedom with which they answer me? Matawhero stood up and led a haka last week to blow off steam. Someone might tread Riti's sore leg for nothing, and how can I go through the top of the piano sequences? Think of Little Brother's bawling! Think of Mohi's wild cuddles! What about Seven and the axe? What if I tell an Inspector to blow his nose by mistake? Oh what have I done, what have I done? . . .

Sometimes I feel too old to pay the price of stepping out of line; yet I must do what I believe or nothing at all. Life's too short for anything else. And it'll be shorter still with this conflict. How can I get out of this hell?

Ah my mistakes . . . my mistakes! Ghastly soul that I am . . .

Go and do it . . . or perish.

Work or perish.

There's no other way.

It's Thursday morning now and I know why they haven't come. I've had time to complete my scheme. As I sit before nine with my feet in hot soapy water to comfort and compose myself I think of de Maupassant's thought to put at the beginning. "Words have souls, but that soul is not manifest until its word is graciously set." Now I feel better. There's a reason for everything and they'll be here this morning for sure. In any case I have washed my cream jersey the evening before and force-dried it during the night and for the fourth time I do these shoes. So, except that I cannot settle to the ironing, all is precariously well.

I look judiciously at the brandy before I leave the kitchen and decide against it. For one thing there are the breath risks, for another there is the loss in precision whereby I might tread someone's fat finger for nothing, and for another it might suddenly let me down. I've got to get out this door without it, I've got to come to terms with the delphiniums without it, and these legs, veins and all, have got to take me through the carpenters to the pre-fab under their own power. If they've got such a thing.

Once more I cross the new-laid concrete to the main building to wish my dear Head good luck, and for the fourth time running Percy crosses to the pre-fab to wish me good luck.

"Why," he asks, winding his way between the sand and the water near the door to the piano stool, "this pathological attitude to Inspectors?"

"Haven't you got one too?"

"Madame! Surely you've learnt not to take Inspectors seriously by now."

"I've learnt not to blame them by now. Eugene taught me not to blame others for our own misfortunes. If I'm nervous it is because of my own failings. The mistakes have been mine all along."

"If you didn't expect anything you wouldn't be nervous. You'd be sitting in another teacher's room at this minute, aidling away the taime like me." He sways a fashionable foot.

"Oh it's not that at all. I know I'm human enough to expect. But it's not that. I'm nervous because I'm . . . because I'm . . . because I make so many mistakes! I'm one mass of mistakes!"

"You do fool yourself. You're nervous because you hope to be approved of, and you may not be. Don't ever say ai haven't traid to save you. You're a marked man. If only you would get that into your head and accept it, you wouldn't be keyed up now. You may be the Senior's whait-haired boy but it doesn't mean that he will *be allowed* to approve of you. Face the facts and save yourself."

Work or perish.
Which?
It is Friday morning now and the last day of the term.
"Do you really think," I ask the Head when I go to his room before school, "that they will come today? The last day of the term *and* raining?"
"I can't help thinking but what they will acknowledge their appointment."
I leave him and cross the concrete to the pre-fab. I have not cleaned my shoes this morning and there is paint and chalk on my cream jersey. I should have stayed in a smock. I haven't opened my scheme for one last anxious look and I didn't turn the iron on and then off again this time. I do not even wish the Head good luck. I'm not insensitive to rhythm.
"Can you smell my breath?" I ask the fashionable Percy, who gets himself mixed up with my Little Ones going about their preparation of the room for the day.
"Can you smell maine?" he counters.
A knot of Little Ones bursts through the others to me and shoves forward a new girl.
"Can you though, Brother?"
"Only," he replies amused, "some strange fragrance."
"Her name it's Katherine," they offer.
"They calls her Ding-dong."
"Sometimes they calls her Hangman."
"The kids they calls her Dopey."
One glance at her shows me what she is. A white-skinned soul of the New Race with no top layer to her mind like me.
"Will you tea with me tonaight in town?" asks Percy.
I hear the invitation; I'm not deaf.
"I'll forgive Mr Abercrombie this unnecessary week of tension," I say. "I'll forgive him for my shoes being cleaned four times running and this jersey washed mid-week. I'll even forgive him the pressure that forced the completion of my scheme. Who am I to question organic behaviour in Inspectors? I, who preach it?

206

"I forgive the Senior all those things," I go on. "But I can't forgive him the ironing not being done and I'll never wear this cream jersey again."

"Will you dain with me in town tonaight?"

"Why?"

"Because you are talked about."

"I could do with a square meal, thank you, Brother."

"Besides, don't forget it is my last naight."

"Another Sojourner." At least this man feeds me. And takes me out. And shows me off. And yet he has no dreams for me to service. He pays for what I don't give him; whereas the others don't pay me for what I do. Strange imbalance . . . I don't know which I favour.

Work or perish.

A simple formula.

One Inspector comes out and makes his apologies to the Head for the others and leaves again. The rain lifts. There is still a lot of morning left and a little autumn. I can't see the day out here . . .

. . . The poplars along the stopbank spill their yellow paint like children and there is scarlet about. As Sandy with Hinewaka on his back and I wander here with our seventy Little Ones I feel a soft release. As they play in the fallen leaves, I feel at one with the season. I sense that something in me more important than flesh is fruiting. In spite of the inner picture of a man with blue eyes, alone with a dream and a gun, alone in the endless night, I believe that I have after all conceived in the spring just like any other of God's creatures, have carried developing life through the summer until now; here with the falling leaves and the reddened berries, are my dream infant room and my nearly completed books. Although the flesh of my person grieves tightly for what might have been, and my mind buries a son at the Corner, there is, nevertheless, a relaxing of tension in the womb of my spirit, just as in any other animal. And in this at least I am like others.

Some of my Little Ones sing aloud as they walk along the high top of the stopbank and some of them dance below, beneath the trees. And many of them play madly at rolling down the bank into the heaped leaves below. There's a loud rustle abroad and a wildness that I love, and a force of expression in their play that is the "true voice of feeling." And although I know that this sort of thing has lost me my professional status and severed me finally from my kind I feel at last that the price

207

I have paid for it in tears and disgrace and brandy and loneliness, in deprivation and tragedy, is a small price; if it can be called one at all.

I get on with my work; I get on with my work.

But only because when I return to it after the havoc of the hurricane in my soul I find, standing waiting within the doorway of my mind, Mr Abercrombie; his hands out of action behind him. He's always here when I come back, too. Indeed, he even asked the Head at a Headmasters' meeting how Miss Vorontosov was keeping. Now is that not a wonderful thing for an Inspector to say? What more do I need to take up my brushes again than this courtesy inquiry? What a big thing it is in my existence! A man asking how I am keeping. For one long moment, for the time it took him to ask and for the Head to reply, he has been thinking of me. Think of that! Thinking of me!

Such a tremendous impetus! I all but burst with inspiration. I will make him proud of me. I'll do all the research he wants. I'll present to him some day the best part of myself in these tender little books and in my Organic Teaching Scheme. I'll show him that his inquiry was worth it.

With what magic it lifts me out from the despair the storm has brought! I hurry outside to my brushes in the delight that fathers thought!

The autumn days now are as heavy as the laden trees. So is Guilt; both at home and at school. But although he no longer leaves me at the border where the cabbage trees used to be and where the loveliest infant rooms of all time are rising almost in spite of the carpenters, but dogs me in the drawing room where Paul lay in his coffin for all of one night into the dawn, he does not defeat me. My precious work guards me everywhere. Sitting over a pork chop for one in the kitchen I go over it all again, marvelling at the simplicity of it all; wondering why it has not been done before. Indeed, it seems, along with the sound of my knife and fork, I hear in the world behind my eyes the sound of rusty hinges. As though some opening were taking place in my infant room. As though some lid, heavy with orthodoxy, tradition and respectability, were being prised open.

Now suddenly, I see in mind Mr Abercrombie, standing tall and quiet and grey within the door of the pre-fab, his hands clasped gently behind him. I see more. Sitting tense and alone at my table I imagine a returned professional status. I see myself accepted at last among other teachers and respected by the Inspectors. I see letters in my box at the gate and hear steps across the grass. In the sudden way that hurricanes attack, crying assaults me, my old overdone crying, until, with my knife and fork stayed, I shake with it so that it seems that my wretched person and ghastly soul might fall apart for ever.

But my person does not fall to pieces, disappointingly enough; nor my soul; neither for the time being nor for ever. When the whole storm is over, like the rain passing over my hedges, I find myself concluding what I call my dinner cheerfully enough and in no time I am singing just like other people. As a matter of fact there turns out to be real rain on the roof and I saunter out to visit my blue garden.

In the evening rainlight the delphiniums appear to have recovered from the attack of the tropical storm. They tower grandly over the humble cornflowers, the canterbury bells and anchusa. Long ago they have lost that white-lipped look when I cut them in the summer. The autumn rains have been busy on a root-transfusion. Real penetrating stuff that says more than my hosing. It is like the inspiration the Senior has laboured to bring me in all the "passionate interchange of talk." On the cool wind-swept acreage of the mind he has walked with me; this man. Father to my creating thought. From his visits over the seasons I have known "the fine delight."

Rain is good for roots. It's good for the hair too; rain. For the newest strands of grey; "these most mournful messengers." And some say it is good for the face; it does not burn the flesh. It does not corrode like tears. Thinking of the man who has informed my work, I let it run all over my head like fingers of love. What tornadoes of the person can match the fine delight in the mind?

It cools and thrills, this rain. Sounds and scenes of the past entombing. While intense in the world behind my eyes, intense is the blue of a second blooming.

Winter

"To seem the stranger lies my lot."

*W*INTER.

And look at my garden. Thrashed about and bare. Wet and woeful. The flowers have vanished like the people in my life. As I work on Book Four and add to my scheme, I hear the shouts of the naked poplars along the stopbank and sometimes even the hoarse voice of River herself. Sometimes I leave the magic typewriter or put down my brushes and walk as far as the bridge to relate passion to it in liquid form; reading there the torrents within myself. So much does one alone need to confer with Nature.

Yet you can't be truly alone. It's impossible to draw breath and not know life. Over many years of necessity I have become acquainted with the language of the years and am able to follow her ways and reasons. What if there are no steps for me? I've an intimate in the seasons.

It's true I'm not insensitive to the cold of isolation, but Nature keeps me informed; as I walk through the wintering garden I can translate what is said and am warmed.

"I" writes Mohi
"Got a new shirt.

Miss Vorontosov
got a new
jersey."

There is a contradictory comfort in the winter. There is nothing to
live up to. There is nothing like the spring to throw into relief your
own virginity. I hand over my gales and rainstorms to the elements. If
the winter throws anything into relief by comparison, it is what little
you have left of sky. Impossibly, irrationally and obliquely I'm disposed
to sky. Mysterious ways of God!

Sandy, all grey eyes and freckles and smiles and big feet, strides into
the infant room and shatters the solemnity in the gay way of youth
and calls me and my two visitors, Inspectors coming to observe from
other education boards, to tea. "Sandy," I introduce him to them, "supplies the common sense to this infant room. That is all we were short
of. Now we are balanced."
"And what do you supply?" asks a discreet one, rising.
I look anxiously at Sandy. I clasp my hands. Here is this new reputation I seem to have been building up over the last year in the hands of
a sixteen-year-old. "Sandy," I plead, "what do I supply?"
He pauses mercilessly; looks upward and thinks.
"She supplies," he answers gaily, "the patience."
Dozens of little girls with their feet turned *out*. Scores of little girls
with their feet turned out. Dozens of . . . "Mr Reardon," I say, running over to his room during the Output Period of the morning, "can
you spare me a minute?"
Over in the pre-fab I show him Hinewaka at the low wall-black-
board, one small brown hand holding chalk of all the available colours
in the infant room and the other steadily multiplying dozens of little
girls with their feet turned out.

I'm going to be sorry when this cheerful winter is over. Searing things
like passion and flowers lie underground. Even my lover Guilt takes
time off duty, so does sorrow for my dead. True they do not wholly
vanish but they're mostly hidden. Don't think I crave delphinium's
blue; geranium's sensuous red: the quietness of the grave might fade
and fevers flame instead.

The rains compete with human tears with such successful grief that what little is left to be glad about is thrown in bright relief. So that coming upon a sunshine-shot to do my pondering in, it seems to me by contrast like a wonder wandering in.

Winter is hardly the time to grieve when love is soundly sleeping. Spring is the time when the heart is stung: Spring's the time for weeping.

"To seem the stranger lies my lot," but only in the world before. In the world behind my eyes I'm the life of the party. Everyone comes to me. What are these steps running over the trodden grass through the garden? It is Paul. What is this shuffling step along the corridor at school? It is Mr Chairman. What is this petally fingering of my soul in frank examination? It is the Head's flowers. Who is this restrained length of grey tweed standing within the door of my infant room? It is the Senior. Who is this black-winged lover with his mouth on my hair? It is Eugene. My mind "breeds dark heavens."

"To seem the stranger lies my lot"; hear the sharp hail shrieking! But in the shelter of my mind many low tongues speaking.

Spring Again

"This to hoard unheard."

BUT here is the spring again with its new life, and as I walk down my back steps ready for school in the morning I notice the delphiniums. They make me think of men. The way they bloom so hotly in the summer, again in the autumn, then die right out of sight in the winter, only to push up mercilessly once more when the growth starts, is like my memory of love. They're only shoots so far but I can't help recalling how like the intense blue of the flowers is distilled passion. Living the frugal life that I do I am shocked at the glamour they bring to my wild garden and at the promise of the blue to come.

But I don't break into noisy sobbing as I did a year ago. Nor do I return to the kitchen for brandy to make my legs go. I don't know why not. I should. Is not Eugene still far from me? Is not the bell about to ring? Where's my luxurious self-pity? Why don't I weep in the spring?

I stop where the cabbage trees used to be and where the new infant rooms stand, the carpenters finishing them off inside. But not to tremble about Inspectors and regret the past. I stand laughing here with my arms wide open for the Little Ones to run to me. I'm the coming Infant Mistress of New Zealand. I am that now; in my own view. It's only a matter of time to the formal inspection that was postponed at the end of the autumn. I'll be recognized for what I am. I might even be invited to lecture at the Teacher's Training College on Maori Infant Method. And then I will be part of the world again, part of country again and among my own kind. What have I got to weep about in the spring? True, Eugene has not written to me, but for some reason I am able to sing.

Matawhero and his little cousin appear at the door a little late in bright green blazers. The brown and yellow infant room stares in amazement.

"What say we change the uniform to green," he suggests anxiously. But I'm tired these evenings. My word I am.

True, it is a new term and a new spring. Pussy is back with some kittens. Ginger Rooster cockle-doodle-doos across the playground, there are new lambs in the nearby fields and there's an exciting glamorous feel in my old garden. But I'm tired.

Only infant mistresses in Maori infant rooms will know why I'm tired these evenings. Because along with the new stock on the Roll, an extra two hens and Matawhero's dog, there is an influx of five-year-old Maori boys. Their attention span is about two seconds; their voices are like wild bulls, their new boots weigh about a ton each and teaching them is a simply fantastic performance. For a start there's no such thing as discipline in this *pa* and for weeks the only deliberate training they get here is the slight though accurate obedience I require. Then when they come to expression work which is about the limit of what they can do at the beginning, the only idea in their heads is to take break, fight and be first. At this stage before the European discipline has been clamped down on them or before the inner discipline has been nurtured in them they remain the only clue I know to what the Maori warrior really was like in the past.

Of course they are not all like this, but what with Waiwini's next brother, Matawhero's cousin, the next Tamati baby, Wiki's nephew and Seven's brother, I find myself thinking so. Anyway I have to let these warriors out for a run in the interests of both the others and myself and I have barely returned from the door when in backfires the Tamati baby.

I lift the tiny chin with my finger-tips. "What is it, Very Little One?"

"Seven's brother he punch my stomat for nothing. Seven's brother."

"Well, stay in here with me."

I look across at Seven putting up his spelling on the blackboard. He is one of the loveliest boys on the roll now. "Think of it, Sandy," I say. "All over again with his brother!"

"I'd give him a few damn good hidings, that kid!"

"I suppose you would."

"He'd soon stop throwing his weight about."

"That's just it. I want him to throw his weight about, but in a different direction. And that's just where a thrashing would fail."

"I don't know how you've got the patience, Miss Vorontosov."

"Age, Sandy, age. And of course, grey hair." Waiwini's littlest brother screams from the playground in true Little Brother style. "Nauti," I say to the senior girl dressmaking, "go out and see to that."

"It's Waiwini's littlest brother, Miss Vorontosov. Seven's brother hit him with a stick."

Dennis runs in. "Miss Vorontosov, Matawhero's cousin is fighting Wiki's nephew."

"Good."

Each could do with a thrashing, as Sandy says.

In comes Pepi, a senior boy, with the axe. "Miss Vontosov, can I leave the axe in here. Seven's brother is trying to chop my little sister's neck off." All over again.

"Yes. Just tuck it in behind the door, Sandy," I say. "Please go and bring in all our relations."

Yes, I'm tired these nights all right. My word I am. "I am burdened by the days of wailing and long riot."

"I hate the sky," writes Dennis,
"It is too high.
I don't want to go in the sky
when I die."

The school is at the end of an arduous day of inspection. The Senior is sitting at my table and I on a desk.

" 'I see the mind of a five-year-old,' " reads Mr Abercrombie aloud from my scheme, " 'as a volcano with two vents, destructiveness and creativeness. And I see that to the extent that we widen the creative channel we atrophy the destructive one. And it seems to me that since these words of the Key Vocabulary are no less than captions of the dynamic life itself they course out through the creative channel, making their contribution to the drying up of the destructive one. From all of which I am constrained to call it creative reading and to teach it among the arts.' "

"That," he says sitting back, "is a very profound statement."

"I have felt it profoundly."

The sun is shining in the pre-fab windows into my eyes. I am slightly blinded since he is in line with it and to look at him I must look at the sun.

"Tell me," he goes on, carefully picking his words, "where do you get your ideas from; reading or thinking?"

"From reading and thinking and experience."

"Whom do you read?"

"When I was young Bertrand Russell was my man. He was my man."

"But he's rather deep, isn't he?"

"Oh, no. A lot of his work is accessible."

"But he's a material old beggar."

"He recognizes a spiritual level," I flash with sudden violence. Mr Abercrombie, I feel, is abandoning his classroom technique of self-effacement and I'm getting the Senior Inspector neat.

"Whom else do you read?"

"Herbert Read, of course." If only I could speak calmly like him.

"Oh, the eminent critic."

I'm relieved to find that the Senior Inspector at least knows of Herbert Read. For to me his *Education through Art* is a teacher's bible.

"He's a poet too."

"Which book of his do you read?"

"Mainly the *Education through Art*. He's my man now."

"I've read it three times," he says.

I pause and look into the sun and try to assess the man before me. I can't make out an Inspector being really educated. Herbert Read's book *Education through Art* three times. Hell! An Inspector up to date. An Inspector with whom one can discuss the latest ideas. But the sun digging into my pupils is soon too much and I turn away my face and wonder if the powder is melting away on my terrible nose. God knows I need every grain of it.

"What else do you read?"

222

"I read a lot of poetry," I answer with shame.

I lean forward in sudden intimacy. "That's where all the secrets are!"

But the noise in the room is too much for conversation. "Wait," I cry irritably. "Wait till I send out the new ones." I play the magic attention chord. "Sandy," I say across the spotless silence, "put out our relations!"

"Have you done any of this before?" he asks, touching the scheme. "No."

"Where do you get the ideas from?"

"They're my own ideas," I snap savagely. I haven't risked brandy this morning and I'm uncovered; vulnerable.

"I know. But how do they . . . where do they come from?"

I look vaguely about the room to find out where they come from. I look back over the year. I just haven't any idea where they come from. Then I hear myself speaking with wonder in my voice. "One day you used the word 'caption.'" I look in marvel at the dull pre-fab. "I saw it all! It was floodlit. The whole Key Vocabulary."

He is silent, but he is watching me. I'm glad he is watching me. At the feel of his gaze I begin to change. I begin all over again to feel that unpoetic eloquent articulation of my treacherous person that I have known with other men who have gone. As though I had indeed after all had a tumbler of brandy. What with the warmth of the sun upon me and the coverage of his stern eyes, barriers round my encloistered soul melt away one after the other and I soften into a pale confidence. Is this Paul's "faith in another creature"?

He turns back to the index of my scheme, and runs his finger down the list of subjects. "Where," he asks respectfully enough, "are the other subjects? Number, Nature Study, Word-building, Art?"

"I've got them all in here in this old scheme. In the drawer. But they're not new enough. I can't include them in that cover. Only my best work's in that cover. I can't put rubbish in there. Now that I have satisfied myself about the reading, I'll turn my mind, my whole mind upon the others. I had to fix that up first. That was the worst."

"Have you got Art in that old book?"

"No."

He waits.

"It's burnt!"

He thinks this over. And says nothing.

"I made an Art Scheme for Maori schools once. But I had occasion to burn it."

He waits again before he speaks. What a new lovely rare thing this is to have a man, more informed than myself, questioning me about my work! So brightly am I aware of this moment as one of those I will "hoard from the spring branches." He has no idea what he is giving me. That he is affording me in this shining shape of a moment, surcease from the past. But he must never know what I am thinking. Indeed he cannot. So ugly and blunt and even rude is my conversation in this pre-fab, always. At length he speaks, quizzically. "What did you base it on, that art scheme?" Man-to-man talk that I love. "Copying?"

"Rake the ashes!"

As a matter of fact I based it on the eidetic image. Why can't I say so, man-to-man also? Come, Anna, come, Anna; where's the dignity of your father? I try again. "I've always been," I confide more softly, "an outlaw. The bad boy who wouldn't toe the line. The freak." I seize on the word. "A freak."

He nods in an understanding that is uncomfortable. I can't endure understanding. I'm not acquainted with it. Understanding and sympathy have had too rough a career in my life. And they have been too long dead. It smells like "festering lilies." Violently I flare again. "I haven't got any sob-stories! Like your other teachers! You won't get any bitterness from me!"

He lowers his eyes and says nothing. A whole lot of our new relations have back-fired into the room. I wrench my hands from the pockets of my red smock and clutch the air. "Sandy! Take these children away! Here I am trying to talk to Mr Abercrombie! I can't stand those boots!"

And neither I can. Guilt at the noise on a formal inspection is stifling me. He lifts his eyes again, watching me in silence. Always reading me. How much more of this divining of me can I endure? These stern eyes noting, annotating, assessing. "They're noisy," I excuse myself, "because they sense that I am uneasy. They always know when I'm nervous. They get like this when I'm nervous!" Where are all my brave resolutions about ignoring Inspectors? Where is "my faith in this creature"?

He nods reasonably; his classroom technique all back. "But," he defends himself with practised gentleness, "you have no occasion to be nervous of me. I've never criticized you."

Me. You. Has he so far forgotten the rules as to speak the ominous Thee and Me? . . . But I hate practised gentleness. I'm used to the real stuff when my Little Ones touch me. "You're an Inspector!" I charge. "I know Inspectors!"

He looks down again in silence as though he were in effect thoroughly ashamed of being an Inspector. He lays an elegant hand upon a painting of Ihaka, the leading character in my Maori books, that I have in my Scheme. He has a short jersey, white trousers all but falling off and a bare brown stomach showing the navel. "Look at this," he says with tenderness.

I recognize real tenderness and I swing back madly to happiness to see his hand upon my dream. Selah and reality meet with his hand upon Ihaka. He turns a page and comes upon the Ihaka song I have composed this winter. He hums the music right through then asks, "Words and music by Anna?"

I don't believe what I hear. "I beg your pardon?"

"Words and music," he repeats, actually *shy!* "by Anna?"

My hands creep down and back into my pockets and I look at the floor. "Yes," I whisper. Shy also.

There comes a silence. An encumbered silence like the presence of a third person. I feel the sun upon the top of my head and hear the rustle of pages. It's this transition from phantasy to reality that so appalls me. I have learnt to know Mr Abercrombie, the Senior in the world behind my eyes, over the winter. I am not conditioned to meet this terrifying real one in the world before. In my conversations with him during those hours of rest in the evening his presence was never as powerful as this. In those hours I knew him as the man I wanted him to be. And that accommodating soul never presented this spectacle of a dynamo beneath a self-effacing technique. Men's careful coverings of themselves never worked with me. It only makes me sense more tremendously the latent vigour beneath.

I didn't ever answer roughly to the Senior in our interchanges behind my eyes. Not like this. It's just that I am so frightened of what he hides. I haven't practised being unafraid of what he hides. He hid nothing during the winter conversations. There was no brain-lightning to hide. This man, this big man in grey clothes, with the grey hair and stern-lined face is a completely different person. Ah the treachery of phantasy!

I start when he speaks. He never spoke unless I arranged it in my own private world. I look up, surprised.

"That Current Rhythm, your time-table, on the board there. I've never seen anything like it."

"What is so unusual," I reply aggressively, "in arranging . . . in allowing, I should say . . . a child's day into spans of output and intake? It's only breathing. Deep breathing of the mind!" Calm, Anna, calm. The dignity of the Vorontosov, remember. "It's his native right to breathe normally."

He rubs his face with his hands in the way I have come to know. He is too close; too real. Yet somehow I must accommodate my words to my feeling for him. But I cannot. "You've made me talk again," I accuse.

"I had hoped to."

"I'm not used to approval. I don't know what to say."

"Just say nothing."

In the precarious way of spring the sun has gone and the sky is darkening. It is much easier on my eyes. But I'm tired of the strain of this conversation. I'm unaccustomed to communion in reality. As the clouds spread their shadows about us two I remember I'm ugly and my hands dreadful. I lower my face.

"It's a wonderful experience to come into this room," he remarks humbly; even, believe it or not, shyly! Real humility and not technique.

I know what to do this time and say nothing. But I turn my face from his view. He closes the cover of the Scheme. "May I take this home? I want to go into it." He is sincere as a five-year-old.

Surely I can answer gently this time. Here before me, right here before me, is at least the origin of the companion of the dawns in Selah. The man who has stood between me and Memory so bigly; the man who has walked with me on the windswept acreage of the mind, summer, autumn and winter. Here, actually before me near enough to touch, true enough to see and hear, is that father of my creating thought. Gently, Anna, gently. Say, Yes, Mr Abercrombie; certainly.

I look up and quite accidentally meet his eyes; for the very first time since I have known him. They are harsh, keen eyes, unwavering. They are clear, steady eyes. How could Percy say such unfair things about a man who looks at you like this? Two-faced, art left behind for administration, kindness a technique and from necessity a yes-man? I meet no man of that kind here. Someone frightening, yes, but sincere.

"I'm not even a teacher," I hear someone say. It is I.

With effort, it seems, he orders his hands out of temptation behind him. "You're a wonderful teacher!"

But it is not until he is walking away down the path to the gate with the Head, later in the rain, that I remember I have not even given him his completed books. I run hard after him, followed by half the infant room, holding them under my smock so that the rain won't smudge the colour on the covers. Overtaking him, I push the brilliantly coloured, vividly-lived things beneath his own coat. I undo the buttons to do it, and hide them against his body. His large, elegant body. "Don't let the rain touch them," I say. "The colours will run."

The books that owed their life to him in the first place are back with him at last; and my scheme is in his bag. Could there be anything more for me than this? . . .

"I'm proud of all your work," he says with this new astonishing shyness, the rain falling all over him like the Little Ones. "Thank you for all you have done."

The rain drips from my chin and wets my shoulders. Every drop has an importance, belonging to this moment. This "hot imprisoned moment."

"I wish you were not an Inspector."

"So do I."

"He told me," says the Head with awe in his voice, after we have seen off all the Inspectors, and are walking back down the path to a severely earned cup of tea, "that the work in your room was of a very high standard. And unique in his board."

I go home and clean the keyboard. It has a winter of dust upon it.

"I want you to do something for me, Madame," says the Head one afternoon a week later when a brilliant report I find in my mailbox takes me running back to school.

"Now's the time to ask, Mr Reardon." I sink into his chair.

"It's not for myself. Or maybe it is. When your letter comes with your grading I want you to give it to me unopened."

"But I've got nothing to be afraid of! Look at my report!"

"I want you to give the envelope to me."

I open my mouth and shut it again.

"Just give me the envelope and forget you ever received it."

I open my mouth again and fail to speak again.

"Now do this one thing for me. I ask it."

Still nothing.

"I ask it."

"But I've got . . ."

"No questions, Madame."

"But . . .!"

"I'm asking you something. Do it."

"How can I . . .?"

"Do it!"

"But why?" I fight. "You can't possibly tell a woman to do a thing like that without giving a reason! Don't you know woman yet?"

He strides to the blackboard. "Because grading is so utterly irrelevant, Madame. No breathing, feeling person can be assessed by a number. The thing is fantastic!"

"Are you going to open my grading?"

"Me open it? I'm not even opening my own!"

"But you've got to. You won't be able to apply for another job. And you're ready for a school ten times this size."

"And what if I am ready for a school twenty times this size? I'll move on when I have finished what I am doing here and not one moment before. And what I am doing here is to make this school habitable for the white children who belong here. And who drive past this gate every day. They have a right to their own school. It's their district. The white parents are involved in endless trouble over transport. I'm a white man. When these two infant rooms are completed and when our warriors recover from smashing telephone cups, climbing high-tension poles, skating on the bridge and riding their bikes across the footway, and risking homicide by removing the blocks from the footway of the bridge, my white children will come back. I'm lonely for my white children."

I am silent.

"And to think of what my own race is missing by their little ones not being with you. If they only knew what they were driving past."

I sigh. I'm lonely for my white children too. Darling little pink and white things.

"Reduce me to a number!" he returns to the initial topic. "Reduce you and all your imaginative teaching, and energy and grace and rages and style to a *number!* Madame. You will pay me the courtesy of handing me that envelope. Unopened."

"I always obey men."

Such joy turns out to be something of a burden and I am constrained to take it outside and unload it on the flowers. I sit out there in the evening under that tree where I often have my tea, watching the parade within. All the times the Senior has appeared standing loftily like a poplar within the pre-fab door, his hands so reasonably behind him. All the concentrated and abstract argument with the educationists he has brought. The fine nuances when he has touched my arm to come to tea or held my hand overlong in greeting or when I have encountered inadvertently the cold, steady eyes. All the tender and sweet places when he has sat on a low chair beside me, a howling child in my arms; the precarious places where he has dangerously discussed my scheme; and the hilarious places when I told him to tuck his shirt in. All these pictures that are so unarguably true.

"I really believe," I confess to the delphinium, "that he is a man with vision."

Vision, Anna! How can you be so loose with that word? He's married! Marriage means a lot in New Zealand circles. Some value the emotional stagnation. What could a married Inspector know about the brilliance of vision? What, for that matter, could any orderly administrator know about the meaning of life? The only meaning of life; communication? Mediocrity means everything to them. They cultivate it and eat it and live on it and thrive on it; personally, domestically, professionally and nationally.

"I have faith in 'this creature.'"

Anna! You make the mistake of living by love! All your rules of behaviour and of morals and of work are confused with it. Love is not wholly respectable, you know. It's not seen openly in Inspectors. For one thing it clogs organization and for another it's no good in thinking. Passion too: there's no place for it in a schoolroom. Except in the storeroom. If only you could live in the world before your eyes, and not in the unreal world behind! Then you'd see the things under your nose!

"Moreover, he is aware of me."

Oh, Anna! they say. He's too old for that! Too old to renew in the spring. "An idle poet, here and there, looks round him; but for all the rest the world, unfathomably fair, is duller than a witling's jest. Love wakes men, once a lifetime each; They lift their heavy lids, and look; and lo, what one sweet page can teach, They read with joy, then shut the book."

This is not what I had expected from delphinium. I rise and move over to geranium, flashing away in red willing love for me. They know all about man-woman interchange; about the "slow rude muscles" of it.

"Look," they say, "at all this juice and all this joy." Look where the sap runs. The sap has to run for joy. Your passion is young, Anna. You've never used it. Not to mention your person. And your face has been looking really lovely lately, what with happiness and expensive cosmetic. Sorrow has turned down the lines but the laughter at school has curled them up again. Look where the sap runs; the sap has to run for joy.

As for this orderly, correct Inspector . . . surely you don't expect him to take one step further within the doorway of your mind. He's an integrated balance man, Anna. We'll go so far as to say he is reasonable. Why, he hasn't even taken his life over you! How can you overlook such a discourtesy! The man has no sense of poetry whatever!

One day after school when I go to the gate I find a letter there. Lifting it up I observe another beneath it. I take that too, but although it has a foreign stamp and a handwriting I know, I don't open it. Because the first one is official and from the Board of Education.

I run back through the trees to the house and down the hall to the kitchen where I can have this moment in privacy away from prying eyes of the flowers. In this wonderful envelope is my grading. It will be a spectacular increase, catching me up with teachers of my generation, even surpassing them. Professional and social standing will return to me and honour among my own. Letters will become a habit in the mail-box at the gate and steps across the grass. I will even be in the position to apply for a lectureship in the Training Colleges where I can plant the Key Vocabulary. And in this wider world I will find commensurate expression of my absolute faith in the Senior. It will no longer matter that he does not make love to me in the storeroom, or that he leaves me to go home to his wife. Just let me express this faith of mine in another creature. Let me give it all away and about. As for his blindness to the woman that I am . . . I can take that easily enough by now.

I burst into tears of fulfilment before I open it so that when I do I can't see. I brush my eyes clear and hold it further back. And when I do finally make out the content I think for a few moments it must be the tears blurring it still, because what I read is that there has been no increase of grading whatever.

Carefully and coolly I replace the notice in the envelope. It is not torn. I take the Gloy from the cupboard and seal it down again. Not too much so that the Head will see it is wet. Just enough to hold the flap down. I have not worked with paper for years not to know how to do a simple operation like rehabilitating a mere envelope. Then I rehabilitate my face too, with powder, run over to school to the Head where he is still busy in his room, toss it on the table with a smile, and return.

. . . For a few days I teach quietly on, neither speaking to nor touching my Little Ones. I explain to Mr Reardon that I chance to have "one of my heads," and send Sandy to Mr Abercrombie's office to borrow my books and Scheme back temporarily. It's all very simple. No trouble at all. Oh yes, and there's that other job.

"I want a first-class, single-berth, deck-cabin on the *Monowai,* please."
"What, again?"
"Last time, Mr Passenger-Manager."
"Your name, again?"

"Anna Mistake."

"Beg your pardon?"

"Anna Mistake, I said."

"You'll need to get your clearance, Miss Mistake."

I laugh. "I've had that for a year."

That's done. Now there's this matter of handing back the house; and of putting the furniture into storage . . . anything else? The car to be handed to a dealer, something to be done about Paul's bike. . . . The piano to be farewelled and the formal letter of resignation. . . . One must at least attempt courtesy; there's no occasion to be discourteous, especially when the defection is my own. . . .

Neither is there any hurry. I no longer need to count the hours and days as jewels entrusted to my keeping. I have done my work; mistaken or otherwise, it is done. The hours and days belong to anybody now. I'll take time off for coffee in the Tip-Top before I go and see about that furniture. And some more coffee before the car dealer, and maybe another after. See? I've finished my work.

Such as it is. And whatever its destiny.

"Although half my life has gone" I have not let the years slip from me without fulfilling "The aspirations of my youth to build Some tower of song with lofty parapet." Neither "indolence, nor pleasure, nor the fret of restless passions that would not be stilled" nor "sorrow and a care that nearly killed" have kept me from accomplishment. "Though half-way up the hill" I am able to look down upon the Past lying beneath me with tranquillity.

I have built my tower of song with lofty parapet.

I have built my tower of song.

"What's the matter with her face?" asks Mohi.

"What do you mean?" defends Sandy.

"That's why, she's ugly! She used to be pretty that other day. Now she is ugly!"

"She is not? Where?"

"Round here." He points to the area around my eyes.

"Her nose it's got long," observes Seven.

"Her hair it is curly like a circus," notes Bleeding Heart. "Ting-a-ling!"

232

"She's skinny," adds Blossom.

"Her legs they are skinny."

"Her head it is skinny."

"That's why, she's bald, ay!"

"Yeah, ay!"

"Her eyes they's like a morepork!"

"That's why she's old."

"She's not old. My Nanny's old an she's not ugly."

"Her flesh it's like the ghost!"

"Yeah, yeah! She the ghost, ay!"

"Yeah . . . see. Her flesh is ghost."

"Her mouf it is too big."

"She got fox teef."

"Her ears they flap."

"Course. She got ghost flesh. Miss Vontopopp."

"She come in our room in the dark!"

"Mitt Wottot?"

"She can't talks that's why."

"Miss Poppoff!"

"Miss Vorontokok!"

"Hey! Miss Foffopop!"

"Mitt Wottot!"

"See? That's why she can't talks, ay."

"No. That's why she can't talks."

"She the ghost."

"Yeah, ay. She the ghost."

I don't go to school the next day; even though our Lord the Bell is calling his loudest and the children's voices calling their loudest. I rise too late and my clothes are not ready . . . if that will do for a reason. Then I take the next day off also to get over the night before. And if that won't do for a reason then it's because I must somehow get this corrosive humiliation out of my mind before I can get on with my living . . . And if that won't do either then it's because I have to wait until my grand rules of loving flow back into me once more . . . and to me, anyway, this is a reason valid enough.

As for that other letter, from overseas, that the mail-box has been waiting for over the letterless years . . . I'll open that at sea. The grading letter will do for the time being. If that is what mail is like.

I have built my tower of song; such as it is, and whatever its destiny. . . .

I wake, as one can never, this side of the grave anyway, avoid, late in the afternoon of the next day. I rise and take some headache pills and dress carefully. Then I take a spade and my twins, the books and the Scheme, and without acknowledging the appearance of Waiwini in her barefoot and instinctive way, dig a grave in the garden where I used to take tea. I lay my twins in two white boxes and we carry them, Waiwini and I, across the grass and through the mourning flowers and lower them into it. I lament truly at the head of the short grave, as truly as Nanny, Waiwini chanting the sleep song; the song of the long, long sleep.

Then we fill in the grave industriously and I lay upon it some unblossomed buds of the delphiniums that have ever made me think of men.

There is only the Head left to see now. Soon I will be making my way to that other country and a job in the laundry with soap-suds all day long. Where I will no longer be burdened with Guilt. Soon this weight will be off my shoulders. I'm so fond of water. The sound of it running is like the conversation of children; and the eddying of it like their dancing. I will go away from scorn and noise, and "the living sea of waking dream; where there is neither sense of life, nor joys. But the huge shipwreck of my own esteem. And all that's dear . . ."

"I'm glad to see you about again, Madame," says the Head, rising and offering me his chair. Here he is working away at the blackboard in his century-old classroom with the new rooms for others outside. He's always here when you come back.

"Oh my heads are growing worse as I grow older."

He hides a smile.

"Oh," I lift my voice, "you can laugh at my 'heads.' But they're my big interest. I'm very proud, actually, to have developed them to such an impressive level. I see flashing colours now when they start."

"Sit down. No! Come and see the new rooms! They're finished. You can go into one tomorrow. And Rangi with the upper primers into the other. And you'll never see the old pre-fab again. It's going away elsewhere. Tomorrow possibly."

You should see this new block! Believe it or not, it's all colours outside. Blue, yellow, buff, with dark red doors. It's not unlike the buildings the little ones draw. In fact you would think it had come straight from the brush of Mohi or Wiki. Except that they add legs. Not one whit is it like the buildings I had anticipated—orderly correct respectable prison—to which I had preferred the pre-fab and its idiosyncrasies. This is different. It would be like walking straight into the paper on the infant-room easel. Wholly related to the young mind. Wholly related to my own, for that matter. It's the kind of thing I paint . . . I mean have been painting . . . in Selah. Marvellous advance in educational building thought!

"The architect said," explains the Head, " 'I like it and the kids like it and that's all that matters.' "

But neither for you nor for me.

And inside! It's a page out of a picture book materialized. One entire wall in each is glassed to the north. Around the other wall, above the low wall-blackboards, the pinex is rich yellow; higher still there is wall-paper of Nursery Rhymes and, believe it or not, cowboys and Indians. Cowboys and Indians, mind you! The ceilings, uneconomically high, are in different shades of primrose; the supports a lovely lemon. And here low along one wall the doors of the children's cupboards are every colour. You'd think the Little Ones themselves had painted this. Lovely mind of men way in the background in their dingy offices. I feel, not for the first time, a glow of pride in New Zealand educational advance.

"I say, look at the finish on this woodwork, Madame! By Jove, these chaps know their job."

"Plenty of space for dancing. They won't have to dance on top of their tables any more."

"Four of these classrooms are going up every day, according to the architect this afternoon. There's a lot to be said for the thinking behind this."

I'm wondering however what Sammy Snail is going to do about his favourite rafter. And how Pussy and the Ginger Rooster are going to like it. I hope they don't desert us like the white children. I mean . . . I suppose they will be now. Their career in the infant room is over. Like mine. Sammy Snail and Pussy and Ginger Rooster and I no longer qualify. As to that we're all deserting. If that's important.

I look at my Headmaster, delightedly opening cupboards. For others. As usual. "The committee," he says, "have decided to make a big thing of the opening. Although you will go in tomorrow morning the opening—official opening, will be in the afternoon. To suit the Board."

"Will the Board attend?"

"A lot has happened while you were away. And a grand dance in the *pa* in the evening. Buses from town. And there's nothing for you to do this time. The *pa* is supplying a Maori programme."

I am silent for some time; until a more mentionable thought comes to me. "Oh I wish one of these were for you. After all your battling. If only dear old Rauhuia could have seen this."

"I've got over that. If ever I had a dream it was to stand my Infant Mistress up in a room worthy of her." He looks around and up and about. "Dreams do come true."

"Look. No doors between the rooms. They both lead out into a common porch. Communication without doors. Fancy them working that out among the plumbing and foundations! There's real knowledge and imagination somewhere at the top."

"It's just made for you, Madame. All your ridiculous ways will fit in here. Anyone would think it was ordered in accordance with your methods."

"But there's no storeroom. Don't they mean teachers to powder up privately before they go to tea? Or to cry in secret when a child draws a hundred little girls with their feet turned in? Or to kiss Inspectors? That's in accordance with my method."

He laughs.

"You know," I warm up, "there's only one thing I've got against Mr Abercrombie. I could never lure him into that storeroom to kiss me."

We both laugh like anything. "You'd have to kiss his waistcoat button."

"That would do. There could be all sorts of passion exchanged between me and a waistcoat button."

236

"Oh, Madame, keep on the rails! I suppose that's why they haven't included storerooms."

"It's a damn shame."

"Mr Abercrombie will do me. Really I don't think I could go on to a bigger school and leave him. I don't know. But whenever he comes in he leaves me with a light satisfactory feeling. As though I am doing well. He comes and looks earnestly at everything I ask him to. There's something about him that makes you disposed to work your best. And he listens. I get a lot off my chest when he comes. I have a feeling of freedom. At the close of the Headmaster's Refresher Course last week he said he wanted to leave a thought with us. The first was that although teaching was not a thing that lent itself to the spectacular result we were to remember that it was fundamentally an essential work and could not be done without. The other was . . . he said, 'You must bear in mind constantly that you are the real heads of your schools. Whatever is suggested to you in method and content in these courses, it remains with you yourselves whether you practise it. You are the Captain of your own ship.'"

"Paul and Percy said about him the very opposite."

"Oh, they used to listen to the gossip at the Institute Meetings. You do well to keep clear of them. It's a teacher's big interest in life to tear the Inspectors to pieces. Well, well . . . I stand you up in this lovely classroom tomorrow morning, Madame. Think of it! W. W. is coming to the opening. He did want to house you well."

Up comes one of my fathomless sighs. I look round this dream infant room. "Neither for you nor for me."

"What's that?"

"I—I mean, I'm sorry it's not for you."

"Oh, forget it. As long as I see you in it."

I return to my rickety old pre-fab. Here on the back wall is this panorama of the life-background of my deceased books. Every colour known and unknown to God and Man on it. Where is it going when the pre-fab goes? Where indeed is the pre-fab going? I can't very well bury a wall. But it will soon be extinct also, when the pre-fab is dismantled and put up somewhere else. It is most unlikely that carpenters will see fit to replace the separate panels in their right order to maintain the coherence; and the picture itself will be by then thoroughly faded and knocked about in transit. Its fate is already written. But it served its purpose for the time that I wanted it. And it has had its moment of life. There's nothing to grieve about. After all it was born and did not miscarry like Whareparita's twins. Moreover, on later reflection, I do not see it to be art of any importance.

Suddenly I do not want to see any more of this dinghy. Yet can I resist one last look at my far hill? I lean over the piano as I have so often in the past year, and examine it for answers. It is blue today with the intensity and sensuousness of petals and eyes. The Senior is fair, I find myself thinking. It was because my work was inadequate that he gave me no grading. All the subjects in the curriculum were not included in my new scheme. Indeed the Art was absent altogether. Also he must know by now that the Head does all my Rolls and Records. And what about my refusal to do a workbook? Besides I have seldom been other than violent when he has been here. I must look drastic to a visitor. How can he know about the tenderness between me and my Little Ones when we are on our own? He is satisfied that I am not a good teacher; if indeed he considers me a teacher at all. I don't. I'm satisfied that I am no more than a vague incompetent artist, inadvertently and regrettably, let loose among children; if not a lunatic of the uncertifiable class. Or a five-year-old with long legs. After all there is only a very fine line between the three. As for his commendations spoken to my face, and written on my report . . . he meant them; to the extent that kindness emphasizes the isolated good in a teacher. I know that all his kindness has been real, otherwise I would never have worked as passionately for him as I have. A synthetic ritual kindness could not support the inspiration that has·exalted me. And that is the measure I use. The sum total of my efforts have just not added up enough to justify grading. And I do not blame him for my own many unwieldy and solitary mistakes. One does not blame another for your own misfortunes. You carry the capacity within yourself. One must not blame another.

I suppose I had better go home now; if you can call it home. Have I a home? The most important thing in life, one of them, so Eugene said, was a home and background. Where is my home and background? Am I like Paul without them? I do not think I am like Paul without them. "Reverence for conscience" is my home and background. It's just that I often lose sight of it. So led aside am I by the argument of my person.

As for the Gift that God has put in my hands . . . to believe any longer in such a thing would be just one more monotonous mistake. Plainly there is no gift in my hands. If that's important enough to grieve over. How long it has taken me to see this fact right beneath my nose. That I am not a teacher after all and that no creative gift has been put in my hands . . . these ugly, ringless, unmarried hands. . . . Ah well, at least I know now. Which is something. It's still not too late to rise to all sorts of success in a laundry.

I collect my pen-box that I have left on the table I don't know how long ago, years ago it seems; unnecessarily I hide my chalk, my precious pre-war chalk and for the last time lock the piano.

I'll have all kinds of fun in a laundry . . . for the last time I lock the piano.

"Where are they taking the pre-fab, Mr Reardon?" I look in his door. He is doing my Attendances.

"Miles up into the backblocks. There's a class up there that has been home for a term waiting for this building."

"Oh."

"If you're thinking about the wall picture, it's not going."

"What do you mean?"

"I mean that the picture is mine, of course. I've had that out with the architect long ago."

"You mean that you want it?"

"I mean simply that it's mine."

"You—you mean that you . . . you honour my work?"

"I'm simply saying that the picture is mine."

For the first time since I opened that letter in the kitchen, nightmares and stomach-aches and funerals ago, very hot tears break. . . . I turn my back as fast as I can and work out something else to say. I whisper, "Do you want a bike, Mr Reardon?"

"A *bike!*"

"There's a man's b-bike over at the house . . . you know. It was Paul's. He sold it to me. Green. But I didn't pay for it. Then I sold it to Rauhuia and he didn't pay me either. He put it back inside my gate before he went to hospital. Could you do with it? Eight pounds Paul wanted."

"What makes you want to sell it now, suddenly, at this late date?"

I've disciplined the tears and turn again. "As a matter of fact I could do with the money. When I die, I'll repay Paul. If we meet again." I look up at the face of my headmaster, inclined in unlikely attention, thinking of something else.

"Do you know I think we are going to have one of those visitations from the Pacific again? A tornado . . . I can tell by the sky."

I'm still looking at him, noticing the sudden flicking of the papers on his table. "If we meet again."

There is still time before the tornado to walk down to the Corner to take leave of my friends, already lost into the endless night. As I make my way up the wild-weeded pathway I hear their voices clearly. It has occurred to me, remarks Paul hollowly, that you might have, might have . . . shall we say . . . immortalized me with an epitaph. "O that was right, lad, that was brave." Rauhuia's gruff Maori voice rises from six feet below ground: You have carried out my wish, dear Lady, he says. You have left the school wreaths still rotting upon me. I never cared what happened to my carcass.

And there's time for my farewell. No failure slinking out the gate here. As I close the garage doors for the last time an éclat of sensational clapping breaks from the flowers, from the little gate at the back that leads out into the plain to the front one that has been padlocked and unpadlocked over the year as regularly as my passage overseas has been booked and unbooked. It's true that when this unexpected homage reminds me of the year we have lived together, the tears, so successfully disciplined over the last week, disobey me momentarily. But I'm not so disorganized by them that I cannot bow. I bow proudly to the vociferous applause from the garden round the house first; to the delphiniums, geranium, dahlia, gladioli and creeper, and then, hearing more clapping behind me I turn and bow to the back; to the sweet pea beneath Selah window, the nasturtium under the tank, the canna lilies at the bottom of the section and the cheeky phlox. Such clapping from my flowers! But they were always on my side. They spoilt me, actually. This way they've always had of making me feel I'm right . . . that I'm a success. Darlings . . .

"Remember me to the rose and the hollyhock when they come," I say.

Speech, speech! they call, clapping.

I look down, embarrassed. I'm shy. Speech! they yell, stamping their roots.

"Ladies and gentlemen," I begin formally. "Thank you for all your kindness and appreciation. I've enjoyed my association with you, and I have profited from it. I feel I could have done more for you as a garden but . . . I—I . . . at least a quarter as much as you have done for me. I feel that this association with you through the seasons has been very one-sided. I—I've got only one thing to ask: that you preserve my confidences. There's much that a woman does not wish broadcast. And when you remember me, do not recall, as is your way, only the effective in me. Think of the mistakes too. I always have. Indeed it is in relation to this that you have been at fault. I don't know that it is a good idea to inspire a person beyond their capacity, as you have me, since the only answer is downfall. But that's my only criticism of you as flowers: your seeing only the best in a person all the way.

"As for the future . . . if you can call posthumous existence a future . . . and with both work and fevers over I am, after all, no more now than posthumous . . . I see only rest. Don't suppose I am sad. As a matter of posthumous fact I'm cheerful. Tranquil almost. To think of the unnecessary grieving I have done for those people I know down at the Corner! If the truth were known they have been grieving for me instead that I should be left above ground. What a blessed rest to be going backward rather than forward!

"Now, if you will excuse me, I'll get on that plane. I want to thank you for all the talk and comfort and understanding you have afforded me over the last four seasons . . . five I mean . . . and although I have plainly proved myself unworthy of it I could not have done what little I have for my Little Ones without it: I could not have lived so comprehensively without it. Indeed I could not have lived at all. If that's of any moment.

"So . . . Goodbye. Remember my hours with you, my year with

you, and—" I speak the word for the first time—"give my love to the Head."

More sensational clapping! Three petally cheers! And I drive off from the gate to the sound of hundreds and thousands of flower throats singing "For she's a jolly good fellow . . ."

Monowai does not shudder from the ocean waves like my little over-crowded dinghy. He strides ahead, come-what-may, sincere, making the best of the circumstances; like a strong Headmaster, his course set determinedly before him. True, he churns up endless foam in his wake, endless flowers in his wake, but he forges forward, in the direction he sees he must. Kind, firm, attentive; his mind on a dream before him.

Reflectively I refold the pages of Eugene's letter; and as I do so one of my historic fathomless old-time sighs arises. True, here is this desired question; the question, unspoken, that has threaded my life like a recurring phrase through a sonata. But even yet I have not heard it voiced.

How hard it is to answer. I've had no practice. I reopen the pages to find again a particular phrase. "Vodka for two and a son, my love."

I answer in the only way I know how. "I have been faithful to thee, Cynara! In my fashion."

In my fashion . . .

"What is it, what is it, Little One?"

A big man, ugly enough without the heavy horn-rimmed glasses, kneels to my level and tips my chin. Tears break away and set off down my face.

That's why somebodies they tread my sore leg for notheen: some-bodies.

He sits on a low chair in his study, takes me on his knee and tucks my black head beneath his chin. Outside the snow falling: on "a city in the twilight, dim and vast" . . .

"There . . . there . . . look at my pretty girl . . ."

About the Author

SYLVIA ASHTON-WARNER was born in Stratford, New Zealand, where she was educated at the Wairarapa College and later at the Auckland Teachers' Training College. She married a teacher and for seventeen years was an infant mistress in Maori schools. In her own words: "I always wanted to travel and to end up in New York or Paris to live, but instead followed my husband in his work beyond the frontiers of civilization among the Maoris." She has now retired and devotes herself to her main interests, painting and music.